D0466153

Unseen Magic

EMILY LLOYD-JONES

GREENWILLOW BOOKS
An Imprint of HarperCollins*Publishers*

Unseen Magic

 Printed in the United States of America. For information address HarperCollins Children's Books, a division of HarperCollins Publishers, 195 Broadway, New York, NY 10007.
www.harpercollinschildrens.com

The text of this book is set in Carre Noir Pro.
Book design by Sylvie Le Floc'h

Library of Congress Cataloging-in-Publication Data

Names: Lloyd-Jones, Emily, author.
Title: Unseen magic / by Emily Lloyd-Jones.
Description: First edition. | New York, NY : Greenwillow Books, [2022] | Audience: Ages 8-12. | Audience: Grades 4-6. | Summary: "Eleven-year-old Fin has never felt safe until she and her mother move to the magic-infused town of Aldermere in the Pacific Northwest, but when the town is suddenly overrun with disturbances Fin is the only one who knows why—and she's the only one who can stop the havoc"—Provided by publisher.
Identifiers: LCCN 2021043706 | ISBN 9780063057982 (hardback) | ISBN 9780063058002 (ebook)
Subjects: CYAC: Memory—Fiction. | Fear—Fiction. | Doppelgängers—Fiction. | Tea—Fiction. | Single-parent—families—Fiction. | Magic—Fiction. | LCGFT: Novels.
Classification: LCC PZ7.L77877 Un 2022 | DDC [Fic]—dc23
LC record available at https://lccn.loc.gov/2021043706

22 23 24 25 26 PC/LSCH 10 9 8 7 6 5 4 3 2 1
First Edition
Greenwillow Books

This book is dedicated to my Aunt Lynden.

Thank you for driving my cousins to the farm so that we could build forts in the woods, get chased by territorial sheep, and make hilariously bad home movies. Those are some of my fondest memories.
Seriously, I love you all.

Unseen
Magic

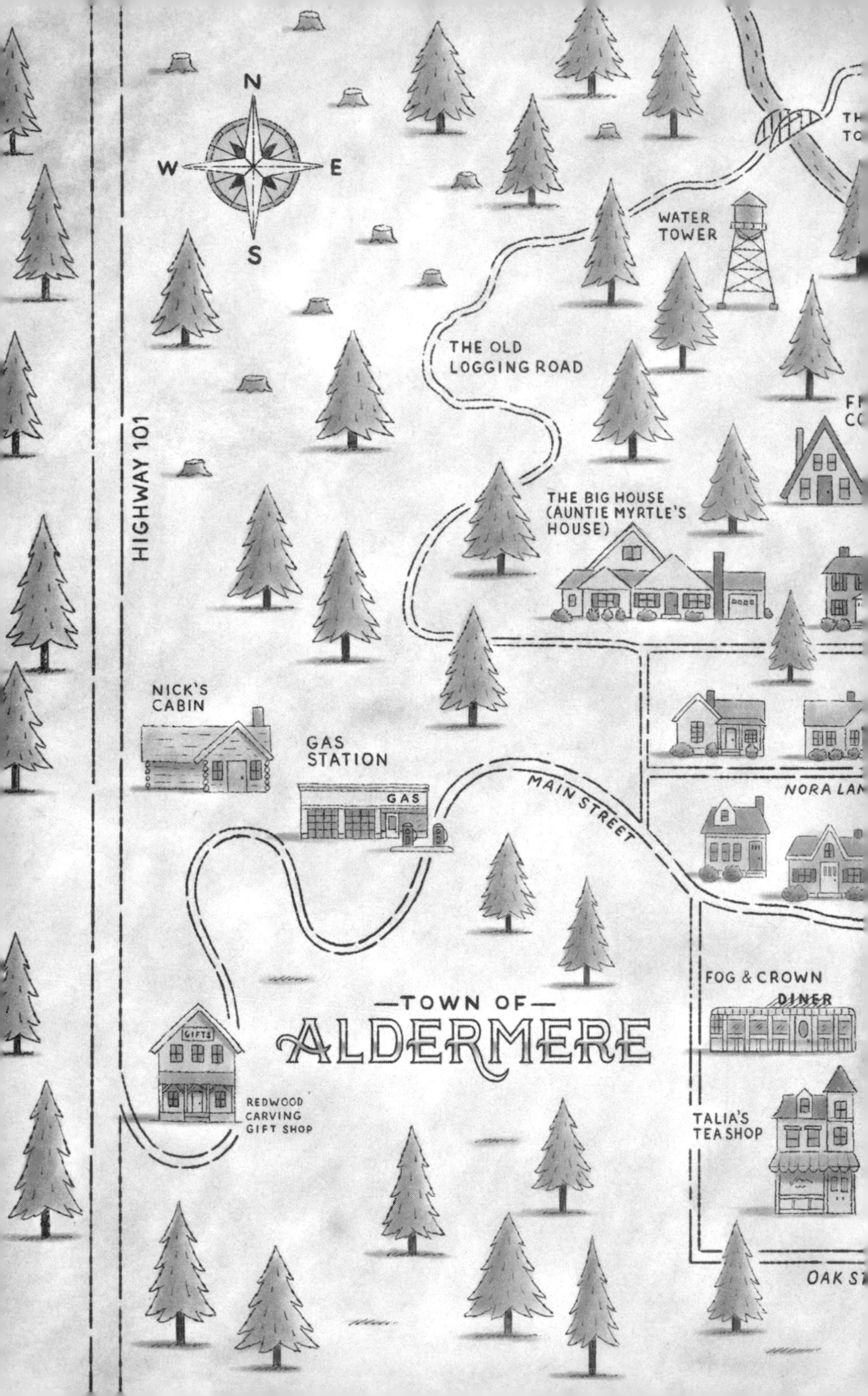
N
W
E
S
HIGHWAY 101
WATER TOWER
THE OLD LOGGING ROAD
THE BIG HOUSE (AUNTIE MYRTLE'S HOUSE)
NICK'S CABIN
GAS STATION
GAS
MAIN STREET
FOG & CROWN DINER
—TOWN OF—
ALDERMERE
GIFTS
REDWOOD CARVING GIFT SHOP
TALIA'S TEA SHOP

REDFERN →
BOWER'S CREEK
REDWOOD STREET
ALDER BOOKSHOP
BOOKS
ALDERMERE INN
MRS. BRACKENBURY'S HOUSE
THE MAGIC SHOP
MAGIC
ALLEY
MAIN STREET
ACK
FT SHOP
THE ACK
BREWED AWAKENING
FIRE STATION
WATER TOWER
CROWBERRY PLACE
WATER TOWER

ONE
The Tea Shop

The tea shop tended to vanish.

It always reappeared—but never in the same place twice. It occupied a corner of Main Street for a good two years, until a tourist tried to force the front door open. Then the shop snapped out of existence, leaving a very confused tourist standing in a bed of overgrown ferns. And once it vanished, it was often days or even weeks before the tea shop's new address became known.

Finley Barnes knew the trick: like all magic, you could only see it if you knew where to look.

She touched a hand to the wooden gate and pushed it open. The rusty hinges creaked so loudly that three ravens looked up from their perch on a neighbor's garbage bins. The lids had been thrown back, and the ravens were happily ripping into the plastic bags.

"Looks like someone didn't pay them this week," said Eddie Elloway. He stood a few feet from Fin, watching the ravens with interest.

"Maybe they forgot," said Fin. "Not everyone remembers the ravens."

Eddie snorted. "They should. Then they wouldn't wake up to garbage scattered all over their yard." He reached into his jacket pocket and withdrew a lumpy napkin. He'd crammed several bread crusts inside, the edges still sticky with almond butter and honey.

He tossed one of the crusts onto the sidewalk. Or what counted as a sidewalk in Aldermere. Tree roots had cracked the pavement, and moss filled in the edges.

One of the ravens perked up, bouncing in place. Then it leaped, wings slicing through the air, and landed about ten feet from Eddie and Fin. It edged closer and swallowed the bread crust, wariness giving way to hunger.

"We're two feet away from a Don't Feed the Wildlife sign," said Fin.

Eddie had lived in Aldermere his whole life; he gave the sign a casual glance. "Ravens don't count. Besides, those signs are for tourists who might try and feed bears. Or worse. Before you moved here, a bigfoot found someone's old campsite, and it took forever to convince her to leave."

"I'm still not sure I believe you about the Bigfoot," said Fin without conviction. "I've never seen it."

"Not *the* Bigfoot," said Eddie. "*A* bigfoot. There's a difference. And if you don't believe me, ask Nick over at the gas station. He was the one who relocated her. Anyways," he said, as if this concluded the conversation, "it's not like the ravens will leave any food behind."

It was true; the ravens had eaten every crumb and were eyeing Eddie as if hopeful for more.

Fin turned toward the tea shop. "You coming?" she called over her shoulder.

But she knew the answer already. Eddie preferred the sweeping space of the outdoors, the fresh scents and wildness. The tea shop was warm and dark and quiet. Fin loved it for exactly the reasons he never would.

He shook his head. "Are you sure you want to . . . ?"

She wasn't sure. Fin was never sure of anything. That was her problem.

"The science fair is less than two weeks away," she said. "I won't do a good job if all I can think about is how I have to talk in front of people."

She felt the fear like a living thing—her stomach shriveled up, her fingertips went cold, and words fled her mind. And the waiting was the worst part. She was jittery and distracted, the constant worry like a song she couldn't get out of her head. The more she tried not to think about the science fair, the more she did.

"Just one last time," she said. Eddie dug more crumbs out of his pocket and tossed them to the flock of ravens.

No, not a flock. An unkindness. That was the right term.

The tea shop's door was heavy, and Fin had to use her hip to shove it open. There was a circular streak across the floor where the door dragged. The first things Fin always saw were the rows of bookshelves lining the hallway. The shelves held leather-bound tomes and modern paperback romances—Talia's collection.

The tea shop's main room looked as though it had once belonged to an apothecary. There was an old wooden counter, and behind it, the tea kept in mason jars with handwritten labels. Sunlight glinted off chamomile blooms, the tight curls of dried oranges, and the dark brown Ceylon leaves. Atop the bar sat a heavy mortar and pestle. It was made of rose quartz crystal—pink, with veins of white.

When a person ordered a cup of tea, Talia took down the jars of herbs and blossoms and sifted a blend into the mortar. A customer whispered a memory into the tea—and then the memory was gone. It was the price that such magic demanded. Fin didn't know what memories she had lost to the tea shop; it wasn't like she missed them. As for the tea itself, Talia placed it in a thoroughly modern stainless steel ball, steeped it for five minutes, and then the customer drank it in the tea shop. A simple trade, one Fin was glad to make.

Just breathing in the scents of the tea shop—bergamot, spice, honey—made Fin feel better. As if a weight were being lifted from her shoulders.

"Talia?" she said quietly.

She had never seen the tea shop empty before. There was no sign of the older woman.

She stepped a little closer to the counter, unease roiling in her stomach. For a moment, she wondered if the tea shop was closed—maybe Talia had forgotten to lock the front door. The idea of being somewhere she shouldn't be sent a shiver through Fin, and she clenched her teeth against the desire to leave.

It would all be better once she got the tea.

She just needed to do something—like ring the bell at the counter or call out. But her fingers were cold and she didn't trust her voice to be loud. She rose on tiptoe, peering over the counter.

And finally she heard a noise.

A groan—and the sound of it made Fin jump. It seemed to be coming from the back room. Fin had never been there; a metal nameplate read EMPLOYEES ONLY—STOREROOM. Today that door was open a few scant inches.

The groan came a second time.

Fin stepped closer, heart throbbing. She placed her fingers against the door and pushed.

"Talia?"

She hoped to see Talia in the storeroom, looking for some obscure blend. But instead Talia lay, unmoving, on the floor.

Talia's hair was iron gray, and her tan face was wrinkled like crumpled linen. But for all that she must have been old, her eyes were bright and sharp as cut glass. Now those eyes were filled with pain. Her leg was at an odd angle, an antique stool was on its side, and a broken jar lay beside her.

"Talia." Fin stepped carefully around the glass. "What happened?"

"Reached for the Lapsang souchong on the top shelf," Talia said tightly. The corners of her mouth pinched into a pained smile that turned into a grimace. "The stool broke."

Sure enough, one of the stool's three legs had come

loose. It had rolled away into a corner.

"Listen, Fin," said Talia. "Go next door. Tell Frank to call an ambulance."

Fin's heart felt as if it was trying to scale her rib cage and escape through her throat. It wasn't just the sight of Talia, indomitable Talia, on the floor. The thought of knocking on an unfamiliar door, asking someone she didn't know to call 911—Talia might as well have asked Fin to walk into oncoming traffic.

"Fin," said Talia. In Talia's raspy voice, Fin's name sounded like a plea.

Fin nodded, once. Then she turned and ran from the room, across the tea shop proper, and into the front yard. Eddie would know what to do.

To her relief, he was still feeding the ravens. Some of Fin's panic collapsed in on itself, and she breathed easier. "Eddie," she gasped. "Talia's hurt—we need to get Frank to call an ambulance."

Eddie dropped the last of the bread crusts. One bold raven darted forward, snagged it, and flapped away. "What?"

"Talia fell," said Fin. "She said to get Frank to call 911."

Eddie stood a little straighter. This was the difference between them: unexpected things set Eddie aflame with excitement, while they doused any bravery from Fin.

"I'll go," he said, and jogged toward one of the nearby houses. Fin watched him, then turned back toward the tea shop. She had left the front door open, and sunlight spilled into the dark interior. It made the place feel strange . . . too open. Part of Fin wanted to retreat, to just leave, but she couldn't do that. Talia needed her.

Fin hastened to the back room. Talia had managed to pull herself upright against a wall. "Did you find Frank?" she croaked.

"My cousin Eddie's taking care of it," said Fin.

Talia nodded. She closed her eyes for a few moments, breathing hard through her nose. Fin stood there, feeling awkward and useless. "What—what can I do?"

Talia opened her eyes. Her face was chalky white with pain. "The EMTs—they might not be able to find this place. The magic . . ."

Fin understood. "You want me to stick around just in case? Show them where the tea shop is?" she asked. "*Can* I show them? I mean—"

"Check the drawer behind the counter," said Talia, her voice strained. "There's a spare key. As long as you carry it, the tea shop will let you guide people in and out."

The cash register was an antique; it looked like an old typewriter, with its worn metal keys. Fin checked the drawer beneath it. There was a roll of tape, bits of twine, scissors, old pens, and a normal key. It was attached to a key chain of a glittery crescent moon. It was oddly heavy in her hand.

Fin hurried back to Talia. "I found the key."

"Good, good," said Talia. "You've been a great help, dear. Thank you." She gave Fin another pained smile. "Go out the back door; tell the EMTs to use that one. I just told the shop to lock the front."

Only in Aldermere could such a sentence be uttered and believed.

The silver lock matched the key in Fin's hand. It was a deadbolt, and Fin was quietly grateful that most of her old apartments had come with such a lock, so she knew how to use it. She unlocked it with an easy twist of the lever and stepped outside.

The back door led out onto a small porch—and beside that, a gravel driveway. The fresh air was a relief against her skin; for once, the tea shop was too small and dark, as if Talia's pain had filled up every corner.

Her legs shaking slightly, Fin walked to the driveway. The gravel was clogged with dandelions and tufts of grass. Eddie stood on the sidewalk, face shining with sweat. Fin waved at him, and he caught sight of her.

"Did you find Frank?" asked Fin. She wasn't sure what

she would do if Eddie hadn't. The inn was a ten-minute walk away—maybe if she ran . . .

"He was home," said Eddie. His gaze went to the tea shop. "What are we supposed to do now?"

"Wait?" said Fin, making it sound like a question. "We have to wait," she said, more decisively. "Just in case the EMT people can't find the tea shop."

Realization sharpened Eddie's features. "Oh, yeah." He bounced on his heels, impatient and eager. Fin sank to a crouch so he wouldn't see that her knees were unsteady.

They waited, and every moment dragged.

It took the EMTs about thirty minutes to arrive, which was pretty fast. They must have been nearby. Fin heard the whine of sirens first, and she walked closer to the street, the key still clutched between her fingers. The ambulance pulled up to the curb, and two people got out: a young woman and a slightly older man. They glanced around as if bewildered.

Fin took a step closer. "This way," she said, but her voice was too quiet and they didn't hear her.

"Hey," called Eddie. He waved, and this time the EMTs heard. Eddie pointed at Fin, and she gestured toward the back.

"There's a back door around here," she said, and the EMTs' gazes snapped toward her. The older man blinked twice, then nodded. There was a flicker of confusion as he looked at the tea shop—that was probably the first time he *saw* it.

He wouldn't know magic for what it was. Most people never did. Even the tourists who believed in Aldermere's reputation mostly came for tarot readings and postcards featuring Bigfoot. Magic wasn't bright flashing spells or turning people into toads. It was quiet and creeping, and it had a way of stealing into the cracks of the sidewalk and into the very water.

Everything happened quickly after the ambulance arrived. Fin led the EMTs around to the back, where they found Talia on the floor. Fin watched as Talia was loaded onto a stretcher, carried up and into the ambulance. She thought she should have taken Talia's wrinkled hand in hers and given it a friendly squeeze. But that was what a brave person would have done, and Fin had never been brave.

When the ambulance's doors slammed shut, Fin stood on the broken sidewalk and watched it drive away. It turned a corner and vanished from sight.

Fin couldn't move; the bitter taste of fear lurked on the back of her tongue. And despite the fact she should have been sorry for Talia, she felt sorrier for herself.

Talia was gone.

The tea shop was closed.

And there was no magic to banish Fin's fears.

TWO
Before

Fin hadn't always lived in Aldermere.

Bakersfield, San Diego, Barstow. The details were all tangled up in her memories—rough old carpets, the smell of neighbors smoking, and the sound of her mom sliding the chain lock home. Her mother worked in shops or restaurants, and they never stayed too long in one place. Sometimes Fin wondered if her mother was an ex-spy. It would explain why they were always moving, why her mother kept glancing over her shoulder. Before Aldermere, a year and a half was the longest they'd remained in one location—renting a place in Modesto.

For a while, there hadn't been the chaotic jumble of boxes in the car's back seat, nor the paperwork of getting Fin into yet another school, nor Mom coming into her bedroom at three in the morning, telling her to put on shoes. They had left their last apartment when the moon was half full; Fin remembered dragging her small suitcase behind her, hefting it into the car's trunk, her mind still fogged with sleep. Her memories were a jumble of trees in the headlights, the taste of orange juice they'd bought from a gas station, and the soft fuzz of the radio as they left all the stations behind.

Fin had known almost nothing about Aldermere, only that it was a tiny town just east of the Redwood Highway. It was shrouded by an old-growth redwood forest, far from any cities. Northern California was a different world: all narrow, twisting roads and red-barked trees that smelled of spice. They drove for so long that it seemed as if they might simply drive off the edge of the earth.

Mom, who had grown up in Aldermere, had only ever mentioned it in whispers at bedtime, when Fin begged her for stories. They always sounded like wild fairy tales: Mom and her older sister, Myrtle, traipsing through forests, crossing rivers on abandoned train tracks, finding keys and strange teeth in creeks. Fin's grandparents had lived and died in Aldermere, leaving Aunt Myrtle their home, but Mom and Fin had never visited. Not for holidays or birthdays or summers.

But now . . . now they were. They were going to Aldermere.

"Fin, darling," Mom had said. "Where we're going—there are a few things you should know. A few rules."

Fin was used to rules. Most of the places they stayed didn't allow pets or loud music.

But these rules were different.

Doors must be labeled or they can lead anywhere.

Pay the ravens or keep your garbage bins inside.

Never keep a knife that's tasted your blood.

Always drop a bread crust into Bower's Creek before going into the water.

Don't use the old toll bridge north of town—there is a price, but no one knows what it is.

Burn nothing within the town borders.

The rules had the wicked, lulling cadence of a fairy tale—the kind her mother used to spin out when Fin couldn't sleep.

"And most important," said Mom, "don't look for the tea shop."

"What tea shop?" asked Fin, confused.

"Aldermere can be dangerous, Fin," was all Mom would say. "Don't ever let your guard down."

Fin fell into silence and watched as the car's headlights shone upon a green road sign.

ALDERMERE
POP: 239

As the car took a right turn, the headlights illuminated a deer standing on the grassy highway shoulder. It was a small, graceful doe. Fin had never seen one in the wild, and she pressed herself closer to the window to get a better look. But as her eyes focused on the deer, Fin's heartbeat quickened.

The deer's shadow looked *wrong*. It was the shadow of a much larger creature, one that stood on two legs and had thick, curved antlers like those of a moose. Its arms ended in long, jagged points.

Fin blinked. It had to be the headlights distorting the deer's form, she told herself. But before she could look again, the lights slid away. The deer vanished into the dark.

The car jounced, the pavement rough and uneven. Fin found herself clutching at her seatbelt as they pulled up to a driveway. Despite the late hour, Myrtle Elloway had greeted them at the front door. Fin had never met her aunt Myrtle, but there had been a trail of birthday cards, flecked with glitter, usually with a twenty-dollar bill tucked inside. Aunt Myrtle wore a fuzzy robe belted at her waist, and she held a steaming mug. To Fin's surprise, the older woman handed the mug to her. It smelled of warm milk, vanilla, and nutmeg.

The mug also had a chip in its handle, and that made Fin feel more comfortable. People didn't give chipped cups to guests—only to family.

"You're late," Aunt Myrtle said to Mom.

"I didn't even know we were coming until yesterday," replied Mom. "How did you . . . ?"

She hadn't called ahead, Fin realized. A swell of shame rose up in her belly; she didn't want to be somewhere they weren't wanted. She wouldn't learn the word "imposition" until a year later, but even then she knew what it meant.

"Never mind that," said Aunt Myrtle. "Come inside."

Fin saw little of the house in the dark; all she glimpsed were wooden floors and the gleam of sea glass dangling from the ceiling. They bustled out of the house and across an overgrown lawn. And all the while, Aunt Myrtle talked. "What are you now, eight?" she was saying. Fin nodded. "Good—my son's nine. He'll be glad to have someone new around. Do you like to draw? Paint?"

A small cottage sat within the fringes of the forest. It was wide at the base and came to a point at the roof. The wood was dark, trimmed with white paint, and there was a porch without a railing. The whole thing looked rustic and strangely inviting. It looked like someone's home.

Aunt Myrtle unlocked the front door, then handed the

key to Mom. "Thank you," Mom whispered. "I won't—it'll only be a few weeks. . . ."

Aunt Myrtle raised a hand, as if to wave away Mom's words. "It's fine. If you decide to stay, the neighbor's a metalsmith. I can ask her to make a new sign for the door."

"I'm sorry," Mom said quietly. "I know you didn't want me to come back."

Aunt Myrtle made a disgusted sound. "It wasn't *you* I didn't want here."

Again, a flutter of fear rose up in Fin's belly. *Me,* she thought. She must be the one Aunt Myrtle hadn't wanted—that's why they'd never visited.

To distract herself, Fin looked at the metal nameplate beside the front door.

GUEST HOUSE, it read.

Beneath the plate, someone had stapled a small sheet of paper. The drawing looked as though it had been done by someone Fin's age. There was a house and two stick-figure people beside it, smiling widely. And beneath the drawing were the words *Angelina and Finley's Home.*

Fin wanted to believe it.

The truth was, Fin didn't know when she had started being afraid.

It had crept in slowly. Maybe all fear was like that—like rot in old wood, working its way into the foundations of a house. All Fin knew was that by the time she was five or six, she had a list of things that were to be avoided at all costs. She wrote it down in crayon, and added to it as she got older. The list became a strange little talisman that went with her from apartment to apartment, school to school, tucked between the pages of an old paperback mystery she kept in her backpack.

1. *Ringing phones*
2. *Knocks at the front door when takeout hadn't been called for*
3. *Knocks at the front door when takeout was called for*
4. *Report cards*
5. *Asking for things*
6. *Adults who look angry*
7. *Goldfish—at least the kind with the bulging eyes*
8. *TALKING ALOUD IN CLASS*
9. *Being unwanted*

Fin knew where the last one came from: a conversation she hadn't been supposed to hear. She'd always had a knack for listening at doors. She couldn't remember when she'd started, but she knew why she still did it—if there was trouble, then Fin could prepare. Grown-ups tended to hide things until they boiled over, spilling secrets and troubles like a pot left on the stove too long.

Fin had overheard Mom and Aunt Myrtle only a week after they had come to Aldermere. The sisters were inside the cottage, murmuring while Fin was supposed to be playing in the yard. Instead, she'd crept beneath an open window and listened.

"—much in savings," Mom had said. "I'm sorry."

"I've been talking to the Butlers," said Aunt Myrtle. "There's an opening at the inn. It'd be cleaning rooms and working at the front desk, but it's something."

There had been a silence, a hesitation. "I wasn't planning on staying here," said Mom quietly.

"Oh, hush," said Aunt Myrtle. "Of course you'll stay. You're family." There was a pause. "Why you left—was it because of Finley?" Myrtle's voice was soft, kind, but Fin's heartbeat tore into a gallop.

"I got a call from her school," said Mom. *Her* voice was sharp, like she was angry, and Fin cringed. "One of the parents at pick-up saw—" A harsh exhalation. "I suppose it was only a matter of time until we had to leave again."

Fin stepped back from the window feeling sick and

shaky, like she had the flu. She looked at the cottage, at the place she hoped would be hers. Her mom said they'd left because of her. There was something wrong with her—one of the parents had seen it at school, and she didn't even know what it was. Maybe it was because Fin was afraid. She'd read enough books, seen enough movies to know that courage was important. Monsters had to be slain, fears had to be faced. And Fin couldn't muster up the courage to even answer the phone.

She turned and walked away from the cottage. She didn't want to hear any more.

Aunt Myrtle had told Fin it was safe to walk around Aldermere—even at eight years old. People looked out for kids around here. But Mom had always drilled into her that she needed to stay close to home. So Fin compromised by lingering in Aunt Myrtle's front yard, watching a couple of ravens chase a piece of garbage fluttering down the street.

Aldermere was like no other place they had lived: the redwoods were thick and their needles carpeted the ground; tiny mushrooms sprang up along fallen branches and in between blades of grass; the cottage was cozy with its old appliances, tall windows, and lofted bedroom. Most of the things in the cottage had been there before Fin and Mom moved in. It had been a vacation rental, a place for tourists to spend a weekend. Fin wondered if Aunt Myrtle would be mad if they stayed too long and she couldn't rent out the cottage. Maybe they'd have to leave soon, find another apartment in some crowded city and—

"What are you doing?"

Eddie's voice made her flinch. She looked up, flushed. "What?"

Eddie stood a few feet away. He wore jeans that were tattered at the edges, rolled up around his ankles, and a T-shirt with a band name that she didn't recognize. "You want to go for a walk?" said Eddie.

Fin shrugged. For all that he was her cousin, they hadn't ever known each other. He was a school picture that came in cards—all freckles, sharp chin, sandy hair, and dark eyes. He looked like the kind of person who wouldn't be afraid to slay a monster.

"We could go to the coffee shop," said Eddie. "You been there yet?"

Fin shook her head.

"Is that a 'No, I haven't been there' or a 'No, I don't want to go'?" said Eddie, grinning.

She hadn't known what to make of him, but he had been smiling like either answer was fine.

"No, I haven't been there," she said. She hesitated a few heartbeats longer, then said, "And yes, I'd like to go."

Part of her had been scared to go to the coffee shop, because if she went—it might be wonderful. And by the sounds of things, Mom didn't intend for them to stay. Maybe whatever flaw Fin had, whatever was wrong with her—it was what drove them from place to place. From home to home.

The thought was so gut-churningly scary that Fin had tried to shove it out of sight, to cram it beneath Eddie's chatter. He'd started talking about a snake he'd caught behind their house, and she was grateful for it.

"Big thing," he was saying. "But they're not aggressive. They sun themselves on the cobblestones that Mom put out back. She doesn't like them—once, I brought one in the house, when I was, like, five, and she ended up standing on the table for an hour when I accidentally let it loose." He sighed happily. "Good memories."

"You let a snake go in your house," Fin said, disbelieving.

"It sort of slipped free. I got it eventually." As they walked through town, Eddie studied her. "You like animals?"

"Yes," she said. "Well, some of them. Not, like, spiders and big dogs. But birds and stuff—yeah."

The coffee shop was on Main Street—it looked like an old house that someone had converted into a business.

There was a porch with wicker chairs and a hand-chalked sign that read BREWED AWAKENING.

Eddie checked the door before they entered—sure enough, there was a metal nameplate that read COFFEE SHOP. Fin shook her head; back then, she had been confused as to why every door had a label. Her mom had said something about doors leading places they weren't supposed to, but it hadn't sunk in.

The coffee shop smelled of sharp espresso and old wood. The walls were lined with chalkboards listing different blends of coffee and tea. There was a glass-paneled display of baked goods—pink and yellow conchas, empanadas, bagels, and a scattering of cookies. A girl with dark hair sat at the counter. She looked Eddie's age—nine years old. She was doodling on her wrist with a blue ink pen, and drawings went all up her arm. When she looked up, she smiled. "Hey, Eddie. Who's the new girl?"

"My cousin," Eddie said. "She and her mom just moved here. Finley, this is Cedar."

Fin forgot the girl's name within five seconds of hearing it. She'd never been great with names or directions—it was like trying to hold on to sand. And then she'd hate herself when she had to ask again, because it seemed to make people sad that they weren't more memorable. Mostly Fin pretended she knew people's names and nodded along when they spoke. It was easier for everyone that way.

"Welcome to Aldermere," the coffee shop girl said. "My parents are out for five minutes, but if you want I can get you some tea! I'm allowed to pour tea." She gestured at the blackboard and the drinks scribbled in chalk. Fin didn't know the language of coffee—of shots and lattes and cappuccinos—and she wasn't allowed to drink them, even if she had known how to order. There were other things: mattes, smoothies, blends of herbs and roasted nuts. Fin found herself glancing at the jars of loose tea with a certain amount of confusion.

The coffee shop girl laughed. "Don't worry, it's just tea," she said, patting one of the mason jars. "Nothing extra. If you're looking for something more, check the tea shop."

"I thought it vanished again," said Eddie. "Some kid broke a window or something with a baseball."

The coffee shop girl heaved a sigh. "Has anyone found it yet?"

Fin felt as though she was listening to half a conversation—and her half wasn't making a lot of sense. "The tea shop vanished?"

Coffee Shop Girl looked at Eddie, a wordless question on her face.

"She's good," said Eddie, nudging Fin with his elbow. "Not a tourist. Her mom's a local."

"Okay," said Coffee Shop Girl. Fin wished she wore a name tag.

"The tea shop vanishes sometimes," said Eddie.

"If anyone tries to force their way inside," continued Coffee Shop Girl, "it goes poof." She moved her fingers, as though to mime a small explosion. "Security measure."

"The only people who can find the shop are those who already know where it is," said Eddie. As if this made sense. "So every time it goes missing, there's a few weeks when everyone panics."

"Talia runs it," said Coffee Shop Girl. "Older woman, silver hair, bright red lipstick."

Fin listened, raptly attentive. "What do you mean, the tea here isn't extra?" she asked.

Coffee Shop Girl leaned on the counter, tapping one plum-colored nail against the redwood. Fin had never been allowed to paint her nails, and she eyed the color with a bit of envy. Coffee Shop Girl said, "Our stuff is good tea. My mom blends it herself—she imports a lot of it from fair-trade farmers in South America and stuff. But it won't change you."

Fin blinked. "Change you?"

"Make you smarter, faster, stronger," said Coffee Shop Girl. "More beautiful. If you want any of that, you go to Talia."

It had to be a joke. People couldn't change themselves, not in the ways this girl was saying. Not with *tea*.

"It's temporary," said Eddie, as if he needed to be the bearer of bad news. "Lasts . . . a few weeks? I don't know."

"Mrs. Liu goes there for her arthritis," said Coffee Shop Girl. "When insurance stopped paying for her meds, she started paying Talia instead. She says the tea keeps her limber, and she doesn't have to deal with insurance companies anymore." She frowned. "I wonder if she's found the tea shop yet. Someone has to find it soon."

"Talia'll invite someone over," said Eddie. "Probably Mrs. Liu or even my mom—she doesn't drink the tea, but they trade romance books. And then word'll get out." To Fin, he added, "That's how it always works."

Fin hadn't believed it, not yet. It had all sounded like fairy tales, like *magic*.

Back then, Fin hadn't yet glimpsed Aldermere's true nature. She hadn't walked through an unlabeled door and found herself in a broom closet across town; she hadn't stood on the edge of the creek and watched a long-clawed hand drag a bread crust beneath the water; she hadn't drunk tea that tasted of sunshine and Ceylon—tea that made her feel fearless for the first time in her life.

She hadn't believed in magic—not yet.

As she walked out of the coffee shop, Fin mustered the small amount of courage she had. She looked over her shoulder at the girl and said, "It was nice meeting you."

The girl beamed at her. "You too. Finley, right?"

"Just Fin," said Fin. The other girl had made it sound so effortless, so she tried to ask the question herself. "And—your name was . . . ?"

"Cedar," said the girl. "Cedar Carver, because my parents are terrible." She flashed Fin a smile, as if to indicate that her parents weren't actually terrible—which was why she could joke about it.

Fin had smiled back, tried to make it look natural. But somehow the joke had her stomach in knots, and she was so intent on looking nonchalant that by the time she was through the door, she realized she still didn't remember the girl's name.

THREE
The Big House

"I don't give refunds," said Aunt Myrtle as Eddie pushed the front door open. Fin followed closely at his heels.

Her heart was still unsteady. The sight of Talia being wheeled away on a stretcher was all she saw when she closed her eyes.

It was *fine*. Talia would be *fine*. She'd fallen; people did that all the time, didn't they?

"No," said Aunt Myrtle into the phone. It was a landline, like all the phones in Aldermere. Cell phones only started working about twenty miles south of town. It had nothing to do with magic; there were simply no cell towers within range of Aldermere. Aunt Myrtle saw Eddie and Fin, and all the irritation melted from her face. She gave them a smile, gesturing toward the kitchen. "Snack," she mouthed. Then, into the phone she said, "Because I read tarot—I don't do weather predictions."

Eddie laughed quietly as he led the way into the kitchen. It was a tight fit: the kitchen was narrow, with low counters mostly filled with old mail, potted plants, and seashells that needed cleaning. The big house was always cluttered, but it was a comfortable, lived-in clutter. There were herbs drying in bundles hung from ceiling rafters, scuffed wooden floors, and secondhand books piled up in the corners. Eddie walked to the old fridge and pulled it open. "Protein ball?" he asked, pulling a plate out. The balls resembled unbaked cookie dough, but Fin knew better than to trust them. They were probably filled with chia seeds and oat flour.

"I'm good," said Fin. She wasn't lying. Her stomach was still too unsettled to think about food.

Eddie shrugged and popped one into his mouth. Fearless, even in this. He chewed and said gummily through his mouthful, "She added bits of almond this time. More crunch."

Fin made a face, mildly amazed and disgusted.

"You want some juice?" asked Eddie, grabbing a glass jug.

Her throat was dry and the organic cranberry juice

sounded good, but Fin shook her head. She wasn't even sure why she refused—and the moment she did, she wanted to take it back.

"So now what?" she said quietly, so Aunt Myrtle couldn't overhear.

Eddie drained half a cup of juice. "Now *what*?"

Fin gave him a hard look. "What are we going to do about the science fair?"

"Finish our poster, hopefully," said Eddie. "And then get started on our terrarium. You want to be in charge of digging up plants or catching lizards?"

"Eddie," said Fin, exasperated. "I'm being serious."

"Yeah, you're right," replied Eddie. "There's no way you're catching lizards. You're on plant duty."

She crossed her arms. As much as she loved her cousin, Eddie had never truly understood. When she'd tried to explain the one time, he'd looked baffled. "If you're scared, why don't you think about something else?" he had asked.

Fin didn't know how to explain that asking her not to think about something was like asking her not to breathe. She could only manage it for so long before all of her thoughts came rushing back. And then she wondered if something was wrong with her, because no one else she knew was followed by a low, constant background noise of fear.

It wasn't even a fear of monsters or being kidnapped or anything else that would be understandable. No—Fin couldn't pick up a ringing phone, couldn't answer the door if she didn't know who was on the doorstep. Her voice would crack if she had to speak to a stranger; she fretted over homework again and again until she was sure every answer was right. And those were only the fears she recognized. There were other, nameless fears. Ones that lurked in the moments between waking and sleeping. They were half-remembered nightmares, ones that broke apart when she tried to recall them.

Fin thought of the science fair and a full-body shudder rolled through her.

"I don't know if I can do this," she said.

Eddie nudged her gently with his shoulder. "Come on. You read a few lines off a notecard. You stand by a terrarium for two hours and tell people what species of plants and lizards are native to Northern California. Then we watch River and his amazing mechanical windmill he built out of toothpicks that actually turns wind into electricity to power a clock win the fair because he always wins." Eddie tilted his head back, eyes slipping shut, as if he were imagining a world in which River did not go to their school. He looked rather happy about it.

"I don't want to win," said Fin, which was an utter lie. "I just want to get through the speech without throwing up on someone." Which was true.

"I love your goals," said Eddie. "Now, we do need to start that poster. Want to work on it tonight?"

Fin shook her head. "It's Tuesday," she said. "Can we do it tomorrow?"

Understanding lit in Eddie's eyes. "Oh, yeah. Delivery day. Well, tell Mr. Hardin I said hi." He grabbed another protein ball.

The sound of heavy footsteps proceeded Aunt Myrtle. She walked into the kitchen, looking as she always did—swathed in a loose skirt, folds of fabric draped elegantly about her shoulders in a shawl. Her feet were bare, toenails painted purple.

"Someone wanted a refund, Mom?" asked Eddie, picking up another protein ball. He popped it into his mouth.

"It happens sometimes," said Aunt Myrtle. "Some people don't like what the cards say."

Aunt Myrtle was the kind of person who made salads of foraged dandelion greens and freshly grown turnips, every mouthful bright with lemon and basil. She would drive for an hour down the winding forest highways until she reached the beach, where she collected broken seashells and shards of abalone, fashioning them into wind chimes that she sold to the gift shop. She painted watercolor postcards. And she occasionally read tarot for the tourists who came by the Foragers' Market.

"Why do you only read tourists' fortunes?" Fin had asked once, when she had watched three teenagers go giggling from Aunt Myrtle's table. She wasn't sure what to call a group of teenagers. A herd? No—a gaggle. Definitely a gaggle.

Aunt Myrtle had answered, "Because people around here know better. Out there, in the world, fortunes will be like ivy with no soil to grow in—they'll wither away. But here, prophecies grow like weeds. It's why I never look at my future—or my family's. You never know what might happen."

Now Aunt Myrtle poured water into the electric kettle. It was the most modern thing in the kitchen. There wasn't even a microwave—things had to be heated up on the old electric stove. "You two going to work on your science fair project?"

"I need to go to the Ack," Fin said. "Tuesday deliveries."

Aunt Myrtle nodded. "You be back before eight, okay? I don't want either of you out after dark. Not with what happened."

Eddie and Fin went still. She had asked Eddie not to mention going to the tea shop for fear that Mom would find out and be mad. Fin and Eddie managed not to share a guilty glance, but Fin knew it was more out of luck than any skill at deception.

"Why?" said Eddie. "What happened?"

Aunt Myrtle shook coffee grounds into a filter. For all that she looked like the type who should have been drinking tea with flowers floating in the water, Aunt Myrtle was fiercely addicted to coffee. "Oh, yes, I forgot you were in school. Mrs. Brackenbury was mugged earlier today."

She might as well have said Mrs. Brackenbury had grown wings and flown to the ocean. Fin had known places where she had to be aware of muggers—she even had a dim memory of her mother handing over her purse to a strange man in a parking lot. But Aldermere was *safe*. It had fewer than three hundred people, most of them old and retired. Tourists came and went, but they wore shiny hiking boots and bought overpriced redwood forest calendars. Kids were used to running around in Aldermere without fear of dangerous traffic or strangers . . . because it had precious little of either.

"She got mugged?" said Eddie blankly. He and Fin shared a confused glance.

Aunt Myrtle nodded. "Someone took her shopping bag and ran off. She didn't see who it was."

"Mrs. Brackenbury is, like, ninety," said Eddie. "Who robs an old lady?"

Aunt Myrtle regarded her son with a small smile. "You'd be surprised, sweetheart." She kissed Eddie on the crown of his head, and he looked both pleased and a little embarrassed.

"She going to be okay?" asked Fin quietly. She thought of Talia, on the floor of the tea shop. But Talia hadn't been mugged; she had fallen.

"Mrs. Brackenbury wasn't injured," said Aunt Myrtle. "More startled than anything else. She'd been doing her weekly errands: went to the grocery store, talked to a few friends, visited the tea shop, and then someone knocked her down. She said that if she found out who took her shopping bag, she'd send Mr. Bull after them."

Mr. Bull was Mrs. Brackenbury's old and lumpy bulldog. He spent his days napping on her front porch and begging passersby for ear scratches.

"Terrifying," said Eddie, managing to keep a straight face.

"So that's why I'd like you both home before dark," said Aunt Myrtle. "I don't think either of you have anything to worry about, but better safe than sorry."

Fin's deliveries rarely took longer than an hour, so it wouldn't be a problem. "When's my mom supposed to get home?" she asked.

Aunt Myrtle sighed. "She's working a late shift, honey. She said there were leftovers in the fridge, or you could eat with us if you want."

Fin nodded. She knew she'd eat dinner in the cottage; she didn't want to overstay her welcome.

She slipped out of the kitchen before anyone could notice she was leaving.

FOUR

Deliveries and Gossip

There were people who thought the magic had appeared after Aldermere was founded. They were wrong—Aldermere had been founded *because* of the magic.

No one knew where the magic came from. One of the older lumberjacks, Frank, claimed it was to do with magnetic poles. Some shift in the world, a glitch that made impossible things possible. Others said it was because this place was untouched by technology—which was a lie. Fin knew nearly every house had a landline and most had computers.

There had been a previous town farther inland—Redfern. That town had been abandoned in the early eighties when its magic had vanished and reappeared ten miles west.

Aldermere had been built up around the displaced magic. Aunt Myrtle had mentioned that Gas Station Nick had mapped out the new boundaries of the magic—Fin wasn't sure how. He had discovered that the magic flourished in an area of about seven square miles, most of it reaching into the redwood forest.

Magic wasn't like in the movies. There weren't any spells or chanted words. No, the magic of Aldermere was strange and uncontrolled—but those who had lived within the boundaries of the town had figured out some of its quirks.

If the ravens of Aldermere weren't given a shiny trinket, or bread or some other tasty treat each week, they'd go hunting for their own treats in the offender's garbage bins. Often the contents would be strewn about the street, making for an unsightly mess. Mayor Downer had once put forth the idea of trying to drive the ravens out of Aldermere, but everyone else agreed it would be an exercise in futility.

Then there were the doors. Unlabeled doors could lead anywhere. Fin hadn't believed that until she'd tried to use the restroom at the coffee shop, not having noticed that the bathroom sign had fallen off. She had stepped through and found herself in a broom closet at the inn. Eddie once commented it was a lucky thing that people could only go astray within the boundaries of the magic, or else they'd be popping up all over the world.

There were other things, as well: prophecies supposedly always came true; something that lived in Bower's Creek would occasionally eat wandering pets; the tea shop vanished and reappeared; drinks had to be consumed in less than six hours or they'd turn into kombucha; the abandoned toll bridge had a price but no one knew what it was; and if a person cut themself on a knife, the blade would try again. Sometimes people would exchange used knives for holidays, to avoid bad cuts—or if they had the money, buy a new knife. Luckily other utensils didn't seem to have any particular taste for human blood.

None of this was ever explained to the tourists.

Three types of tourists visited Aldermere: the cryptid/ magic hunters, the hikers, and people who needed a place to stop while road-tripping along Highway 101.

The first type were the most worrisome. They came to find Bigfoot and other mythological creatures, often armed with cameras and compasses. Some believed in magic, while others simply *wanted* to believe. They came for tales of cryptids, for redwood carvings, for plush squirrels with antlers, for the tiny magic shop that sold crystal balls and card tricks and tarot readings. Most of Aldermere's residents scoffed at those who came to town looking for magic and walked away with postcards instead—but no one stopped selling those postcards, either.

As for the hikers, they were good to have around. They sported athletic wear, bought maps of the local trails, stayed at the inn, and didn't spend too much time within the town itself. And the road-trippers were usually bleary-eyed, drank plenty of coffee, and asked where the nearest public restroom could be found.

During the summer months, there was a steady flow of people coming in and out of town. Some locals complained, while others welcomed them. Because like it nor not, most of the town's businesses were kept afloat by such visitors.

When Fin was ten, her aunt had asked her to deliver a package to Harry Hardin—the owner of the town's only grocery store: ALDERMERE GROCERY & ACK. It was probably supposed to say GROCERY & TACKLE, but the other letters had long since rusted away. It had become town shorthand to say "the Ack" instead of "grocery store."

In addition to reading tarot and fashioning wind chimes out of broken abalone, Aunt Myrtle also painted watercolor postcards and sold them all over town. "Would you be a dear and run this over to the Ack?" Aunt Myrtle had said as she handed over the package.

Fin had carried the box to the grocery store. She would

have asked Eddie to go with her, but he'd found a fallen birds' nest and was trying to put it back in a tree. Mr. Hardin was behind the counter, and he had smiled at her when she'd slid the box onto the counter.

"Cheers," he had said. He had a faint British accent and wrinkles etched around his mouth. He had lived in Aldermere for years now, a permanent fixture behind the grocery store's counter. "Would you mind doing another errand? Mrs. Liu needs a prescription, but I haven't had time to run it over to her. Her hip's acting up again."

Fin hadn't known how to refuse, even though the idea of another delivery made her stomach tight with nerves. So she had taken the paper bag and the address and walked out of the store. The walk was a short one—all walks in Aldermere were—and soon Fin found herself on the doorstep of a simple white cottage, with an ancient woman pressing a wrinkled five-dollar bill into her hand and saying how much Fin looked like her mother, and how dear it had been for Fin to bring an old woman her medicine, and—

Fin had slipped away before the older woman could invite her in for cookies and conversation.

And so, when Fin had gone into the grocery store a few days later for milk, Mr. Hardin had asked if she would take a bag of food to another one of the town's older residents.

"How about this," he had said. "Your mother's got an account here—I'll add a little bit to it for every delivery. Sound fair?"

Mom worked at the inn. She often came home a little tired and worn, but it was better than the other places she'd worked for. A few times, Fin overheard Mom talking to Aunt Myrtle about trying to save money, but the inn didn't pay much. If running errands for Mr. Hardin helped her mom, Fin would do it.

And so for a year now, Fin had stopped by the grocery store on Tuesdays and delivered packages for Mr. Hardin. Most of the time it was small stuff: medicines, favorite cookies, special orders of fishing equipment, and letters that mistakenly came to the store. Mail had a tendency to go astray in Aldermere. They were normal deliveries—until they weren't. Once, Mr. Hardin gave her a live rabbit to be brought to a young man at the edge of town; another time, a sealed paper bag was to be left in the woods behind the coffee shop.

Everyone became accustomed to seeing Fin flit about town, running errands for Mr. Hardin. Knocking on unfamiliar doors never became any easier, but she did like the sense of purpose. It made her feel like she could belong in Aldermere. And the extra money for groceries helped too.

The Ack looked like most of the businesses in town.

The buildings were all reclaimed redwood, with uneven floors and windows with old-fashioned panels. She'd once asked Mr. Hardin why so much of the town looked like a Wild West film. "Tourists expect it," he said. "The biggest Northern California exports were logging and history. Now, we've mostly got the latter."

Today she stepped through the doors of the grocery store and found Mr. Hardin on a stepladder, replacing an overhead light bulb. A cat was winding around the lowest step, making plaintive sounds. "—just fed you," Mr. Hardin was saying.

The cat glared, tail twitching. Then it hunched over and made a hacking noise.

"No," said Mr. Hardin, alarmed. "Do not do that in the store!" He began to clamber down the ladder.

Fin stepped back, disgusted, as the cat coughed something onto the floor. It looked like a dead mouse—or it would have, if the creature didn't have ten legs sticking out of its tiny, furry body.

Mr. Hardin reached down to scoop up the creature with a paper towel. "I told you to stop hunting the whintossers," he told the cat.

"I thought those things stayed underground," said Fin, wrinkling her nose. Of all the strange creatures in Aldermere, the whintossers were among the most harmless. They used all of those feet to dig intricate tunnel systems, then nibbled the roots of ferns. Sometimes they got into people's gardens, but a sprinkle of cayenne pepper usually sent them scurrying away.

"They do, for the most part." Mr. Hardin dropped the towel and dead creature both into the trash. "But the cat keeps bringing them inside. Last week a tourist saw him chewing on one and thought we'd glued extra legs on."

Fin glanced at the cat. "Have you named him yet?"

He shook his head. "Moment we name him, we'll be his."

She frowned. "Wouldn't he belong to you?"

Mr. Hardin let out a breath that was half huff, half laugh. "Maybe with a dog. With cats, it's the other way around."

Fin didn't argue; she'd never had any pets—besides a potted plant that she'd left behind in Modesto. And she was pretty sure succulents didn't count. "Do you have anything for me today?"

Mr. Hardin vanished into the stockroom, then returned with three small boxes. "Two for Mr. Madeira. They were supposed to go to his house, but my wife found them near the gas station. Along with some feathers."

Sure enough, two of the boxes had a few ragged holes in the side—about the size of a raven's beak.

"And this one is for your mom, actually," he finished.

Fin took the three boxes, stacking them from biggest to smallest. Eddie kept joking about her using a little red wagon or something to carry her deliveries, but so far she'd managed.

Mr. Madeira only lived two doors down from the big house. He cooked for the inn and often gave her scones instead of tips. This time of the day, he would be working in the kitchen, which meant she'd only have one stop: the inn.

She gave the cat a scratch under his chin, then carefully walked out of the grocery store. She liked Aldermere best in the hour that most people were having dinner—it was quieter, fewer people walking about. It was why Fin picked this time to do her deliveries; there was less chance of running into anyone.

"Hey, Fin!"

Cedar was sitting outside Brewed Awakening. Fin liked delivering things to the coffee shop. Mr. Carver had warm brown skin, an easy smile, and tattoos on both forearms. His shirts were always rolled up to the elbow as he pulled shots of espresso and chatted with customers. He would offer Fin a hot chocolate whenever she brought her deliveries. Mrs. Carver was taller than her husband, her blond hair always short, and she jogged the length of Aldermere every morning.

Cedar looked more like her dad. Her dark hair was chin length, and it reminded Fin of old movie stars. She always looked effortlessly comfortable with herself, which only made Fin feel more awkward. Now Cedar waved at Fin, gesturing her over. Fin pasted on a smile.

Fin didn't *not* like people. She just liked them best at a distance. She found far more comfort in her own company, in the mystery books she checked out from the school library, even in the games she sometimes played on Eddie's computer. Pages and pixels were easier to deal with. She didn't spend hours afterward worrying that she'd said the wrong thing.

"Hi, Fin," said Cedar. "You have deliveries today?" She nodded at the packages in Fin's arms.

Fin nodded. "Yeah, it's Tuesday." Then she cringed because it was such an obvious thing to say. But if Cedar noticed Fin's awkwardness, she didn't say anything. Fin took half a step back, but Cedar didn't notice that, either.

"Anything for us?" Cedar asked.

"Not today," said Fin.

"You have any plans for after you're done?"

Fin hesitated. This sounded like a leading question, but Fin wasn't sure where it was leading to. Maybe Cedar was trying to get out of working in the coffee shop, or maybe she wanted to know if Eddie was around. People liked to hang around with Eddie at school; he was always cheerful and friendly.

"Homework," Fin finally said, because it was the truth. "Math. And I need to talk to Eddie about our science fair project."

Cedar looked crestfallen for all of a heartbeat. Then her face was smiling and natural, her posture relaxed. "Ah. Of course you're paired up with Eddie—you two are best friends, right?"

"He's my cousin," said Fin.

"Still," said Cedar, her smile a little wistful. "Must be nice." She gave Fin one last nod. "I'll see you at school, okay?"

"Yeah." Fin turned and hurried toward the inn. She breathed a little easier when she was on her own.

The inn was Aldermere's biggest business. It had been bought by some far-off wealthy businessman from San Francisco a few years back. He'd renovated the old buildings, employed a few more of the townspeople, and made the occupants of Aldermere simultaneously grateful and resentful. Mom had worked there ever since moving to Aldermere—first at the front desk, then as a manager. The hours were long, but it was a steady job, Mom liked her coworkers, and there was a free meal every day.

Fin carried the boxes up to the front doors, balancing them on one knee as she struggled to reach for the handle.

The door swung open, and Fin looked up.

Bellhop Ben stood over her. He was tall and lanky, with ash-blond hair and eyes more dishwater gray than blue. "Finley," he said with a smile. "Need some help?"

"I've got it," she said, but she allowed him to hold the door open for her. She shifted the packages, trying to take a tighter hold on them. "Is Mr. Madeira working tonight?"

"He's in the midst of the dinner rush at the moment," said Ben. Then he shrugged. "Or what counts as a rush in September. I think there's like three guys in the dining room."

When Fin first met Ben three years ago, she had thought him like any adult. Only recently had she realized he couldn't be much older than the kids who went to high school on the bus with her. From a few scattered conversations, she knew he'd grown up in Aldermere with a single mom. He'd gone off to Santa Rosa for community college, but when his mom got cancer, he returned without graduating. After his mom passed away, he'd remained in Aldermere and started working at the inn.

"I can take those boxes," he said. "It isn't like I've got a lot to do around here."

Fin shook her head. "I've got it," she said again. She knew

the inn as well as her cottage; sometimes she did homework in the staff lounge or helped her mother fold towels. It was something to do, and she got to see Mom.

Ben nodded. "So, everything all right?" Something in his voice made her think it wasn't a casual question.

Fin froze in mid step. "Are you talking about Mrs. Brackenbury?"

Ben's gaze was steady on her. "No, I mean, I was on my way to work when I saw ambulance lights. You and your cousin were talking to some EMTs near the tea shop. I thought someone must've had an accident or something."

A chill slipped down her ribs, settling in Fin's belly. "Oh," she said. "I—yes."

Ben leaned against the front desk. "What happened?"

It was natural that he'd want to know, Fin told herself. It was town gossip, the kind that everyone loved to indulge in. But even as Fin tried to remind herself that she'd done nothing wrong by going into the shop, she felt as though he'd shone a spotlight down upon her. She squirmed a little, her gaze going to the far wall. "Talia fell," she said. "A stool broke."

"Ah," he said, understanding. "My great-aunt once broke her hip in a fall and had to stay in the hospital for a week. You know if Talia broke any bones?"

Fin shrugged. "No idea."

"Well, I hope she comes back soon," said Ben. "I know a lot of people around here depend on her tea." He stepped back behind the desk as a woman wearing hiking boots and carrying a backpack walked into the lobby. Ben flashed Fin one last smile and then turned to the tourist.

Grateful for the reprieve, Fin hurried down the hall toward the kitchen. She could hear the clanging before she nudged open the door with her foot. It swung open easily, and the smell of garlic mashed potatoes and roasted meat made her stomach grumble. She almost regretted not taking one of those protein balls from Eddie. Almost . . . but not quite.

Mr. Madeira was barking orders to a server, but when he saw Fin, his face softened. "Finley! Those for me?"

"These two," she said. "Where can I put them?"

"Just set them under the table behind you," he said. "If those are the knives I ordered, I can start cleaning them tonight."

"More knives?" asked Fin.

Mr. Madeira scoffed. "We've got a new hire. Didn't realize that knives are a one-use thing if they cut you. Kept right on using it."

Fin winced.

Mr. Madeira nodded sympathetically. "She'll be all right. I mean, we found the finger in time." He kept right on working as he talked, throwing salt and pepper onto a steak. "Didn't know which knife it was. Couldn't risk another accident, so I had to buy new ones."

Fin set the two heavy boxes down, her arms aching with relief. Her mother's package was light, at least.

"Wait!" Mr. Madeira nodded to one of the servers—a harried-looking young woman. "Put together a to-go box. Roasted chicken, potatoes, asparagus." He looked to Fin. "That all right?"

"You don't have to," she began to say, but the server was already moving. Her fingers were a blur as she packed up the box, then slipped it into a paper bag. She held it out to Fin.

Fin hesitated, then took it. Technically, both she and her mom got one free meal a day from the inn—but it was normally day-old leftovers, not fresh dinner fare. And while Fin didn't like the feeling of charity, the thought of cold lasagna back at home wasn't quite as appealing as herb-roasted chicken and vegetables. "Thanks," she said.

"Thank you for the knives," he said with a grin. "Now I can stop using these dull things I dragged out of storage."

Fin hastened out of the kitchen, letting the doors swing shut behind her. She left behind the clanking of dishes and the sound of Mr. Madeira grumbling at the steak, and set off toward the back offices.

Fin wasn't quite sure of all the things Mom did as assistant manager—some days she helped out with laundry, others, she soothed customer complaints, and sometimes she lurked in the office for hours at a time with stacks of paper. The door was labeled with a metal nameplate: ASSISTANT MANAGER OFFICE. Fin knocked, then opened the door. Mom sat behind the desk, typing at her computer.

She looked up at Fin, a brief smile tugging at her mouth. Then her lips pulled taut, and it reminded Fin of when she helped out at the inn sometimes, of making beds and pulling sheets tight across the mattress.

"Hey, Mom." Fin set the package on the desk. "Delivery."

Mom picked it up, turned it over. "Ah, good."

"What is it?" Fin asked, hoping maybe it was something exciting.

"New business cards," said Mom. Fin's shoulders slumped a little. "Let me guess—you were hoping books?"

Fin shrugged. "We haven't gone to the bookstore in a while."

"I know." Mom's lips pursed. "And I will make time, once Sofia gets back from maternity leave. Until then, I'm running the inn." She sat a little straighter, her fingers folding together. "Fin, you should know that Frank came to the inn to speak with his niece. She's working as a server."

Fin blinked, surprised. "She wasn't the one that lost a finger, was she?"

"No," said Mom. "She's fine."

"Well," said Fin, "that's good." For all that the town was small, sometimes she had trouble parsing the tangled threads of relatives and friends—everyone was connected to everyone somehow.

Mom nodded. "Frank said that Talia had an accident—that Eddie ran over to ask him to call an ambulance."

Ice formed in Fin's stomach. She forced her face to remain impassive.

Mom fixed Fin with a stare as piercing as one of those needles that were shoved through dead insects. It made Fin want to look away, to spill every secret she'd ever had. Mom let the silence stretch out until it was painful.

"You went to the tea shop," said Mom, finally. "Again."

Fin winced. "It was only . . . I had a delivery and—"

"Don't lie to me." Mom's voice went a little ragged. "I know why you went there. I know why everyone goes there." She rose from her seat and walked around the desk. She took Fin by the shoulders and squeezed gently. "I know why. But you can't. It's dangerous, sweetheart. It costs too much—and it isn't going to help anything."

Fin bit down on the tip of her tongue.

Mom didn't understand. Mom had no fear of picking up phones or answering doors. She was . . . she was . . .

Normal.

Fin forced herself to think the word.

"Listen," said Mom, more gently. "I want you to go home, okay? Did you hear about the mugging?"

Fin nodded, glad that the subject of the tea shop had been dropped. "Aunt Myrtle told us."

Mom reached out, pushed a strand of Fin's hair behind her ear. "Good. If you want to have dinner with Myrtle and Eddie, I'm sure it'd be all right."

Fin held up the paper bag. "Mr. Madeira gave me takeout."

"Okay, sweetheart," said Mom, a little too wearily. Fin hated when she sounded like that: worn thin with exhaustion and worry. Fin wanted to fix it, but she didn't know how.

"I'll see you later." Mom kissed Fin's forehead, giving her shoulder a squeeze. It made Fin feel a little better.

Fin slipped out of the office. Her steps were quick, her eyes focused straight ahead. The day pressed down on her, and all she wanted was the familiarity of her cottage. Her heartbeat was unsteady, her hands clammy around the paper bag's handle.

She half walked, half jogged through Aldermere, past the familiar broken sidewalks and watchful ravens. There was a path around Aunt Myrtle's home, and she took it rather than going through the house itself. A glance at the window, and she saw Eddie and Aunt Myrtle sitting at their dining room table. Fin knew that table: it had been built of an old door, the knob taken out and the square edges polished soft. It was heavy and dented and comfortable, and if she walked inside, they'd ask her to sit down and join them. She didn't.

She walked down the darkening path, across the backyard with its ferns and moss, to the guest cottage that had been Fin's home for three years. The paper label from that first night had been exchanged for a metal one: ANGELINA & FINLEY'S HOME. It was reassuringly permanent, and Fin let her fingers trail over the lettering. Part of her was still scared to love this place, because to love a place meant hurting more the next time they moved.

She unlocked the door, then stepped inside. Her hands moved on reflex—locking the door behind her, flicking on the light, and shrugging out of her light jacket.

The cottage was small, an A-frame with a single bedroom, a little kitchen where she dropped the bag of food, a cozy living room with a tiny woodstove, and a loft. Mom had the bedroom and Fin had the loft. Mom said she didn't want to climb down a ladder every time she needed to use the bathroom, and Fin had been glad to take the space. It was private and hers, a safe sanctuary with bookshelves built into the walls and a window overlooking the forest.

Fin climbed up the ladder, and something pinched along her hip, poking through her worn jeans pocket. She reached into her jeans pocket and withdrew a key. She blinked in surprise.

Talia's spare key. The one for the tea shop. For a moment, she thought wildly of tossing it into the woods, of chucking it as far as she could. If her mother found it, she'd be angry.

Reason reasserted itself, and she forced herself to take a few breaths. The key was unmarked; Mom wouldn't know what it was for. And besides, it wasn't like Mom searched her things. She could put the key on one of her bookshelves until Talia returned from the hospital. She remembered what Ben had said about his great-aunt staying in the hospital for a week with a broken hip. A week wouldn't be so bad. Fin could last a week. Then she could return the key to Talia, buy her cup of tea, and remember what it felt like to be fearless.

FIVE
Overheard Conversations

Mornings were always early.

The moment her alarm went off, Fin stumbled down the ladder and into the minuscule bathroom. Mom had come home sometime around eleven at night, and Fin only had a dim memory of hearing the key in the lock. Fin was used to waking up on her own and making a breakfast of whatever leftovers she found in the fridge. This morning, it was cold lasagna—which wasn't bad. A little drizzle of olive oil and some salt, and she was almost awake by the time she'd eaten half of it.

There wasn't a school in Aldermere; the town wasn't big enough to merit one. Fin, Eddie, and the other town kids walked down to Highway 101, where a bus took them north to the next town over.

Fin walked into the big house through the back door. Eddie was at the dining room table, head on the wood next to a half-eaten bowl of mushy oat bran. Fin set her backpack on the other chair and his head jerked up. "—'m awake," he said, blinking blearily at her.

"Sure you are," she replied, smiling. She liked being better than Eddie at one thing, even if that one thing was being awake early. It made them feel a little more equal. "You going to finish that?"

Eddie picked up a spoonful of oat bran and dolefully shoved it into his mouth.

"You should get a move on, Eddie," said Aunt Myrtle, bustling through the dining room. She still wore her nightgown and a terry-cloth robe belted around her waist. She held out glass containers to both Fin and Eddie. "Here, take some protein balls."

Fin dutifully put the protein balls into her own backpack. Sure, they were weird, but she'd probably eat them if she got hungry enough.

"Listen, you two," said Aunt Myrtle. "This weekend I'm spending two nights in Eureka. And your mom will be working late again, Fin. I was thinking . . . maybe you and Eddie could watch the house?"

Fin blinked. "Us? Alone?"

"You're old enough," said Aunt Myrtle reasonably. "I trust you. And besides, even when she's at work, your mom is only a ten-minute walk away. I'll leave the emergency numbers next to the phone and make sure there's plenty of food in the fridge. Both your mom and I would feel better if you were in the big house, keeping an eye on things."

It was a big responsibility to watch the house in her aunt's absence. "Okay."

Aunt Myrtle smiled. "You're good kids. You'll do fine."

The back door swung open, and Mom stepped into the dining room. She wore a crisp white shirt and slacks, her hair pulled into a ponytail. "Morning," she said briskly.

"Good, you're here," said Aunt Myrtle. "Angie, can we talk upstairs?" She started down the hallway, then added, "Don't forget your backpack, Eddie."

Eddie grumbled into his breakfast.

Mom kissed Fin's hair, then followed Aunt Myrtle upstairs.

"So," said Fin. "They're leaving us in charge of the big house?"

"Well, it'll give us time to work on our science fair presentation this weekend," Eddie replied.

Fin just looked at him. "You're the only person I know who'd work on school stuff instead of eating candy and playing video games."

"We'll do that too," said Eddie. "After we grab four or five native plants and maybe two lizards. I'll find the kind that won't fight each other. Somehow I feel like a lizard battle royale wouldn't get us a great grade." He glared down at his breakfast. "Maybe if I find a really rare kind of lizard, I can finally get first place over River and his oh-so-great energy-converting Popsicle windmill."

Fin snorted with surprised laughter. "Good plan."

Eddie ate another bite of oat bran. "I'm going to beat River. This year. I can feel it."

"Sure," said Fin amiably. She rose from the table. "Listen, I'm going to use the bathroom and then we'll head out, okay?"

He made a noise of acknowledgment, but she was pretty sure he was still imagining himself with a first place ribbon.

She walked up the stairs, one hand on the dented railing, but her footsteps slowed when she heard voices. She'd forgotten that Mom and Aunt Myrtle were up here. The sound of her own name made her go still, her foot frozen over one step.

"—thought Fin was done with the tea shop." That would

be Mom. "I don't know what to do, how to keep her from going there."

"Listen, Angie. I have a counselor friend up in Eureka," said Aunt Myrtle. "I was going to ask if maybe she'd use a sliding scale. Then it wouldn't cost so much."

Fin could hear her mother's hesitation in the silence.

"You can't expect this to go away. Mental health disorders aren't something that vanish if you ignore them. You've tried ignoring it for far too long."

"I know," said Mom, and she sounded exhausted. "I'd hoped she'd outgrow it, maybe if the constant moves stopped . . . but I suppose we should try this."

"My friend specializes in child psychology," said Aunt Myrtle. "She's nice. If I ask, she'll probably be amenable."

Chest too tight, fingers too cold, Fin took a step back down the stairs. Then another. And another. Until she stood at the bottom, and her back was to the wall and she tried to breathe.

A counselor. Fin knew what that meant. She'd read about them. A counselor was the person kids were sent to when they were screwed up.

Fin's hands clenched.

She felt like there were two versions of herself—the girl who flinched at the sound of ringing phones, who worked up every fearful moment in her head, who listened at cracked doors and windows.

And then there was the girl she wanted to be. She caught sight of that girl only in glances, in moments when she walked by a window and barely turned her head. She saw a girl with flashing brown eyes and a half smile, who looked like she knew all the secrets of the world. She was the kind of girl who read old mystery books in the cafeteria without fearing what anyone would think. She raised her hand in English class, because she'd done the reading weeks ahead of time. She didn't necessarily have more friends, but she didn't crave them. That version of Fin was comfortable with herself.

Fin couldn't ever be that girl. She tried—she tried so hard. To do the breathing exercises like her mother had taught her, to push past the fear, but that only ever seemed to make it worse.

And now even Aunt Myrtle thought she needed a counselor. She thought Fin had a *disorder*.

She wanted it to stop. To have a week, a day, an hour—just a minute—when she wasn't afraid.

She thought of the taste of Ceylon tea, of leaning over a crystal mortar and pestle and whispering a memory.

Fin had never stolen before. She was far too aware

of how it would feel to be caught, too anxious of the consequences. But she wouldn't steal now either. She had a key, so it wouldn't be breaking into the tea shop. She would pay the normal price.

She would . . . make the tea herself.

SIX
The First Heist

Fin had been nine years old the first time she'd found the tea shop. It had taken her a year. Mostly because she wasn't looking for it.

It had been a cold autumn day. Mist clung to the ground and fog to the trees, and the grass was stiff with late-morning frost. Fin wore her heaviest coat; it was secondhand, the fabric thick and rough. It looked like some kind of army coat, and when Fin put it on, she imagined herself as a spy or warrior. Someone fearless.

Eddie had asked her for a favor—Aunt Myrtle had some books that needed to be returned to a friend. He'd been sidetracked rescuing a lizard caught by the neighbor's cat. So Fin followed Main Street away from the big house, the paper bag full of borrowed books tucked against her chest. She walked by Mrs. Liu's home; the older woman was sweeping redwood needles from her porch. Mayor Downer was on the other side of the street, surreptitiously glancing around before taking a ruler to someone's lawn, measuring the height of the grass. She'd been sending out notices to townspeople who had overgrown lawns, but most of those official-looking letters ended up in the trash. A few ravens sat on a roof, watching sunlight glint off the ruler.

Even after a year, Fin still didn't feel like she entirely belonged in Aldermere. She loved it—the magic and the strangeness—but she still felt slightly out of step with all of the town's other residents. She glanced up at the street signs.

Oak Street. That was where Eddie had said to go. *That's where Talia's tea shop is right now.*

Talia. The moment Fin thought the name, it was as if a heat wave rose from the pavement. The air rippled, and then she saw it for the first time.

The sign for Talia's tea shop was only a few feet away.

It was true, then. The tea shop was magical.

Fin had pushed open the wooden gate and walked up to the front door. There was the usual flutter of fear when she knocked at the door, but this time it was accompanied by a little eagerness too. She liked uncovering mysteries, and this tea shop promised all kinds of mystery.

"Come in."

The tea shop looked like an old apothecary's shop, full of old jars and vintage furniture. Fin tiptoed inside, the bag of books clutched tightly in her arms. "Hello?" she had said tentatively.

A woman behind the counter had gray hair and a stripe of red-orange lipstick across her mouth. She must have been Talia. When she saw Fin, she nodded. "Hi there."

"Hi," said Fin. "I—I brought these." She shoved the bag onto the counter and Talia reached inside, pulling out a paperback.

"Oh, Myrtle sent you," Talia said a little more warmly. "Are you her niece?"

"My mom and I moved here a year ago."

Talia nodded. "And why did you come in here?"

Fin frowned at the bag of books. "My cousin Eddie—Aunt Myrtle asked him to deliver these, but he was busy—"

"I didn't ask why Edward didn't come in here," said Talia. There was no sharpness to her words, but Fin felt scolded nonetheless. "I asked why you did."

Fin shrugged, unsure of what else to do. "I—he asked me to."

Talia set the book down, then leaned over the counter.

Her eyes were bright and keen, like those of a bird. "I'm going to tell you a secret. No one comes in here unless they have a reason. And no one stays away unless there's a reason. There's always a reason." The way she said it reminded Fin of how Mom had uttered the rules of Aldermere.

"Is it true?" asked Fin abruptly. Before she could lose her nerve. "That these teas are magic?"

Talia glanced over her shoulder at the hand-labeled mason jars full of dried flowers and teas. "I suppose that depends on your definition of the word." The way she spoke was matter-of-fact, like this was a real conversation instead of an adult indulging a kid. It made Fin feel a little bit braver.

"I heard," said Fin haltingly. "I heard that these teas . . . can change a person."

"Is that what you want?" asked Talia. "To change?"

"I want . . . ," Fin started, then faltered.

The truth was, Fin wanted a lot of things. She wanted more books; she wanted a certain shirt she'd seen another girl wearing at school; she wanted time to herself; she wanted to be able to ask for things without wondering if she was doing something wrong; she wanted Mom to be home more; she wanted—

"Everything to stop being scary," she finally said.

Talia nodded. Then she reached for one of the mason jars. Fin watched, unsure but fascinated, as Talia measured out a scoop of brown-leafed tea. A heavy mortar and pestle sat atop the counter. It was made of some pink crystal—rose quartz, she would later learn. As she worked, Talia spoke. "I cannot make the world less scary," she said. She talked like one of Fin's teachers, as if she was imparting a lesson. "But according to some, fear is rooted in the self. I can help with that." She spooned the tea into the mortar. "But there's a cost. There's always a cost."

Fin wilted. "I don't have any money." Mom didn't make enough to give Fin an allowance like Eddie had—and Fin had stopped asking for one, because it made Mom look sad.

"You can't trade money for magic," said Talia. "Not real magic, anyway."

"Then what does it cost?" asked Fin, confused.

Talia touched the edge of the mortar. "A memory."

That couldn't be right. "Memories?"

"A single memory," Talia corrected. "You get to choose. But you should know, the bigger and more important the memory, the longer the magic will last. You give me the memory of you picking weeds out of your aunt's garden, and the magic will last maybe two or three days. But if you give me the memory of an important day, the magic can last as long as a month."

"I get to choose?" said Fin. That didn't seem so bad. Everyone had things they wanted to forget. For a moment, that memory of Mom and Aunt Myrtle discussing Fin flashed into her mind—Mom saying that they'd moved because a parent saw something at Fin's school. She could forget that, if she wanted. But no, she decided. As much as that memory prickled at her, she had to hold on to it. If there was some great flaw inside Fin, something that drove Mom to move again and again, then Fin should know. It was the only way she could try and change herself.

"Yes, you will choose." Talia's voice was a little warmer, more understanding. "Magic isn't something you can force upon a person. Pick your memory, and the magic will do the rest."

Fin hadn't chosen many things in her life—a few outfits, that succulent she'd owned in Modesto, what used books she picked up at the store. But big decisions—those were out of her hands.

Again, her mother's words had come back to her.

"Don't look for the tea shop."

Mom had told her not to do this. But Mom was normal; she didn't understand.

"What do I do?" Fin had asked.

"Whisper the memory into the mortar," said Talia. "I

won't listen. I don't need to know. Then I'll brew the tea and you will drink it here."

Fin had been too short to reach the counter. She stepped atop a three-legged stool, forearms flat against the counter, as she stared down into the mortar. The tea leaves were curling and brown and they smelled like spice. Fin closed her eyes and whispered a memory.

She didn't know which one. It was gone the moment it passed her lips.

The tea had tasted a little bitter and sweet. Talia asked her if she wanted milk, but Fin refused it. She drank it down in three scalding gulps, the way she'd first dunked her head beneath water at a swimming lesson. Best to get it over with.

The tea warmed her from the inside out. She felt lighter, as if she'd dropped something she hadn't realized she was carrying. She tried to think of something that scared her.

Goldfish. Big, bulgy-eyed goldfish. She wasn't even sure why she was scared of them, but she was.

When she conjured the image, there was no accompanying rush of nerves. Her heartbeat didn't quicken, her fingers didn't twitch. It was just a thought—and for once, it held no sway over her.

She walked home, her steps light and chin held high.

Fin had been so absorbed in her own happiness that she barely noticed Mayor Downer shouting at a raven, a ruler clutched in its beak.

Friday after school, Fin sat at the table in the big house and listened to Aunt Myrtle bustling around upstairs. She was packing a bag for her trip to Eureka, telling Eddie that he needed to remember to water the pitcher plants she kept on the kitchen windowsill. Mom had gone to her night shift at the inn. Fin worked on math homework; it kept her out of the whirlwind of packing and reminders. Finally Aunt Myrtle kissed Eddie goodbye, waved at Fin, and drove away in her rusty Ford Fiesta. She would be back on Sunday, she told them both. And Mom would return from work early Saturday morning, probably to sleep for most of the day. Dinner was leftover mac and cheese made with strange white cheeses and homemade egg noodles.

Eddie went out into the yard while Fin remained in the big house, pretending to look through the bookshelves for at least half an hour. That seemed like enough time. Then Fin pulled on her heavy army coat and stepped quietly out the front door. The crescent-moon key was in her jeans pocket, but she still touched it to be sure it was there. She glanced from side to side, then hurried across the yard.

"What are you doing?" asked Eddie.

Fin jumped.

Eddie stood under the shadow of a redwood. He had a small blue-bellied lizard carefully held in one hand. The lizard looked rather resigned about the whole thing.

"Nothing," she said.

Eddie raised both brows. He'd spent hours trying the one-brow thing—Fin knew because she had once watched him when their Wi-Fi was down. But he'd never managed. So two-brow incredulity it was. "Where are you going?" he said.

"Nowhere," was her reply.

Eddie looked at Fin. So did the lizard.

"All right," he said.

Fin began walking. Eddie followed after.

She stopped. So did he.

"What?" she said.

"You're doing nothing at nowhere," he said. "Sounds like fun. I'm coming."

She glared at him. Fin didn't make a habit of glaring, but Eddie was safe. Eddie was family. And besides, she knew the glare would have absolutely no impact on him. Disapproval slid off him like oil across a hot skillet.

"Come on," he said. "With Mom off to Eureka and your

mom working, I've got no one to talk to. I promise whatever this is, I won't tell anyone."

She considered. Eddie liked to talk, which meant he wasn't ideal for keeping secrets. But she also didn't know how to leave him behind.

"Fine," she said. "I'm going to the tea shop." She began walking again, and Eddie fell in step beside her, the lizard still in hand.

"You want to see if Talia's back? She isn't. We would've heard."

It was true. The only force in Aldermere as powerful as magic was gossip.

"No," said Fin, and hesitated. "I still have her spare key and—and I never got the tea I need to help me with the science fair."

Eddie blinked. "You're going to steal it?" He sounded more impressed than reproachful.

"No," said Fin. "I'm going to pay for it. But—I mean, I've seen Talia prepare it before. I'll just do it myself, take it home, and drink it."

"Are you sure you can do that?"

"Talia sends tea home with people," Fin said, a little defensively. They walked down Main Street, past the Ack and Mrs. Brackenbury's porch. Mr. Bull was napping on the front steps. "I know that Mr. Madeira keeps some on hand for his wife." Fin had heard other people say that Mrs. Madeira had dementia. It wasn't something medicine could fix, so Mr. Madeira found a different solution. It was whispered, far away from the inn's kitchen, that Mr. Madeira was trading some of his own memories so his wife could keep hers. "And Mrs. Liu has some for her arthritis. Talia probably never sent any home with me because she knew that Mom doesn't like the tea shop."

Eddie absentmindedly wiped dirt from his fingers onto his already-muddy jeans. "I never really talk to Talia much. I mean—I don't even know when you started going to the tea shop."

"Yes, you do," said Fin, raising her eyebrows. "You sent me there."

"I did not," said Eddie. Then he appeared to think it over. "Did I?"

"It was the time Aunt Myrtle wanted you to return romance books to Talia but you had a lizard rescue."

"Oh, yeah," he said brightening. "The neighbor's cat, Tobin, got ahold of him." The lizard currently in Eddie's hand glanced around dejectedly.

The day was a bright one, the autumn sunlight streaming through the overhead foliage and illuminating dust motes and pollen. A few cars were parked outside Brewed Awakening—Fin glimpsed a car full of camera equipment and frowned. Likely a Bigfoot hunter or one of the other cryptid chasers. They were more worrisome than the hikers. They'd also probably find that locals would be less than friendly once they started trying to hunt for monsters in the woods.

Fin veered left onto a gravel side street, and the tea shop came into view. It looked as it always did: an old Victorian house, with peeling paint along the eaves and overgrown ferns at the porch. Fin ducked into the shadows and picked her way through the ferns to the back door. Fear tingled up her fingertips and wrists, a fluttering sensation that made her light-headed. She felt as though the whole world was watching, waiting for her to break the rules.

There was a moment of quiet. Fin looked at the door, then at Eddie. Eddie had one hand in his pocket, and the other held the blue-bellied lizard. "You really going to do this?" he asked.

Fin closed her eyes. She thought of words like "counselor" and "disorder." She thought of Aunt Myrtle quietly telling Mom that Mom wasn't the person she hadn't wanted to see again. She thought of all the little sharp edges inside her, the ones she could never make fit, no matter how hard she tried.

The name plate on the door was small and metal. TEA SHOP, it read.

Fin slid the key into the doorknob and twisted it.

The door opened easily, and they stepped in.

The interior was dark, and it took a few seconds for Fin's eyes to adjust. The scents of Ceylon and old wood settled her, and she breathed a little easier. Things would be better soon. *She* would be better soon.

Eddie shut the door behind them. It was dimmer than Fin remembered, and the shadows made everything more ominous. Fin didn't dare turn on a light, just in case someone saw.

"I've never done this before," said Eddie. "What does Talia usually do?"

Fin thought about it. "She would get the tea down, put it in that mortar, I'd whisper in the memory, then she'd put everything into a tea ball. I'd drink it here, then I'd go home."

The shelves behind the counter were stacked full of mason jars, each hand labeled with a different blend. Fin's gaze slid past the sunset orange of rooibos, an Earl Grey studded with lavender, delicate blossoms of chamomile, curling peppermint leaves, dried fruits, rich brown mattes, and stalks of lemongrass. Some of the jars held desiccated honeycomb, and one even contained a spider that might or might not have been alive.

Fin ignored them all, her attention on a jar of Ceylon. It was what Talia always used for her tea, and Fin wasn't sure if the blend made a difference. She glanced around; she'd never been on this side of the bar before. There were shelves full of random objects: scissors, wooden boxes, a metal pail with FOR ASHES scribbled across the front, balls of twine, a single knitting needle, and finally a wooden footstool. Fin dragged the stool over, then rose on tiptoe, fingers straining for the jar.

"You want me to grab it?" asked Eddie.

"You're shorter than me," said Fin, arm burning as she reached even higher. "Don't think you could—ah!"

Her fingers nudged the jar and it fell forward, tumbling end over end. Fin caught it—barely. She clutched it to her stomach, heart thudding in her chest. When she could breathe properly again, she stepped down from the stool and set the jar on the counter. She measured out the tea—enough to fit into a steel tea ball, she hoped. When Talia did this, it all looked effortless.

Eddie tucked the lizard into his shirt pocket. His wiry arms were used to reaching for tree branches and rocks, and his palms were creased with calluses. He picked up the jar and managed to slide it back into place with a well-placed jump.

"Can you stand over by the chair or something?" said Fin.

Eddie frowned at her. "Why?"

"Because it's awkward if someone's listening," said Fin.

"Tell you what," said Eddie. "I'll stand guard by the back door. Just in case."

Fin waited until he was gone. The memory wouldn't have to be a very big memory—just enough to last until the science fair.

She leaned over the mortar and whispered to the crystal.

The memory was lost the moment it passed her lips.

She straightened, relieved as if she had set down a heavy load. There were a few tea balls beneath the counter and she reached for one.

Something moved outside the window. A shadow fell across the dirty glass.

Her heartbeat picked up, fear making her fingers unsteady. Someone was outside. If they peered through the dusty windows, they might see her.

She scooped the tea into a stainless-steel ball, scattering Ceylon leaves across the counter in her haste. She snapped the ball shut and crammed it into her pocket, then rushed toward the back room. Eddie leaned against the frame of the door, the lizard peering out of his shirt pocket. Fin hissed at him, "There's someone out there. We need to go now."

Together, they rushed outside. Eddie held a hand over his pocket as he went down the porch stairs, and Fin pulled the door shut behind them. She used the crescent-moon key to lock it, then stepped away.

"This way," Eddie whispered, and hurried behind the neighboring house.

Some of the homes were tangled in the redwood forest; the trees loomed high overhead and the undergrowth crept in around the buildings' foundations. The foliage would hide Eddie and Fin from view, but vetch and long grasses dragged at their arms and legs. It felt as if the very forest was trying to get her caught. Her heart hammered against her ribs, and the silver tea ball in her pocket was a heavy weight.

Eddie led them unerringly through the edges of the forest, weaving in and around a few older trees, their roots protruding through the dirt like half-submerged fingers. Before she had lived in Aldermere, Fin had never realized the way the redwoods shaped the world around them. They could block out enough light to cast the world into shadow and churn the ground into new shapes—and when they fell, they created a whole new landscape.

Eddie turned right, and then they came out along the sidewalk. Fin glanced up and down the street, but there was no one. Only Mrs. Brackenbury a few houses down, sitting on her porch swing with her ancient bulldog napping at her feet.

"You sure you saw someone?" asked Eddie, frowning.

Fin remembered the shape of the shadow—narrow shoulders and long head. "Yeah. Someone was by the front windows. I hope they didn't see me inside." She thought of word getting back to Mom and shivered, despite the warm sunlight.

"Probably just someone trying to see if Talia's back," Eddie said dismissively. "Hopefully they won't try to force open the locked door. Having the tea shop vanish now would be . . . bad."

Fin realized what he was thinking.

Talia lived in the tea shop. So when the tea shop vanished, Talia was always inside it. She could step outside, take note of her new address, and tell someone. Word would trickle out until people could find it again.

But if the tea shop vanished with no one inside—

"Would anyone ever find it again?" she asked. "If Talia wasn't in the tea shop when it vanished?"

Eddie shrugged. "No idea. It's never happened before."

A chill unfurled somewhere behind her belly, a niggling dread that she tried to push away.

"Come on," said Eddie. "We should get home before Mrs. Brackenbury asks us in for cookies or something. I heard she's telling anyone who stands still about the mugging, and while she's nice, Mr. Bull always drools on my shoes."

Fin nodded and followed as he turned down the street. She glanced over her shoulder one last time as they rounded the corner.

The tea shop stood there, as solid and still as ever. Windows opaque and dark.

No sign of anyone at all.

SEVEN
Brew with Caution

Fin made the tea when they returned to the big house.

The tea ball had come open in her coat pocket, so Fin had to scrape out the tea leaves, and she was pretty sure a bit of lint got into the tea. But Fin didn't care so long as it worked.

The electric kettle bubbled merrily and its blue light clicked off. Fin picked it up and carefully poured the boiling water into a chipped blue mug. Steam rose in delicate tendrils, and the steel tea ball swung between her fingers on its chain before she lowered it into the mug.

Eddie was rummaging around in a closet. He swore he had an old fish tank in there—they could use it for their terrarium. Fin ignored the distant sounds of old cans, papers, and other clutter being tossed about; she watched as the water slowly turned a deep brown color. The scent of Ceylon filled the air, and Fin breathed it in. Maybe it was her imagination, but she was calmer already.

Once five minutes had passed, Fin pulled the tea ball up, setting it on a saucer. The mug was still warm to the touch, but the tea wouldn't burn her.

Fin drank. The tea had a malty flavor lightened with citrus and a hint of sweetness and spice. When she was finished, she put the mug down and waited.

For the briefest moment, there was that knot at the back of her mind—thoughts of *I can't do the science fair and stand up in front of all those people!* and *Oh, what if Mom finds out I went back to the tea shop?* and *What if someone saw?* and *Counselor, counselor, counselor,* and—

The knot *loosened.*

It was like releasing a fist that Fin hadn't realized she'd been making.

She took one breath, then another.

Fin leaned against the counter. She summoned up the mental image of the phone ringing, of the shrill noise it would make, of having to answer it without knowing who was on the other end. She waited for the telltale thump of her fearful heart—but it never came.

If the phone rang, she'd just answer it.

Fin smiled. A real smile, the kind that crinkled at the corners of her mouth and had made a couple of candid photos embarrassing.

This—this was how normal people felt all the time. She wondered if they knew how lucky they were.

Fin picked up the tea ball. She unscrewed it and dumped the soggy tea leaves into the sink. She hit the garbage disposal and water, listened to the engine grumble to life, then turned it off. She rinsed the ball out, then shoved it into her pocket. She'd put it away in the cottage. And when Talia came back—because she would come back—Fin would return it to her, along with the key. No one would ever know.

Everything was going to be fine.

And for the first time in weeks, Fin actually believed that.

Most of the evening was spent in the backyard. In the waning sunlight, Fin sat on a tree stump with a plant identification book spread out across her legs, while Eddie rummaged around in the undergrowth. The lizard was still in his pocket, and it occasionally popped its head out before vanishing again. It wasn't enough to have ferns or wildflowers, not for Eddie. He wanted this terrarium to be perfect—which meant native and rare plants. Along with whatever lizards wouldn't eat each other. Two plants were safely dug up and transplanted. As for the lizard, it would remain a single occupant for now.

They set up the tank with food and water, and a few sticks for the lizard to climb on, and then they made dinner for themselves. Well, they heated up the mac and cheese. Then they retreated upstairs to Eddie's room, where he played some video game on his laptop while Fin dug out a mystery book she hadn't read yet. She liked the older ones best. The kind with moors and hidden attics and British words. There was a single bookshop in town, and mostly it dealt in donated mass market paperbacks and a few *New York Times* bestsellers that tourists would read. The owner, a middle-aged woman called Amalita, put aside any classic detective stories for Fin. Particularly the ones that always ended up in the fifty-cent bin.

Now Fin reclined on the bed and lost herself in historical London while Eddie attacked zombies in some medieval land. "Come on," he was muttering. "Stop respawning—oh, come on. Healing yourself is a cheat."

"Boss monster giving you a hard time?" asked Fin. She turned a page, the worn paper soft against her fingertips.

"It won't stop eating health potions and getting bigger," said Eddie. "You want a try?"

"I'll pass." Fin preferred the kinds of games where she went on quests to gather potion materials or fetch items for helpless villagers. Monster fights weren't her thing.

When it was around nine, Fin dug out a sleeping bag from the hallway closet. She'd sleep on the floor, atop a foam pad with a borrowed pillow. She'd done it before when the cottage's roof leaked. She took a step toward the bedroom, but a sudden noise made her go still.

A clatter—like pots rattling. "Mom?" she called down the stairs. But Mom was working the late shift again, wasn't she? She shouldn't have been back yet.

There was no answer.

Fin took a step toward the stairs. It was dark; Aunt Myrtle had no hall lights, saying they drained electricity. Fin cocked her head and listened.

Another clatter—this time even louder. Fin jumped. She set the sleeping bag down and poked her head into the bedroom. "Eddie?"

Eddie was in the midst of climbing up a virtual mountain, killing zombies the whole way. "Yeah?" he said distractedly.

"I think something's downstairs."

He frowned, pausing the game. "Something like . . ."

"Something that made a noise."

His frown deepened. "Did you leave a window open?"

"I never open the windows," she said. "Yours don't have screens and bugs can get in."

Eddie rose from his chair and walked to the doorway, head angled so he could hear better. For a moment, neither moved.

"Are you sure . . . ," Eddie began—and then there was a distinct sound of something falling from the counter.

Eddie and Fin looked at each other, eyes wide and faces pale in the light of the computer screen. All of a sudden, that frozen image of zombies mobbing Eddie's character seemed less than comforting.

"What do we do?" Fin whispered.

Eddie glanced around. Then he went to his closet and withdrew a—

"You have got to be kidding me," Fin hissed. "A lacrosse stick? You don't even play!"

"I used it to catch frogs once," he whispered back. "And I don't have a baseball bat."

"Well, that's great if our intruder is a frog!" Fin's stomach turned over. "What if it's the mugger?"

Eddie squared his shoulders. "We have to go downstairs. The only phone is downstairs. You grab the phone, I'll go into the kitchen. If I yell, call someone."

It was a terrible plan, and part of Fin wanted to shut the bedroom door and wedge a chair beneath the doorknob, but even if they did that, there was no way out. They were on the second story and there were no good trees to climb from the window. They were trapped.

"If I die, release the lizard in the forest, okay?" Eddie whispered. "Oh, and tell my mom I love her."

Fin glared at him. "I am not touching that lizard, so you better live."

He nodded and, still holding the lacrosse stick, began to edge toward the stairs. They moved as silently as they could. Eddie knew which stairs creaked, and he avoided them; Fin followed in his footsteps. They descended slowly, ever so slowly, and Fin thought she might shake apart, she was so scared.

This wasn't her normal anxiety, that low buzz that crowded in on her thoughts at all hours of the day. This was well-earned fear—the rational kind.

When they reached the hallway, Eddie gestured her toward the living room, where the corded phone would be resting on the coffee table. Then he took a step into the kitchen. Fin considered grabbing him and dragging him with her, because he was her cousin and she didn't want him to be murdered by some mugger because the only weapon they had was a frog-catching lacrosse stick.

But then he was too far out of reach. So she turned and tiptoed into the living room. There was barely enough light to see by—faint moonlight cast the edges of the furniture into fuzzy outlines and shapes. Fin navigated more by memory than anything else, creeping around the secondhand couch and bookshelves. There was a desk covered in scattered papers; this was where Aunt Myrtle conducted her business and took orders. Fin rested her hand on the phone and waited. Her heartbeat was a steady drum in her chest, pounding so hard she was sure anyone who came near enough would hear it.

She waited. For the sound of a fight, for a yell, for anything.

Eddie said, "Fin? Um. I think it's coming from the sink."

"The sink?" she said, and her hand slipped away from the phone. Sure enough, the kitchen was empty but for Eddie. He held the stick loosely at his side.

"Something's shaking the sink," he said. "That's why a pot fell off the counter."

"Seriously?" said Fin. "That can't be—"

The sink quivered.

"Did something crawl down there?" said Eddie, sounding

more alarmed than truly scared. "Did—did the lizard get out?" He turned and sprinted in the direction of their terrarium, tripping over a broom as he went. Fin remained still, watching. Every breath was sandpaper in her lungs.

She knelt, reached down, and opened the cupboard beneath the sink. There were a few bottles of half-full cleaning supplies: a lemon-scented soap for the floor, wood polish, and scattered rubber bands. The U-bend of the sink looked old, the plastic stained.

It *shivered.*

A bit of dust slipped to the floor. There was something alive down there. A mouse or maybe a whintosser. They had dealt with mice in the past, Eddie putting out cheese and boxes so he could release them back into the forest.

The pipe shuddered harder and Fin recoiled, tripping over her own legs. She fell, gazing at the dark space beneath the sink.

She wanted to cry out, to yell for Eddie. It was like one of those dreams when she couldn't speak loud enough for anyone to hear her—and she was awake.

The wire-mesh sink strainer jumped, shook once, then flew into the air. It hit the counter, traces of food still trapped between the wires, and rolled to the floor. Fin gaped at it—then she saw the *thing* creeping up and out of the sink.

It moved like something boneless, weightless. It reminded her of a video she'd seen of squid gliding along an ocean floor.

One tendril slipped out of the sink's drain, feeling about as if searching for something.

Then another tendril slipped free, and the creature lifted itself up and out of the pipe.

It was dark brown, slick and damp. For a moment it sat there, swaying back and forth. It was not like any animal that Fin had ever seen—it had no mouth, no eyes, no face.

It was not an animal at all. Which meant it had to be magic.

Fin could not breathe. She could not move. She feared if she even twitched a finger, that thing would see her and lunge.

And for the first time, Fin thought she understood why Mom had told Fin to stay away from the tea shop: because magic was not just hungry ravens and doors that led to places they should not. It was dark and slimy and something altogether unknown.

Fin's lungs burned, and she took the shakiest of breaths.

The creature seemed to notice Fin. It had no eyes, but she had the distinct impression it was studying her. A ripple curved along its surface, and its edges solidified.

It raised itself higher, sliding across the sink, one tendril wrapping around the neck of the faucet. As if readying itself to strike.

A shout came from behind Fin. Eddie stood there, his face stark in the pale moonlight, lips bloodless, but his expression hard with determination. He held the lacrosse stick like a spear.

The creature recoiled a few inches, shifting as its form changed.

"Get back," Eddie said, threatening. "You—whatever you are."

The creature glanced from Eddie to Fin, then it hunched in on itself. Coiling like a snake.

Fin scrambled to her feet, ready to run, when—

The creature launched itself into the air, but not toward Fin. Toward the window. The crack between window and frame was a quarter of an inch. But the narrowness did not deter the creature: it squeezed through the small space. A bit of stuff fell from it, landing wetly on the counter.

The creature was gone—and the kitchen was very still.

Fin heard Eddie's ragged breathing a few feet away; he had yet to put down the lacrosse stick.

"What," said Eddie, "was that?"

Fin reached one shaking hand to the counter and reached for the fallen piece.

"Don't touch it! What if it's an alien and infects you or something?" said Eddie, rushing forward. But Fin didn't listen. She picked it up between thumb and forefinger. It slid between her fingers, soggy and slick. She recognized the smell.

"What is that?" asked Eddie.

Fin finally managed to speak. Her voice quavered, and it took two tries.

"T-tea," she said, holding up the leaf. "It's made of tea."

EIGHT
The Raven

The ravens woke to the creaking of a gate.

One of them, a young female, lifted her head from beneath her wing. She cocked her head, listening. The ravens were always listening; it was their nature. They knew when Mrs. Liu burned a slice of toast and tossed it into her yard; they knew when the young man at the inn took his lunch into the courtyard; they knew when the cat at the grocery store sat beneath a picnic table and watched for whintossers.

Ravens listened; ravens remembered. It was their way.

This night, the ravens heard the rasp of metal against rusted metal. A gate swung open with a grumble of hinges, and under the waning light of a half-moon, a thief stepped over a low fence and into the backyard of the Madeira residence.

Half of Aldermere didn't lock their doors at night. Some of the younger ravens tried to sneak into the houses, to seize bags of bread or indulge in the shiny trinkets the humans adorned themselves with. But the elders warned them off—territory was to be respected. It was natural to defend nests, and the ravens knew this. They would not enter the homes, and so long as weekly tribute was given, they wouldn't touch the plastic bins, either.

It was a peaceful life—most of the time.

But not all creatures understood the nature of territory.

A dark form crept into the backyard. The raven heard the crunch of dirt and grass beneath feet, and then the whisper of the doorknob. Someone was walking toward the house, someone who should not be there.

The door opened silently.

And a shadow crept inside.

The raven let out a shrill sound, but her mother hushed her. She ran her beak down her daughter's neck, tugging gently on the half-formed adult feathers. It was a command for silence and a caress all in one.

The raven glanced at the human territory again, the strange contraption of metal and glass and stone. Their nests always seemed so impenetrable, but now there was something inside. Something unwanted.

The raven flapped her wings. It was dark, too dark for comfort, but she launched herself unsteadily into the air.

She liked these humans. Mr. Madeira fed her crumbs, and his mate wore rings that glittered. They should know their nest had an intruder.

The raven alighted on the windowsill. She could not see much—only a dim form moving inside.

She let out another shrill caw and began rapping her beak against the glass.

The creature within the nest went still—then its head turned to look out the window.

A prickle of fear ran down the raven's neck and wings. She had never met the hawks and owls that her parents warned her of—but every raven could recognize a predator. Unease tingled beneath her skin, a thrill of glorious adrenaline. Some ravens chased this sensation; she had heard tales of her cousins teasing hawks by tugging at their tails or taunting the chained-up dogs that a few humans left in their yards. But she could not understand why anyone would choose this; panic flared beneath her ribs, and the raven flapped her wings, trying to make noise, to make herself bigger.

A light came on inside.

The raven blinked, startled by the sudden illumination. She did not see where the creature fled to, but one moment it was there—and the next it was gone. The humans within were awake, moving about the place where they made food. Mr. Madeira glanced from side to side, frowning.

They were safe.

The raven ruffled her feathers, satisfied. The intruder was out of the human's nest. She could return to her tree, she could—

A branch snapped.

The raven's head jerked up and her small heart throbbed in her chest. Only now did she realize that if the invader was not inside the nest—it was outside.

She flung herself into the air, but hands clamped down across her wings and held her. She bit and scratched, but it was to no avail. The clamor must have alerted the humans, because a porch light came on.

Mr. Madeira strode outside, holding one of the sunlight devices in his hand.

But when he checked beneath the kitchen window, all he found were a few black feathers. He didn't see the figure in the shadows—the raven held tight and bundled away.

NINE
Monster Hunt

Neither Fin nor Eddie slept that night.

They went up to Eddie's room, closed his window, locked the door, and then sat in the middle of the room with a flashlight. During previous sleepovers, they'd brought up a lantern and strewn blankets about, so that it felt like real camping. Eddie had even dragged his own blankets onto the floor. It had been fun.

But this . . . This wasn't fun. They sat on the floor because it was the farthest distance from the doors or windows.

Neither spoke; there wasn't anything to say. And besides, Fin could guess what Eddie would want to do—talk to his mom. Aunt Myrtle knew magic, had grown up with it, treated it like an irritating raccoon that kept blundering into her garage and had to be shooed out with a broom. Mom had grown up with it too, but Mom had left Aldermere and made no secret of distrusting the tea shop. She would scold Fin for returning there, for unleashing the magic.

It was only when the first rays of dawn began to creep through the curtains that Eddie rose and crossed to the window. He peeked outside, then nodded to Fin. "I don't see anything out there."

"You think it went into the forest or something?" asked Fin. That was her hope—maybe the creature would vanish.

"It could have," said Eddie, "but it can't have gone too far. I mean, the town boundaries do stretch into the redwoods, but only about seven miles inland. If that thing crossed a boundary . . ." He made a collapsing gesture with his hands, like a house falling inward.

Hope burned hot within Fin. "Maybe . . . Maybe it will. That would be the best solution, right? For that tea . . . thing to try and leave town. The magic would go away. It would just be tea again. Harmless, completely normal, soggy tea."

"Maybe," said Eddie, but he sounded doubtful. He looked at Fin. "How did that even happen?"

Fin shrugged. "I did everything that Talia does. I brewed it, steeped it for exactly five minutes, tossed the tea leaves down the garbage disposal—"

"They're supposed to go in the compost," said Eddie.

"I don't think that really matters at the moment," replied Fin, flushing.

"I mean—if that thing was made of tea—"

"Which it was," said Fin.

"Then why aren't there tea . . . monsters crawling out of everyone's compost?" asked Eddie. "That seems like something people would notice."

"Maybe I steeped it too long."

"And the tea got angry with you?"

Fin threw up her hands. "I don't know what went wrong!" She took a breath, and then another. "One good thing came out of this."

"What's that?"

"I don't feel anxious," said Fin. "I mean, I'm scared of being eaten by a tea monster, but I think that's normal under these circumstances."

There was a moment of quiet. Then Eddie snorted with laughter. "Normal circumstances. Yeah. That's exactly how I'd describe this."

They made breakfast. Eddie swore he wasn't dealing with anything magical until after he'd eaten. Fin had long ago learned how to cobble together pancakes, but the only flours they could find in Aunt Myrtle's kitchen were barley and almond. Fin could have retrieved the pancake mix from the cottage, but at eight in the morning on a Saturday, her mother would still be asleep after her late shift. So she and Eddie made do. The eggs were from a neighbor's coop, and Fin had to brush a stray feather from one before cracking it open. The pancakes had a slightly denser texture than she was used to, but it was food. And it didn't matter once they added plenty of maple syrup.

When it came to cleaning up, both of them stood before the sink and eyed it doubtfully.

"Okay, you turn it on," said Eddie.

"Why me?" Fin said, turning to him. "It's your house."

"It's your tea monster," he replied. "And besides, aren't you supposed to be fearless now?"

It wasn't that the tea made her fearless. It was like being able to take a full breath after being underwater for too long. It was mostly dizzy relief, the sensation of constriction and weight gone from her shoulders. She wasn't *fearless*; she just wasn't *afraid*. But she knew Eddie wouldn't understand, so she didn't try to explain.

"Fine," she said. She stepped up to the sink and glanced down. The mesh strainer was still on the counter, and Fin stuck it in place before turning on the faucet. It spat water for a moment, then steadied out into its usual flow.

The water vanished into the sink easily. There was no sign of a blockage, at least.

"Well, that's one thing," said Fin. "We don't need to tell your mom we ruined her sink."

"Only that you unleashed a tea monster," he said.

"I thought you said *we* unleashed a tea monster!"

"Trust me," he said, "I'm going to get in enough trouble with *your* mom when she finds out that I helped you steal from Talia. We don't need to add my helping create Franken-Tea on top of it."

They rinsed off the dishes, set them in the rack, and ventured outside. Eddie led the way through the bushes to the place beneath the kitchen window. "You think we can track it?" asked Fin. Eddie had studied animal tracking with Frank.

Eddie made an uncertain noise. He knelt beneath the window, shoving aside a thick bit of overgrown vetch. He looked around the dirt and grass, and then he reached down and picked up something. "This look familiar?"

Fin took it from him. It was a slimy brown leaf. She sniffed it. Tea—definitely tea.

"Okay," said Eddie. "Okay. I can do this."

Five minutes later, they walked away from the house wearing boots and jackets, and Fin carried Eddie's lacrosse stick. She wasn't quite sure how it would help them, but it felt better to have something in her hands. Eddie found another tea leaf in the grass, sniffing it for good measure before moving on. Fin trailed in his wake. Her mind was whirling, trying to come up with plans and backup plans.

A tea monster. An actual tea monster. This couldn't happen every time Talia made the tea, because otherwise Aldermere would be overrun. Fin had made a mistake. She must have missed a step.

Eddie found another tea leaf on a mossy rock. Then another between the roots of a tree. "This clump's bigger," he said. "Come on. Look at this grass—it's all tamped down. Someone wandered around here." He knelt beside a broken branch.

Fin kept the lacrosse stick raised. "What do we do if we find it?"

He glanced at the stick. "Hope that it likes sports?"

"I'm serious," Fin said. "Do we . . . I don't know. Can we trap it somehow?"

"Like with a really big tea ball?" Eddie suggested.

Fin glared at him.

"Sorry," he said. "I'm trying not to freak out. Pretty much

the only way I can do that is with badly timed humor. Or at least that's what Mom says."

Fin thought of Aunt Myrtle and shook her head. She loved her aunt, but right now that love was laced with resentment. "She wants me to see a counselor."

"Who?" Eddie asked, surprised.

"Your mom," said Fin. "She thinks I need counseling. She wants me to see someone up in Eureka. I overheard her and Mom talking." She gripped the stick a little harder. "She thinks there's something wrong with me."

"We're hunting a tea monster with a lacrosse stick," he replied. "I think there's something wrong with both of us."

Fin smiled, but it wasn't real. Eddie didn't get it—he'd always been talkative and friendly, so easygoing that he could still crack jokes when they were out in the woods with a monster running amok.

They did not find the tea monster. They did find another lizard, which Eddie popped into his shirt pocket; signs that a bear had wandered by; a flower that Eddie claimed was native only to Aldermere; and a bit of shoelace. Eddie was pleased with the lizard. His jeans were damp and muddy at the knees, but he had the satisfied look of a collector who had come across a rare prize. Fin shook her head; the only thing she'd ever collected were old mystery paperbacks.

They walked deeper into the woods, until the sounds of the town and highway had all vanished. Redwood forests were always quiet and oddly still, save for the occasional garter snake that tried to slip away unseen. The fallen red needles softened every step, and even the birds were silent.

The forests were beautiful—but she knew better than to relax. She had grown up in cities and suburbs, where street signs could tell her where to go and the only predators were people. But out here, if they got lost they would have to find their own way back to town. Black bears were common, and a few months ago, a cougar had lingered in the area.

There were other things that lived in the forest: whintossers; deer that looked normal except for their distorted, strange shadows; a hog-bear that only Frank claimed to have seen; the flocks of ever-present ravens; whatever lived in Bower's Creek; and, of course, the infamous Bigfoot. But today Fin and Eddie saw no sign of monsters.

They lost the trail near the creek.

Eddie stood on the muddy ground, tennis shoes sinking. "Sorry. Wherever it went, I don't know."

Fin let out a sigh. "It's not your fault. You got us farther than I thought we would." She knelt beside the creek, extending her hand to run her fingers through the cool, clear water. She was sweaty; the summer was lingering in the sunlight, reddening her forearms and making her hair stick to the back of her neck.

Eddie caught her by the wrist. "Wait."

Fin looked at him, exhausted beyond words, but then she understood.

She rummaged around in her pockets but came up empty. Eddie did the same and found half of a gummy protein ball with lint stuck to it.

"That was in your pocket?" said Fin, aghast.

Eddie shrugged. Then he tossed the protein ball into the creek. It spun around, bouncing merrily along the current. It floated toward the dappled shadows of trees upon the water.

The thing that lived in Bower's Creek always kept to the shadows.

Fin and Eddie waited, watching, to see if a clawed hand would reach up and seize hold of the food. If that happened, they would have to go around. There was a fallen log about half a mile east of town, and they could cross there.

No one knew what lived in Bower's Creek. At one town council meeting, Aunt Myrtle had said it could be a malevolent mermaid or a siren, Frank insisted it was a swamp monster, and Mr. Carver murmured about a miniature kraken. But one thing was certain: like all magical creatures, the thing was hungry. And not particular about what it ate.

No one could prove it ate people. But there had been an older man living on the edge of Bower's Creek who had vanished five years ago. And once in a while, a pet would go missing. There would be a search, but more often than not, the animal would never be found again.

The protein ball floated away and out of sight. Whatever lived in the creek wasn't here. They were safe.

Fin unlaced her shoes and waded through the shallows. The water was breathtakingly cold but clean against her sweaty skin, and she cupped her fingers and splashed a little on the back of her neck.

"We should head back," said Eddie. "Your mom'll probably be awake by now, and she'll want to know where we are."

It was true; Aunt Myrtle and other Aldermere parents tended to allow greater leniency than Fin was used to, but her mom still liked to know where the kids were playing.

They took a different route back to town, winding through a trail kept neat for hikers. It was packed with dirt and dead redwood needles, and more than one garter snake slithered reluctantly off the sun-warmed path. As they approached town, Fin heard the sound of bustle and voices. They walked out of the trees, past the edge of the inn's parking lot. There was a rumble of voices nearby, and Fin remembered it was Saturday.

On Saturdays, from the months of May through October, the Foragers' Market opened up along East Redwood Street. A few local shops made their presence known: Brewed Awakening always set up a small table where Cedar and one of her parents sold coffee and herbal tisanes out of paper cups, the bakery set up a table of fresh breads and sweets, and the Ack brought over snacks and fishing bait.

But more common were those people who lived off the grid and sold foraged fare. Among the offerings were turkey tail mushrooms in jars of vinegar; balls of homemade cheeses rolled in California bay leaves, fennel, and garlic; jars of dogberries, thimbleberries, huckleberries, salmonberries, and blackberries; bags of edible greens from the forest floor; candied spruce tips wrapped in parchment paper; fresh breads flavored with nettles and sorrel. Sometimes Aunt Myrtle convinced Eddie and Fin to bring a folding card table down to Main Street so she could sell a few seashell wind chimes or offer to read tarot for the tourists.

Eddie and Fin trudged into the market, burrs clinging to their pants and sweat dampening their foreheads. Fin's forearm stung where she had accidentally brushed a nettle, and all she wanted was a shower and a sandwich. "I'm going to talk to Frank about tracking," said Eddie. At Fin's sharp look, he added, "I'm not going to say anything about a tea monster. I just want to know where creatures would go out near Bower's Creek. Like, if it was trying to find shelter or something."

Fin nodded, and Eddie walked toward Frank's table. Frank brewed some kind of frothy beverage out of elderberries and served it to the adults in paper cups. For the kids, he had fresh apple cider.

"Hey, sweetie."

Mom stood a few feet away. She had a bulging tote bag tucked under her arm and a tired smile on her face. Fin's stomach lurched at the sight of her; what if Mom knew something was wrong?

"Hi," said Fin. "What—what are you doing here? I thought you were working today."

"I am," said Mom around a yawn. "Just headed to the inn, actually. But Mr. Madeira texted me and said he didn't have time to bake bread this morning, so I stopped here."

Sure enough, a closer look at the tote back revealed the edge of brown paper—the kind the bakery always used to wrap their loaves. "You and Eddie have a fun sleepover?" asked Mom. Her keen gaze slid over Fin, stopping at the muddied spots on her jeans.

Fin hated lying to Mom, but this was one of those times when it was unavoidable. She had gone against Mom's wishes, returned to the tea shop, stolen tea, and accidentally created a monster. She couldn't imagine how Mom would react—no, she could imagine it. There would be disappointment and lectures and . . . and maybe this would be the final straw. Maybe this would make Mom so angry that she'd decide this place was too magical for both of them.

They hadn't moved for three years, and it had been the best three years of Fin's life. She didn't want to leave, didn't want to be uprooted again.

So she kept the truth to herself. It was safer.

"It was a good sleepover," Fin said. "And this morning Eddie wanted to look for stuff for our science fair project, so we went into the woods."

Mom's eyes lingered on the ragged hems of Fin's jeans. They were dark with damp, the cold creeping through her socks and against her bare skin.

"You weren't near Bower's Creek, right?" Mom asked.

Fin swallowed another lie. "Yeah, we waded in."

Alarm flashed across Mom's face.

"We were careful," Fin said quickly, before Mom could open her mouth and give her the lecture Fin could recite by heart.

Aldermere can be dangerous, Fin—

"We checked to make sure the creek was empty," said Fin. "Before we crossed it."

—Don't ever let your guard down.

Mom exhaled, and it sounded as though that breath carried the weight of those unspoken warnings. "All right," she said quietly. "That's good that you were careful. I want you safe, okay? And I trust you."

That was almost worse than a lecture. Fin's stomach clenched, her insides tight with guilt. Mom gave her a one-armed hug before leaving for the inn.

Fin glanced around the market. There were the usual vendors: the bakery, Frank's drink stand, and a homesteader with blackberry honey. The Reyes twins were standing near a truck selling bundles of foraged mushrooms. Fin waved to them uncertainly. The twins were Fin's age, but she didn't know them all that well. Matty and Izzy were a little intimidating—both attractive and aloof. It was rumored that the twins only spoke to each other and vanished into the forest for weeks at a time. Fin thought it was all gossip; after all, the twins were homeschooled. They were probably normal and just kept to themselves.

Probably. This was Aldermere, after all.

The twins stared back at her, and only Izzy raised a hand in reply. Feeling awkward, Fin turned away—and to her relief, she saw Brewed Awakening's little cart. It was a place to stand while she waited for Eddie.

Cedar was at work, pouring two young tourists cups of coffee and making change. Fin watched as Cedar deftly counted out the dollars, handing them over with a polite "Come again."

The tourists never once looked at Cedar—just took the money and walked away.

"That was rude," said Fin, when they were out of earshot. The entire interaction made Fin glad that her only job in town was to help with the grocery store deliveries. At least people smiled, grateful when she brought their packages. Maybe it was different working in a coffee shop or a restaurant; people treated Cedar with rude indifference.

Cedar shrugged. "Tourists," she said simply. She leaned against the cart, gazing at Fin with interest. "You look more tired than I am, and that's saying something. You want a cup?"

Fin shook her head. "I'm not allowed to have coffee."

"We also have tisanes," said Cedar. "We've got an iced blend of hibiscus and pineapple my parents are trying to move because it never sells in the fall. You want some?"

Fin dug into her pocket and came up with a few crumpled dollars. She passed them over in exchange for a paper cup. It was wondrously cold against her fingers and it tasted like summer. "Thanks," she said. She gulped the rest down.

"Your parents here?" asked Fin. They had to be—Fin

couldn't imagine a kid being allowed to run a cart all by herself, even if she was a year older.

"Yeah, they wanted to run to the bakery stand before they ran out of sourdough," said Cedar. "Someone said it was selling fast today."

"My mom may have bought it all for the inn, sorry," said Fin, wincing.

Cedar laughed. It was a nice laugh—quick and quiet, like a secret. "They'll have to settle for whole grain, then. That's fine, I like that better." She smiled at Fin. "You want a refill?"

"No, I can't—"

But Cedar was taking the empty paper cup from Fin's hand and refilling it with the cold herbal tea. "It's not selling," said Cedar. "You can have it."

"Thanks," said Fin.

Another person walked up to the coffee cart—Mayor Downer. She wore leather shoes and pressed trousers, despite the muddy ground. She looked over the small chalkboard menu before saying, "One cup of coffee, please."

Cedar was already picking up a thermos before the words were out of the mayor's mouth. She poured a cup of black coffee, holding it out even as Mayor Downer pushed a few dollars across the table and picked up the cup without looking at Cedar. She moved on, striding into the Foragers'

Market with a kind of grim determination.

"Why does she even come to the market?" asked Fin, her eyes on Mayor Downer's back.

"Probably to check that everyone has licenses to be here," said Cedar with a snort. "And make people leave when they don't."

"She can try." Fin thought of what might happen should Aunt Myrtle be told that she needed a license to read tarot cards. It wouldn't end well for the mayor.

"Were you and Eddie out playing in the woods?" asked Cedar. She gestured vaguely at Fin's head. "You've got briars in your hair."

Fin grimaced; while Cedar was always friendly, she had a way of making Fin feel awkward and unsophisticated. Fin yanked a small blackberry leaf from her messy ponytail. "Eddie and I were looking for lizards for our science project," said Fin.

Cedar nodded. "Oh. You hear about the break-in?"

Fin went still, the edge of the cup against her lips. "Break-in?"

Cedar seemed to be trying to sound sympathetic, but there was no mistaking the excitement in her voice. "Someone broke into Mr. Madeira's house last night. He only noticed when the ravens started shrieking up a storm."

"He feeds them stale bread from the inn," said Fin. "They flock around his house."

"Mr. Madeira went into his kitchen and found it trashed. Stuff just thrown everywhere, so it took a while to figure out what the thief stole."

That was why Mom had come to the Foragers' Market, Fin realized. Mr. Madeira must have been dealing with the aftermath of the break-in, so he hadn't had time to bake in the morning. "Who steals from a kitchen?" said Fin, frowning. "Don't they go for phones or computers?"

"Not this thief," said Cedar, tapping a finger against her cart. "This one stole all of the tea."

A chill started at the nape of Fin's neck and worked its way downward. "T-tea?"

Cedar gave her a significant look. "Talia's tea. The kind Mr. Madeira buys for his wife."

Fin's breathing was coming a little faster now, rough in her throat and lungs. It couldn't be. It couldn't—

"Do they know what time it happened?" Fin asked.

Cedar shrugged. "Around ten at night."

Ten. The tea monster had crawled out of the sink earlier than that. There would have been more than enough time for it to circle through the woods and break into Mr. Madeira's home.

"Why would anyone want it?" Fin muttered, more to herself than to Cedar.

But Cedar answered. "Don't know. I mean—the tea is special, but no one's ever tried to steal it before. Maybe Talia wouldn't sell to someone and they decided to take it. But since they couldn't break into the tea shop itself without the shop vanishing . . ." She let the sentence trail off.

"Did they see who did it?" Fin asked. Maybe Mr. Madeira had caught a glimpse of the thief, maybe—

"Nope," said Cedar. "Not a look."

The last of Fin's hopes died away.

Because she knew what had broken into Mr. Madeira's home. Not a person, but a thing seeking tea.

Maybe it needed more. Maybe all those soggy tea leaves that had flaked off had left the creature small and injured, and it had needed to replenish itself. It reminded Fin of those video games that Eddie played, when monsters healed themselves halfway through a battle. Or scooped up magic potions and grew ten times their size.

Monsters were hungry, after all.

TEN
The Town Meeting

News spread quickly through Aldermere. Between the Madeiras' home being broken into and Mrs. Brackenbury being mugged, everyone was buzzing with gossip. Some people were sure it had to be a tourist, because it couldn't be a local. The tourists found themselves being eyed with suspicion.

There were no more signs of the tea monster after the break-in at Mr. Madeira's home. Part of Fin was hopeful that the creature would disappear and never return.

Aunt Myrtle came back from Eureka on Sunday, pleased that several gift shops now carried her postcards and a few wind chimes. She said nothing about counselors or appointments and merely kissed Eddie on the top of his head before going into town to buy milk from the Ack. Mom was in the cottage, having spent her Sunday cleaning. The rugs were draped over the porch railing, and when Fin had darted inside for a book she'd forgotten, the entire cottage smelled vaguely of lemons.

Mom had a tendency to clean when she was in a bad mood. Or sometimes even if there wasn't anything else to do. It was why she'd been such a good room cleaner before she'd managed the inn. Fin knew that Mom was worried about some of the tourists leaving early. The season was almost over, and from the months of October through February, business in town would slow to a crawl.

It was the second Monday of the month, which meant a town council meeting. They were held in the only place large enough: the banquet room of the inn. On those evenings, Fin would trek to the inn at a quarter to six and help set up folding chairs. She'd done it ever since her mom started working there, just so they could spend time together. The tradition had been continued even after Mom took over as assistant manager.

Fin liked the meetings; she helped set up the chairs, then got a cup of instant hot chocolate, sat in the back of the room, and listened to her neighbors argue about everything from deer invading gardens to reminders that door labels needed to be bolted on, because no one wanted a tourist to try to use a restroom and end up in someone's basement by accident.

She used the inn's main entrance, striding in through the front doors. Bellhop Ben was behind the counter. He straightened when he saw Fin, as if she was a guest. "Good evening, ma'am."

Fin laughed. "Hi, Ben."

He flashed her an easy grin. "You here for the meeting?"

"Always."

Ben leaned across the counter. "We got some new chairs."

"Lighter?" she said hopefully. The inn's folding chairs were padded with old cushions and two of them weighed nearly as much as she did. She had to carry them one at a time and her arms ached afterward.

"Yeah," he replied. "Super flimsy, though. I feel like we should put a warning label on them or something. They look like they could snap if someone sat on them the wrong way." He shrugged. "Budget cuts, you know how it is."

This was one thing she liked about Ben—he talked to her like she was another adult. There wasn't any condescension or saying she wouldn't understand.

"You coming to the meeting?" she asked.

He shook his head. "Someone's gotta stay at the front counter, keep the guests happy."

The phone rang and Ben reached for it, giving Fin a nod of farewell. She walked down the hallway to the banquet room. Mom had already set up the podium and was connecting the microphone. She saw Fin and smiled. "Hey, sweetheart. Got your homework done?"

Fin nodded. "Just math. It was easy."

"That's my girl." Mom dropped a kiss against the top of her head, then said, "We got some new chairs. We've been keeping them in the left-hand side of the closet where we store the linens."

They worked in comfortable silence for about fifteen minutes, putting the folding chairs in rows, and then arranging a table with hot and cold water. There were packets of tea—the cheap, normal kinds from the grocery store—and coffee and hot chocolate. Fin grabbed one of the chocolate packets, stirring the brown powder into a mug with the inn's logo printed on one side.

This was the part she liked best—the five minutes after setup that was quiet. Just her and her mom. They sat together in the front row, waiting for the townspeople to arrive.

"So how was school?" asked Mom.

Fin smiled. "It was good. Read aloud in class during English." With the tea's magic running through her, the prospect hadn't been as daunting as it might have been. She'd made three mistakes during the reading. Without the tea, those mistakes would have swelled up like balloons, becoming the only things that mattered in that memory, all she could recall. But now—now they were just mistakes. And she could handle them.

"You going to stay for the whole meeting?" asked Mom. "It might be a long one. I'm sure the mayor will have plenty to say about our recent 'crime spree.'"

Fin tried to keep her face normal. That was exactly why she wanted to stay—if there was any news about the creature that had broken into Mr. Madeira's home, she needed to know about it. "I think Aunt Myrtle's making cheese quesadillas," said Fin, pulling a disgusted face. "The kind with the soy cheese. If I go home, she'll want me to eat one."

Mom smiled. "Well, we can't have that." She leaned forward, elbows on her knees, hands clasped around her cup of coffee. "How was your weekend with Eddie?"

Fin considered her answer. "We got a lot done on our science project."

"That's good." Something flickered across Mom's face—

it looked like nerves. "I know that you've been worried about that. And that's why you tried to go to the tea shop a few days ago." She inhaled through her nose. "Listen, sweetheart. I've wanted to talk to you about—well, your aunt knows someone up in Eureka."

The counselor. A cold throb went through Fin at the realization. This was it. This was Mom trying to tell Fin there was something wrong with her, something that needed a counselor to fix.

Fin opened her mouth, desperate for some way to convince her mom that everything was fine, she was fine—

The *tap-tap-tap* of a cane made Fin look to her left.

It was Mrs. Brackenbury, come to claim a front row seat before anyone else. Mom swallowed, reached over and put her hand over Fin's. "We'll talk later," she said. "You should help Mrs. Brackenbury, okay?" She rose to her feet and walked to the podium, straightening the microphone.

Relief swept through Fin. She'd never been so glad to see Mrs. Brackenbury before. The older woman's hair was dyed a soft red-brown and her large-knuckled hands grasped a cane. She tottered to a seat and Fin went to the table and poured a cup of coffee. Regular, two sugars. Fin knew—she'd been watching Mrs. Brackenbury come to town council meetings for years now. She brought the coffee to the older woman.

"Such a good girl," said Mrs. Brackenbury, beaming at Fin. "You helping your mother out tonight?"

Fin ducked her head, but nodded. "Yeah."

"Well, I'm glad that you're here." Mrs. Brackenbury grasped her cane a little more tightly with her left hand. "The streets aren't safe, not anymore. Not when there are muggers around who think it's all right to knock an old lady down and steal her groceries."

"How are you doing?" asked Fin. It had been the right thing to say, because Mrs. Brackenbury looked pleased.

"I'm fine, dear, don't you worry about it. I wish Mr. Bull had been with me—I could have used him like one of those tracker dogs."

Fin tried to imagine Mr. Bull, with his sagging face and snorting breaths, tracking a criminal through the woods. He seemed more likely to find a patch of sunlight and fall asleep. Even so, she nodded agreeably.

The others began to trickle in. Fin took up a seat in the back. She watched as the others took their seats. Mr. Hardin sat down in the second row. Mr. Madeira helped his wife into one of the chairs nearest the exit. There were the Reyes twins, Matty and Izzy, and their moms. Then the bearded and tall Frank, who always looked like a modern-day Paul Bunyan, with combat boots and a pet ferret instead of an ox. The ferret resided in the hood of Frank's sweatshirt, only emerging for food and play. Sure enough, Fin saw a flash of white fur when Frank settled into one of the folding chairs.

The editor of the town paper, Cassandra Catmore, took up her usual spot in the back row. She had a pen wedged into the hair knotted at the top of her head and a tiny pad of paper tapping against her thigh. Her lipstick was matte and dark, making her look like a heroine from a black-and-white film. Next inside were Mr. and Mrs. Carver from Brewed Awakening. Cedar trailed after, her hands shoved into her jeans pockets. When she caught sight of Fin, she seemed relieved.

"Hey," she said.

"Hi," said Fin. "I didn't know you were coming."

Cedar looked down, a little sheepish. "With all the crime stuff going on, my parents didn't want to leave me home alone." She rolled her eyes toward the ceiling, as if to indicate how irritating overprotective parents could be. "Is Eddie here?"

Fin shook her head. "No, Eddie doesn't really do town meetings—not since Aunt Myrtle and Mayor Downer got into a shouting match."

The corners of Cedar's mouth twitched. "Never boring around here, is it?"

"Sometimes I wish it was," Fin said.

Cedar glanced over her shoulder. "I have to go back to my parents. But I'll see you at school." She gave Fin a small smile before returning to the rows of chairs. It was only as she walked away that Fin wondered if she should have invited the other girl to sit with her—but some guilty, relieved part of Fin was glad to be alone again.

The room had mostly filled up during her short conversation with Cedar.

Finally Mayor Downer walked into the room. Fin had never once seen Mayor Downer smile. Eddie said that the mayor wanted to live up to her name. In addition to being the mayor, she was also head of the tourist commission board, the neighborhood watch, and the homeowners' association. She'd ruled the town for years, but as much as people complained about her, no one was willing to challenge Mayor Downer for her throne.

The meeting began with a call to order, agenda review, and the mayor's prepared announcements—which consisted of a reminder to everyone that gates were *not* considered doors and thus labeling gates in the hope of getting a deer or an unwary tourist into the home of a person you disliked was not only considered vandalism, it was also utterly useless. Then there was the usual plea either to keep one's garbage bins indoors or give the ravens their weekly allotment of food, because Oak Street had once again seen a spate of moldy garbage strewn across the sidewalk.

"Lastly," said Mayor Downer, "a fallen tree is blocking the northwest hiking trail. We need someone to clear the path."

"It's almost the end of hiking season," said one of the older men up front. "Do we really need to spend the town budget on unnecessary construction?"

"*Almost* the end of hiking season," said Mrs. Brackenbury in her creaky voice, "isn't the *end* of hiking season. We've got to keep the town nice for tourists."

"Or they could go somewhere else," the man muttered.

"I nominate Frank," said Mr. Madeira.

"That's not how this works," said Mayor Downer with deliberate calm. "We'll have to check the town budget and—"

"I second that," said Mrs. Brackenbury.

"No," said Mayor Downer. "I'll speak to the committee about—"

"The planning committee consists of you," said Mr. Madeira. "Do you need to have a meeting with yourself?"

"There are procedures," said Mayor Downer, her eyes like hard chips of glass. The glare bounced right off Mr. Madeira. He took a sip of his tea.

"We should clear open that trail as soon as possible, so we don't have people going home early," said Mom. Her voice was soothing, and Fin recognized it as her "a customer is angry" voice. "We can't afford that, not before the off-season."

Mayor Downer looked at Mom. Then she nodded. "I suppose we can forgo procedure for the sake of town prosperity," she said. "Frank?"

Frank was sliding what looked like a sunflower seed into his hood. A tiny ferret paw snatched it from his fingers. "I can do it on Wednesday," he said.

"Well," said Mayor Downer, "at least that's taken care of." She took a step back to drink from a glass of water while her assistant announced that they were moving on to public comments and non-agenda items—which basically meant anyone in the town could take the microphone for up to two minutes to complain.

This was the most entertaining part of the meetings, in Fin's opinion. While she often read during things like voting on public works or allocations of funds, she deeply enjoyed listening to the gossip. She wasn't the only one; the entire first two rows of chairs were filled with the town's older residents, some of whom brought knitting or crossword puzzles for the more boring bits of the meetings. People still talked about when Mayor Downer tried to implement a law that would keep lawns under an inch but Aunt Myrtle fought back by sneaking into Downer's yard at ten in the evening and measuring her grass with an ancient wooden ruler. Or when someone said they should try to relocate the creature that lived in Bower's Creek and it turned into a shouting match. Or last year when someone—or something—kept stealing doorknobs and no one could figure out who to blame. That last one had never been resolved.

Of course, tonight's public comments were all about crime.

"—to the dogs," one of the older men was saying at the podium. Fin couldn't remember his name; he lived on the street behind the grocery store. "This place used to be family-oriented, but with all these newcomers . . ." He glared in the direction of the Reyes family. The twins were sandwiched between their two moms—Matty was playing on a tiny videogame device, but Izzy was listening. Both of the twins had black hair; Izzy's hair was tied off in a ponytail, while Matty's swung in front of his eyes as he leaned forward. Fin had wanted to talk to Izzy a few times, but her courage had always faltered.

Izzy made a rude gesture toward Podium Man; Matty grabbed his sibling's arm and yanked it down before the elderly first rowers could turn around and see it.

"Yeah, it's us that's the problem," said Mrs. Reyes—the one sitting beside Izzy. "Not you and your seventeen-year-old nephew who tried to lure the Bower's Creek creature by kidnapping your neighbor's cat and pushing it out into the creek."

"Is that why the Winterborn cat looked so wet last week?" muttered someone in the back row.

"Don't worry, Tobin drew more blood than any monster," someone else answered.

"That's—that's nothing to do with this," sputtered Podium Man.

Mayor Downer tried to regain order of the meeting by waving her gavel about.

Fin used the distraction to rise to her feet; she needed to use the bathroom. At least no one had mentioned seeing a tea monster yet. That was something to be grateful for.

"Point is," Podium Man continued, "that's two occurrences in one week. If it wasn't a tourist, and we can't be sure it was, then we need to root out who would do such a thing as break into a man's house and mug an old lady to steal her purse."

"Grocery shopping," said Mrs. Brackenbury in her creaky voice. "They took my shopping."

Fin slipped out of the conference room, letting the door

swing silently shut behind her. The staff bathroom was down the hallway, near the front desk.

As Fin walked past the desk, the phone rang. She jumped, startled by the abrupt sound. She glanced around, but Ben was gone. And Mom was in the meeting. On any other day, she would have hesitated. But with the tea still singing through her, she simply reached down and picked up the phone. "Hello?"

"Oh, good." Fin recognized the voice at once: Aunt Myrtle. "Hi, Fin. I thought everyone would still be in that terrible meeting. I was trying to get ahold of your mom, to tell her that the roofer is going to come out tomorrow and check the cottage for winter."

"Oh," said Fin. "You want me to tell her?"

"Thanks, sweetie." Aunt Myrtle hesitated for a moment. "Did you go to the meeting? To see your mom?"

Fin blinked at the wall, confused. "I always come to the town council meetings, Aunt Myrtle."

"I know." Aunt Myrtle sounded bewildered. "I just could have sworn I saw someone moving around in the cottage a minute ago. Angie left the light on—must've been a shadow." Her voice lightened. "Well, you have a good time. And if Downer tries to implement her lawn agenda again, you tell her that she can shove it."

"I'll do that," said Fin, knowing she would never do any such thing. "Bye."

Fin set the phone back into its cradle. Her mind was racing.

A light on in the cottage. But neither Mom nor Fin ever left lights on. They couldn't afford to. And it wasn't like someone could wander inside—Mom was one of the few people who kept their house locked when no one was home.

But even if someone got into the cottage, it wasn't like they had anything of value to steal—

Except a key.

The spare key to the tea shop. She'd left it on the windowsill of her loft.

Aunt Myrtle's voice came back to her. *"I just could have sworn I saw someone moving around in the cottage a minute ago."*

Someone was in the cottage. Or perhaps . . . some*thing*.

Fin turned, heart hammering against her ribs and, as quietly as she could, hastened to the door.

ELEVEN
The Second Heist

There were times that Fin wished she had a cell phone.

But cell phones didn't work in Aldermere. Supposedly, a company once tried to install a cell tower nearby, but residents fought so hard against it that the company backed off and never tried again. There were entire swaths of wilderness along Highway 101 without service, and if a person's car broke down, the best they could hope for was to trek to one of the emergency lines set up for such purposes.

Most of the time, Fin didn't care. Cell phones seemed like more trouble than they were worth; her classmates were always complaining of lost phones or broken screens.

But right now she yearned for a way to call Eddie, to

tell him what was going on. She wanted backup.

Her feet pounded the pavement as she ran, cool night air rushing past. Her breath sawed painfully, every gasp tasting of adrenaline.

She ran down Main Street, cutting through the gap between two houses. The forest's long shadows ushered in the night, and darkness tended to fall quickly, even when the overhead sky still held streaks of orange and pink. A raven cried out—perhaps greeting the night or startled by Fin. Fin ignored the bird and ran even faster, ducking down a side street and finally arriving at the big house. The windows glowed a comforting orange, and if she took the time, she knew she could see Eddie and Aunt Myrtle dining at their table.

Fin slowed to a jog, her breaths still coming hard.

She crept around the side of the big house, keeping out of sight. She didn't want Aunt Myrtle to see her, to ask questions.

Sure enough, light spilled through one of the cottage windows.

She hurried to the front door, reaching for the doorknob. Unlocked—which could mean that Mom had simply forgotten to lock it, or that whatever had broken in could pick a lock. She pushed the door open slowly, trying to keep silent. Someone could still be in there. She half expected to see the amorphous tea monster.

But the cottage was empty; she could see into her mom's room. There was no intruder, no monster, nothing at all.

Except the lights were on. Fin knew she hadn't left them that way. She often double-checked to make sure her keys were in her pocket, that her notebook was in her backpack, and that she hadn't left anything dangerous plugged in.

Fin scrambled up the wooden ladder to her room. Her bed was always a little messy—she didn't see the point in making it when she'd mess it up the next night. She hurried to the windowsill.

There was no key. She stood there, gaping at the empty spot where it should have rested.

Fin's mouth moved silently, but she couldn't make a sound.

Talia had entrusted her with that key, and Fin had lost it. No—worse than that. She'd allowed it to be stolen.

Again she thought of creeping tendrils, slick with old Ceylon leaves, and that formless, shapeless thing that had crawled out of the sink. She thought of the tea leaves it had left behind, the brown and soggy bits scattered in the grass.

What if it needed more tea to sustain itself?

It might have gone to the source.

Fin sat on her bed, frozen with indecision, for nearly a full minute. Her immediate instinct was to crawl beneath her covers and pretend that this had nothing to do with her. If she could pretend hard enough, maybe it would be true. She didn't want to get in trouble; she wanted it all to go away, to leave her in peace.

Be brave, she thought. *Be brave.*

The town council meeting would go on for probably another hour. She had that much time.

Fin took one breath, then another, and another. Maybe it was the magic still in her veins, or sheer determination, but she felt steadier. She left the cottage, locking the door behind her, and jogged across the yard. Through the window, she saw that Eddie was helping Aunt Myrtle put away the dishes. She couldn't ask him for help, not without alerting her aunt.

Fin was on her own.

She hurried past the big house. Eddie's lacrosse stick was propped up against the front porch, and Fin veered to her left to grab it. Night had fallen like a heavy blanket across Aldermere, pushed back at corners by a few automatic porch lights. Some flickered on as Fin took off down the street. Gravel crunched beneath her shoes as she hastened toward the tea shop.

When she rounded a corner and saw it, her heart gave an

unsteady thump. The shop was dark, the windows opaque. Fin didn't bother going to the front door—someone might see her. And she suspected that most monsters wouldn't walk in the front door. Fin crept slowly through the overgrown ferns toward the back of the shop.

The door was half open.

"Oh," she heard herself say. Her voice was quiet, thin with alarm. Her hands gripped the lacrosse stick so hard that her knuckles ached.

She stood there for a heartbeat, unsure what to do. She couldn't call for an adult to handle this—if she did, she'd have to tell them what she'd done. And if Aunt Myrtle or Mom found out, they'd send her to that counselor for sure.

Something in the open doorway moved. Fin staggered backward.

She wasn't sure what to expect when the door swung fully open. Perhaps a larger version of the creature that had slunk out of the sink—all slick tendrils and seeking limbs.

But then the creature stepped out of the tea shop. And in the dim illumination of a neighbor's porch light, Fin saw the girl.

The girl who looked like *Fin*.

Sandy brown hair, freckles all across her face, eyebrows that were slightly uneven—one crooked upward. Her chin had the same stubborn jut, and her hair fell across her shoulders.

The only difference was in her eyes. Fin had dark brown eyes; this girl's eyes were silver. Not blue or gray but *silver.* Silver like metal. Silver like—

The girl's eyes glittered like those tea balls that Talia kept behind the counter.

As Fin watched, the girl pushed her hair back over one shoulder. A few strands fell, catching the dim light. As they fluttered through the air, those strands of fallen hair changed from wispy and dry to dark and soggy.

Damp tea leaves spattered to the ground.

This girl who looked like Fin was made of tea.

"You're too late," said the girl.

TWELVE
Tea Fin

The girl stepped out of the doorway, down the two wooden stairs, and walked toward Fin.

She didn't move like Fin. Her stride was firmer, her shoulders thrown back, her stubborn chin pointed forward. Her silver eyes caught and held the light, and when she smiled, Fin recognized her.

This was who Fin sometimes glimpsed in window reflections—those moments when she wondered if she could be fearless, could be brave, could be comfortable in her own skin. This girl did not cower when faced with the world: she dared the world to face her.

It both *was* and was *not* Fin.

"W-what . . . ," Fin said, and didn't know how to finish.

The girl who looked like Fin tilted her head, her smile tightening at the edges.

"You're too late," she said again. "All the tea is gone."

Too late. Too late. The words crowded out all other thoughts. Fin was too late, and this creature had stolen all the magical tea. She'd used it to become this—this thing.

A monster that looked like a girl.

Fin raised the lacrosse stick high.

"You stay back," she said. "Or—"

The Fin made of tea laughed—and it was Fin's laugh: a chortle with a snort at the end. Fin always tried to tamp it down because that laugh was embarrassing, but this girl didn't care.

"You'll what?" said the Tea Fin. "Score a goal at me?"

"You're not supposed to exist," Fin said. "When Talia gets back—"

"When Talia gets back, you're going to have to tell her that she shouldn't have trusted you with that key," said Tea Fin. "Have fun with that."

Fin's jaw went tight. For the first time, anger flared deep within her belly.

"You shouldn't exist," she said hotly. "I did everything Talia did. I paid for my tea with a memory and—"

"You did," agreed Tea Fin. She took a step closer, and Fin took a step back. "Bet you never wondered where those memories went. What happened to them."

It was true—she'd never once considered that. She had thought them gone forever.

"I'm everything you forgot, Fin," said the girl. "Luckily for you, memories aren't so easily destroyed. That mortar carries the echoes of so many. Including yours."

The words fell between them like a lead weight.

Fin gaped at her.

"Now," said Tea Fin, "we're going to split up. I've got things to do—people to find, scores to settle. And if I know you, which I do, you're going to want to help her." Tea Fin gestured at the overgrown grass near Fin's feet. For a moment, Fin didn't look; it was probably a trick, a way to get her to glance away. Then the monster would attack.

A low croak came from the grass. Startled, Fin leaped to one side, heart hammering, and saw the creature—or rather, she didn't see it. The bird was a smudge of darkness against an already dark ground. Its wings rustled, and it croaked balefully at her.

A raven. It was sitting in the grass, small and inky black. A distant part of Fin wondered why the bird didn't fly away.

Fin looked up at Tea Fin. The monster's smile had gone,

and all that was left was something hard. Her silver eyes glinted like steel.

Tea Fin turned on her heel and walked toward the darkness of the trees. She moved like—like something liquid. Fin took half a step after her, lacrosse stick still clutched in her hand.

She had to stop the monster.

"Don't move," she snapped.

Tea Fin didn't stop; she merely glanced over her shoulder. "You need to get that bird to Edward."

It took Fin a moment to realize that she meant Eddie. No one called Eddie by his full name except for the first day of school or if Aunt Myrtle was in a rare bad mood.

Fin knelt, and sure enough, the bird had a crooked wing. And abruptly, she remembered what Cedar had said about the break-in at Mr. Madeira's home.

"He only noticed when the ravens started shrieking up a storm."

Perhaps it hadn't just been the break-in that had disturbed the ravens—maybe Tea Fin had injured them in an attempt to keep them quiet, taken one hostage when it hadn't worked. Had she kept the raven all this time? To keep the other ravens at bay? To intimidate them? Or to distract Fin long enough to escape?

Fin shoved the lacrosse stick under her arm, then carefully reached down and placed her hands around the raven's wings. It croaked weakly in protest, but it didn't try to peck or escape. Fin rose, the bird in her hands, and she looked up.

The monster was gone.

Eddie was in his pajamas when Fin knocked at the back door of the big house. He wore loose sweats too big for him—no doubt bought secondhand—and a toothbrush hung from the corner of his mouth. When he spoke, his words came out gummy.

"Wha," he managed to say.

Fin knew she must have looked ridiculous: hair tangled, lacrosse stick jammed under one arm, and a raven held between both hands.

"It's hurt," she said. "I—I found it."

She added that last bit when Aunt Myrtle rounded the corner. Aunt Myrtle wore her soft robe, and her frizzy hair was braided down her back. "Oh, sweetie," she said, when she saw the raven and Fin.

"I found it on my way home," Fin said. The words may have been a lie, but the quaver in her voice was real.

"Come on in." Aunt Myrtle opened the door wider and

Fin stepped inside. "You know you don't have to knock."

The truth was, Fin wasn't always sure. The big house was a home—but it wasn't Fin's home. Her home was the tiny cottage out back.

They took the raven to the bathroom, where Eddie snapped into action. He retrieved a box and added a soft towel before Fin carefully placed the bird inside. It croaked again, this time sounding more weary than protesting. Eddie filled a small bowl with water and offered it to the bird. It considered the shiny edge of the bowl, nibbling at it with the tip of its beak before dipping into the water and tipping its head back in a birdish swallow.

"Good," Eddie murmured, more to himself than to Fin. "She's healthy enough to be thirsty."

"How do you know it's a girl?" asked Fin, blinking.

Eddie shrugged. "Just do."

Fin didn't question; Eddie's knack for animals was something she'd never understand, but she trusted him.

Aunt Myrtle stood in the doorway. The bathroom was too small for all three of them. "You should take the bird to Nick at the gas station tomorrow before school," she said. "He's worked with ravens before."

"Not animal control or bird vets or something?" asked Fin.

Aunt Myrtle shook her head. "Nick'll decide if that's necessary. He's good with that kind of thing." She trudged down the hallway, and Fin heard her rummaging around in the kitchen.

Eddie leaned closer. "All right," he said quietly. "What really happened?"

Fin lowered her voice. "How do you know I didn't just find her?"

"Because you don't typically walk back from town council meetings alone with a lacrosse stick," said Eddie. "Unless the meetings have gotten way more interesting."

Fin bit down on her lower lip. "It's . . . it's a long story. Can I tell you tomorrow?"

Eddie looked a little hurt, but he nodded. "Okay. We'll have to get up early to bring the bird to Nick before school, anyways. You can tell me then."

All the while, he was still holding out the water to the raven. She drank twice more, then ruffled her feathers.

"My mom'll be home any minute," said Fin. "I . . . I should go."

Eddie glanced down at the bird. "I'll take care of her."

Fin knew he would—that was why she'd brought the raven to him. "Good night," she said. She began to walk out of the bathroom, then hesitated. "Eddie?"

"Yeah?" He looked up from the raven.

Fin swallowed hard. "Lock your doors and windows tonight."

Eddie's skin was both tanned and freckled from hours spent in the sun, but now Fin watched as the color drained from his face. He understood, even if she didn't say the words.

"You . . . ," he began to say, but he faltered. Fin knew what he was trying to say: "*You found it?*"

Fin nodded jerkily.

Eddie's gaze dropped to the injured raven, and his mouth flattened into an angry line. It took a lot for Eddie to get angry, but anyone hurting an animal would set him off instantly.

"I'll make sure nothing gets in," he said, and Fin's shoulders wilted with relief.

Fin walked out of the bathroom and passed Aunt Myrtle. She had a plate with bits of cooked rice on it, probably leftovers for the raven. "You going back to the cottage?" she asked.

"Yeah," Fin said. "I'm tired."

It wasn't a lie. Now that the raven was safe, exhaustion settled into her every limb. Her bed sounded wonderful—provided it was behind a locked door, of course.

Fin remembered the eerie grace of the monster—of Tea Fin—creeping up out of the sink and through that crack in the window. Fin would have to make sure every window in the cottage was secure before she could sleep. At least Mom would lock the door behind her when she came home. Even if Aldermere was safe, Mom would never sleep in an unlocked house.

"You did a nice thing, sweetie," said Aunt Myrtle, patting her on the shoulder. "Saving that bird. I'm proud of you."

The words sank into Fin like splinters, sharp slices of pain that she wanted to dig out. She wasn't brave or nice; she'd stolen tea, unleashed a monster—a monster that had broken into Mr. Madeira's home, injured a bird, stolen Talia's spare key, and made off with every bit of magical tea in Aldermere. It was only a matter of time until people figured it out and Fin would have to let the world know how badly she'd screwed up.

She thought of the disappointed expression on her mother's tired face, and her stomach clenched.

No, Fin thought. Things weren't hopeless yet. Fin knew what the monster looked like, and she would find it again. She would stop it.

Fin walked to the back door. She took a breath of the peppery redwood air and began to step outside.

She froze mid-step.

The cottage was fifty feet from the big house. It had never seemed a long distance, but now it looked as wide as a football field. Fin hadn't understood the true meaning of night, not until she'd moved to Aldermere. Cities always had streetlights, car headlights, distant glows from shopping centers or storefronts. But in the forest, where the branches were so thick they crowded out moonlight, the darkness was impenetrable. The cottage was tucked against the edge of that forest, its windows black and door locked. Because Fin had made sure to lock it.

Her fingers found her house key jammed deep in her pocket. She held it so tightly that its metal teeth bit into her skin.

Go on, she thought. *Step down. Just step down. Do it on the count of three. One, two, three—*

She didn't move.

Things lurked in the dark. Tea Fin and the monster that lived in Bower's Creek and the ravens that slept in the trees overhead and those deer with the strange shadows.

Be brave.

She stepped down from the doorstep, walking as quickly as she could without breaking into a jog. If she could pretend she wasn't afraid, maybe the fear wouldn't be real, either.

The long grass brushed her bare fingers as she walked toward the cottage. The forest loomed ever closer, the tall branches catching what little moonlight fell across the ground.

She was fine. It was fine, she was—

A branch snapped somewhere to her left.

Fin broke into a sprint, her breath coming in a jagged gasp. Her feet slammed against the ground and the grasses dragged at her jeans and shoes. She was too slow, and the cottage too far and—

She stumbled up the stairs and nearly fell against the front door. She tried to shove her key into the lock, but her hands were shaking too badly. She didn't dare glance behind her. She had to unlock the door, unlock the door, unlock, un—

The key slid home and she twisted it. The door came open and Fin stumbled inside, yanking her key free and shoving the door shut with a loud bang. She leaned against it, gasping for air, heart beating so hard that it burned. She covered her mouth with one hand, trying to block out the sounds of her own breaths, and listened. For a footstep, for the sound of wet tea leaves falling against the wooden steps. For anything.

But she didn't hear a thing.

She locked the door, climbed up to her loft, and unknotted the laces on her shoes. She let the shoes drop against the floor with soft thumps. She didn't bother getting undressed; she buried herself beneath the covers. Maybe it was childish to think that blankets could protect her, but she felt better the instant she was beneath them.

She was safe.

Yet even as she calmed, a terrible thought occurred to her. She was safe—but Mom would still be walking home alone.

Fin lay there, wondering if she'd made a mistake by telling no one but Eddie about the monster. If she had, she'd have been in trouble—but also, people would know to be on their guard.

There was nothing she could do now. Nothing but lie awake and wait for her mother to come home.

It took twenty minutes. Twenty minutes that were an eternity. Fin heard someone unlocking the door and rolled over to see the familiar shape of Mom's shoulders and short haircut silhouetted in the darkness.

Fin listened to Mom lock the door and stumble over Fin's dropped shoes. There was something comforting in the grumble of Mom's voice as she picked up Fin's sneakers and tucked them against a wall. Then Mom walked into her small bedroom and shut the door behind her.

Fin lay there, gazing up at the ceiling. She didn't glance at any of the windows.

After all, if she could see anything out there, it meant something could see her.

THIRTEEN

Ravens and Secrets

Fin and Eddie left for school early.

Mom hadn't even been awake when Fin had slipped out of the cottage, backpack slung over one shoulder. They would need the extra time to bring the raven to Nick. Eddie kept yawning and jamming his fist against his mouth. In his other arm, he gently held a cardboard box with holes poked into it. Fin had offered to carry it, but Eddie waved her off.

As they walked, Fin told Eddie everything: about how the cottage had been broken into by the tea monster, about how it had taken Talia's spare key, about the monster coming out of the tea shop wearing Fin's face, about the injured raven and the choice Fin had made.

"I know, I know," Fin said, when she was done. "I should probably have gone after it. I mean, letting Tea Fin go was a mistake."

Eddie squinted at Fin blearily. "Teafin?" Maybe it was his exhaustion, but the word was more crammed together when he said it—like it was a real name.

"I couldn't keep thinking of it as the tea monster," said Fin. "And—well. It looks like me. Exactly like me, except for the eyes."

"It's always in the eyes," said Eddie, with all of the knowledge of someone who'd spent days playing video games. "That's how you tell one of your companions has been taken over by something evil."

"I haven't been taken over," said Fin. "It just—stole my shape."

"Well, maybe it was the only shape it could take," suggested Eddie. "Because you're the one who brewed it into existence, it has to look like you. Like how butterflies and moths change shape. That blobby thing we saw crawl out of the sink—that could be its larvae form."

Fin shuddered. "Thanks for making this even creepier."

"Anytime," said Eddie agreeably. "So it ate all the tea in the town and, well . . . grew up. Into its final evolution or whatever."

"You're making it sound like one of those bad monster movies," said Fin. "The kind that are all black-and-white and have people in rubber suits destroying cities."

"Hey, some of those movies are pretty good," said Eddie. "And I mean, so far it's keeping to the rules of those films. Next she's going to grow to the size of a house and—"

"Destroy Tokyo?" asked Fin. "Trap all of us in a tea ball? Wreak havoc upon the town? Just start eating us?"

"Okay, now you're the one making it creepy," replied Eddie.

"Well, it *is* creepy," said Fin. Their path sloped downward toward the highway. Fin had to lean back a little as they walked down the road. "It looks like me and it broke into two houses and it attacked a raven. All in three days. Who knows what it'll do next?"

"At least Nick can help with the raven," said Eddie.

Nick's full name was Nicodemus Elphinstone, but no one called him that. There were rumors that he couldn't come into town; Fin had overheard people muttering about everything from a bad tarot reading to the creature in Bower's Creek hunting for him. All anyone knew for sure was that Nick lived beyond the boundaries of Aldermere in a hand-built cabin with two tin men made of old soup cans dangling from the eaves.

Eddie rapped on the door. It took another knock before there were sounds from inside. Finally the door opened a crack and a man peered out.

He had a nose that looked as if it'd been broken a few times, a thin scar across his mouth—and his hair and brows were dark. He had the look of a worn-out guard dog. Fin wasn't great at guessing ages, but he looked a little older than Mom and Aunt Myrtle. "Someone need gas?" he asked, voice rough with exhaustion. "Place doesn't open for another hour. Tell 'em they can wait."

"It isn't that," said Eddie, and he held the cardboard box more tightly. "Sorry about this—but we found a raven. She's been hurt."

Nick passed a hand across his face, exhaling hard. He pushed the door open and said, "Come in." Fin saw he was wearing a gray bathrobe, sweatpants, and slippers with adorable pig faces on them. She blinked a few times.

Eddie walked in, but Fin hesitated on the porch. One of her mother's rules was to never enter an adult's home without another adult present.

Nick seemed to see her for the first time. "Ah, the Barnes girl," he said, with a nod. "You've got a head on your shoulders, don't you?"

Fin wasn't sure what he meant by that.

"Tell you what," said Nick. "You can come in or not. Keep the door open, if you like. Prop it open with a planter, if you think it'll lock."

"Oh, come on," said Eddie, from the doorway. He sounded a little exasperated. "It's just Nick. Why are you—"

"Don't talk to her like that," said Nick sharply. "Girl's got the right idea, being cautious. Someday you're going to blunder your way into something you can't get out of, Mr. Elloway."

He took the box from Eddie and strode into his house.

Fin watched him go. She'd never had anyone talk to her like that—like she wasn't being overly cautious. Like being careful was something to *aspire* to. Of course, he was a hermit who lived on the edge of town and sold overpriced gasoline to tourists, but still. She kind of liked him.

Eddie looked baffled; Fin knew he liked his ability to charm most everyone, so finding someone that it didn't work on, like Nick, must have been startling. "You are coming in, right?" he said, sounding unsettled.

Fin thought of the raven; it had been injured because of her.

"Yeah," she said, and stepped over the threshold.

She didn't shut the door, though.

The interior of Nick's house made her feel better. It

reminded her of the cottage—small but clean and organized. Fin walked past a sitting room with a laptop resting on a loveseat. In the next room was the kitchen, with a French press coffee maker and a bowl of fresh fruit. There was a tiny table beneath a window. Nick set the box on the table and pulled it open.

A croaking noise made Fin jump. She whirled around.

A raven sat on a coatrack, tucked in amid a few moldy-looking winter jackets. It hopped down, coming to rest on the nearby table. For all that the ravens were graceful in the air, they had a tendency to bob and stagger on the ground. This raven knocked over a stack of papers as it approached the box.

"Aletheia," said Nick, and there was a note of warning in his voice.

The raven looked at Nick and fluttered its wings. Fin couldn't help but think of kids in school who got caught trying to sneak into the hallways during class. Nick clucked his tongue and the raven puffed itself up indignantly, then turned and hopped back toward the coatrack.

"You have one for a pet?" asked Eddie curiously.

"Ravens aren't pets," said Nick. "Well, the town ravens aren't. Aletheia's a different story. She wouldn't survive in town, not anymore."

"What about our raven?" asked Eddie.

Nick bent over the box, looking over the injured raven.

"Hey there," he said, in an entirely different voice. Softer, almost a croon. He reached into the box, running his fingertips across the raven's back. "What happened to you?"

In reply, the raven made a soft grumbling noise and nibbled at his fingertips with her beak.

"Sprained wing, it looks like," Nick said. "Someone grabbed her badly—you see this in birds when kids try to catch them." He turned his dark, sharp gaze on Eddie. "Was it you?"

"I found her," said Fin, before Eddie could answer. "She was by the tea shop, sitting in the grass."

She didn't mention Teafin. Let him think a tourist kid had done it.

Nick nodded. "I can take care of her here. She won't be the first raven I've returned to the unkindness."

"What about that one?" asked Eddie, nodding at the raven on the coatrack.

The raven, Aletheia, returned Eddie's gaze with interest. She bobbed her head, as if trying to get a better look at the newcomers. "She can't return to the flock," said Nick. He stepped up to the rack, holding out a hand to the raven. She allowed him to run his fingertips through the short feathers near her beak. She even seemed to enjoy it.

"Why not?" asked Fin.

Nick's gaze fell on her. He reminded Fin of one of those private detectives she'd read about—all heavy brows and tragic past.

Fin squirmed beneath his scrutiny, wondering what he saw. Probably a skinny girl with unruly brown hair and hands that could never settle. Even now she was toying with a hangnail at the edge of her thumb.

"Do you know how magic works?" he asked.

The question startled her. "I—I mean . . . I think so?"

"Aldermere is a sanctuary," said Nick. "And to take magic outside is . . . problematic."

"Because magic vanishes once it passes the town borders," said Eddie impatiently. "We know."

"Yes," Nick says, "if it doesn't have something to protect it. In Aldermere, that is the forest. Outside, the magic would need something else to sustain it. Or more likely, someone."

"People can be magic?" asked Fin.

"Not inherently," said Nick. "But people can carry magic within themselves. Think of magic like a plant. Plants need soil, water, sunlight. Take away those things, and the plant will wither. If you take a magical artifact or animal out of Aldermere, it's like ripping a plant out of the ground and then expecting it to survive. It won't. But if magic is in a person—it's more like removing a plant and putting it inside a pot. It can survive for a time."

"For a time?" said Fin.

Nick nodded. "For the magic to keep thriving, a person would have to return to Aldermere. Again, think of it like watering a potted plant. It refreshes the magic, keeps it alive."

Fin glanced down at her raven in alarm. "But we're—right now we're—"

"Outside the town line, yes," said Nick evenly. "It's all right. Magic takes time to fade. This raven"—he touched the box—"would need to be here at least a week before anything went wrong. I'll have her back long before then."

Fin was beginning to understand. "Did that raven, Aletheia, leave Aldermere? Is that why she can't go back to the flock?"

"She didn't leave," said Nick, his voice harder. "She was taken." He turned to face Fin and Eddie, his face grave. "A man wanted to study the ravens. He lured her with food, caged her, and took her. The flock managed to get word to me, but I arrived too late and . . ." He let the sentence trail off. "She'd forgotten."

"Forgotten what?" asked Fin softly.

"The old ways," said Nick. He exhaled hard. "That's

what comes of telling people magic is real—they want to study it."

Eddie frowned. "But if people didn't believe at least a little, the town wouldn't have any business. People come here because Aldermere is weird. If they didn't . . . we wouldn't have a town."

Fin bit her lower lip. They were going to be late for school if they lingered any longer.

"We have to get going," she said, tugging on Eddie's sleeve. He seemed transfixed by Nick's words, and it took a few seconds for him to shake it off.

"Oh, right. School." Eddie squared his shoulders. "Thanks for helping, Nick."

Eddie turned and walked toward the front door, Fin following after. She was walking through the door when Nick said, "Ms. Barnes?"

Fin turned and looked at him. He had the kind of piercing look that made her want to shrink away. As if he could dissect all of her secrets with a single glance.

For a moment, he didn't continue. Then he said, "Some of us pretend for a reason."

She didn't know how to reply to that. She didn't even know what he meant. Maybe he was talking about her, how Fin spent most of her life pretending. Pretending to be normal, pretending that she wasn't always worried, pretending to be someone else.

Eddie was ahead of her, blithely striding toward the bus stop, and Fin wanted to follow after—but she didn't.

"Pretend what?" she asked.

"That the magic isn't real." Nick's dark eyes were intent. "I know tourism keeps the town going, but I've always thought the advertisements were a mistake. Have you ever heard of Glass Beach?"

Fin shook her head.

"It's farther south," he told her. "Near a coastal town. A long time ago, it was a dumping site for garbage, and over the decades, the waves wore it all down. Time and the tides made that garbage into something unique and beautiful. The glass was worn soft and smooth. You could stand on the beach and be surrounded by color."

"It sounds pretty," Fin said.

"It was," said Nick, "until the beaches were opened up to the public, and people began to take the glass. They wanted keepsakes. Most people are not content to observe. And now—now Glass Beach is little more than sand and pebbles. The beauty is all but gone. The same goes for magic. Those like your cousin take it for granted. They think it will always be here. But others understand what a rare and precious thing it is; we know that we have to keep it safe." Nick's voice was low, utterly serious. "Do you understand what I'm saying, Finley?"

She did understand. If it became common knowledge that Aldermere's magic was real, that it wasn't a tourist gimmick like most outsiders thought, then this place would be overrun. And the magic drained away.

Nick said, "If it was a magic hunter who injured that raven, if it was someone trying to study magic—you should tell me now. I can deal with it." The way he said that last sentence made Fin shiver. She didn't know what he meant by "deal with it," and she didn't want to know.

She swallowed. Her throat felt too dry to answer, but she managed. "I don't think it was."

"All right," Nick said quietly.

She turned and ran after Eddie, following him down to the bus stop, her heart pounding.

Nick was right—magic *was* rare and precious, and it had to be protected.

And Fin thought of Teafin, of the way she'd said, *"People to find, scores to settle."*

A chill swept through Fin. She'd been mostly concerned with telling Talia about what had happened, about Mom finding out and sending Fin to a counselor—but what if the stakes were higher than she'd assumed?

Teafin was chaotic and unpredictable. What if she changed from a girl to a tea monster in front of someone with a cell phone or a camera? It was one thing for a tourist to get a tarot reading. It was another to see a girl who flaked tea leaves and didn't hesitate to break into people's houses. If the wrong person learned about Teafin, about what she *was* and what she could *do*, the entire world could find out about Aldermere.

Then it wouldn't just be tourists who hiked, bought postcards, and posted pictures of themselves with the Bigfoot statue near the highway. It would be scientists looking for whintossers or people who might drag nets through Bower's Creek. It would be people willing to sift through Aldermere to find whatever made it different, even if that meant destroying the magic.

Fin loved Aldermere. It was the first place she'd ever had a home, not just a place to stay. Fin couldn't be the reason that its magic was taken away.

She had to stop her double. But she didn't know how. Clearly a lacrosse stick wasn't the answer. Fin couldn't ask Aunt Myrtle for help. There had to be another way to find answers. A way to dispose of tea—

Fin stumbled over a crack in the pavement.

Of course there was a way to dispose of tea. Talia had been brewing it for years without something like this happening. There was probably a step that Fin hadn't known about. If Fin was lucky, Talia might have written those instructions down.

One thing was certain. She had to visit the tea shop again.

FOURTEEN
The Third Heist

Fin barely remembered what happened at school. She took notes without noticing what they were on, and she ate her bagged lunch in the cafeteria with a kind of robotic absence. A girl glanced at Fin, then whispered something behind her fingers to another classmate, probably remarking on Fin's baggy secondhand jeans or her worn sneakers. On any other day, Fin would have felt a pang of shame that she couldn't afford the kind of clothes the popular kids wore. But now Fin didn't care what her classmates were saying. She had other, more important concerns.

Finally she was back on the school bus again—sitting beside Eddie, her backpack clutched against her chest, and

Highway 101 winding through the trees. Eddie was chatting to an older kid who lived north of Aldermere, while Fin gazed out the window.

The bus let them off at the carving shop beside the 101 and Fin followed the other kids up the road to Aldermere. Cedar hung back a little; her dark brown hair shone auburn in the sunlight. "Hey," she said. "You okay?"

Fin wondered if her worries were written across her face. "Yeah, why?"

Cedar's gaze swept over her. "You've been kind of quiet."

Fin broke into a laugh. "I'm always quiet."

"Not with Eddie," said Cedar. "You're always talking with him."

That was true. Eddie was the one person she could talk to without her anxiety getting in the way. "He's family," she said, as if that were explanation enough.

"Is he your only family?" asked Cedar. "Besides your mom and your aunt, of course."

Fin hesitated. "Yeah. I mean, I never knew my grandparents—they died a long time ago." When she finished, Fin felt obligated to return the question. "What about you?"

"My dad's side of the family lives in SoCal," said Cedar. "We get together for holidays and stuff. There aren't a lot of kids, so I mostly hang out with my abuelita. My mom's side is in New Hampshire, so we're not close." She looked a little wistful. "I love my family, but I'm not really *friends* with them. Not like you and Eddie. You two are tight, I get that. But you know, if you need someone else to talk to . . ." She shrugged and let the offer trail into silence.

Unbidden, Teafin rose to the forefront of Fin's mind: the easy step of the monster girl and the way she stood with her arms held loosely at her sides—not with her hands shoved awkwardly in her pockets like Fin usually kept them. Half the time Fin wasn't even sure what to do with her feet.

Maybe the tea girl was a monster, but she was a monster that didn't doubt herself—and Fin envied that.

Cedar drifted away and Fin watched her go. She and Eddie dropped their backpacks off at the big house; Fin had explained her plan to Eddie at lunch, and he'd agreed to go with her. Aunt Myrtle was out of the house and Mom was at work. Eddie found a plate of cookies in the fridge: oatmeal cookies with raisins and extra nut flour that gave them a strangely mealy texture. Even so, Fin took two. They were better than the protein balls.

They walked across town in a meandering path, so no one could guess their destination. Eddie was talking determinedly about the science fair; apparently River's attempt to create a working wind turbine out of Popsicle sticks wasn't going too well, and Eddie harbored a not-so-secret desire to beat him. Fin's interest in the science fair had waned to the point of indifference; she listened so she didn't have to talk.

They approached the tea shop from the back. A few ravens were perched atop the roof, talking to one another in hoarse squawks. They went silent when they saw Fin and Eddie, and a prickle of unease went up the back of Fin's legs. Maybe they resented her because she looked like the girl who'd hurt one of them.

Fin walked up the steps to the back door, reaching for the knob. There was an inch of space between the door and frame; Teafin hadn't shut it. She pushed the door open, and it creaked a little.

Fin walked in first, every step cautious. The shop smelled a little damp, a little abandoned—like old wood with underlying hints of tea. Eddie carefully shut the door behind them; neither dared to flick on a light. They tiptoed through the narrow hallway, past the place where Talia had fallen. Fin gently pushed open the door to the main room. It was empty—no Teafin in sight. Fin heaved a breath of relief. Then she glanced up at the shelves, and her heart sank.

The mason jars had been ransacked. They'd been pulled from the shelves and hastily shoved back into place, their contents gone. One lay shattered on the floor, bits of broken glass scattered among a few tea leaves. Eddie stepped up beside Fin, eyeing the mason jars.

"So Teafin took everything?" he said.

Fin nodded glumly. "It's probably how she grew from small enough to fit in a garbage disposal to—well, me sized. She needed to feed."

"That's a nice thought," said Eddie. "So how do we make her go away?"

Fin gestured at the interior of the tea shop: all dark woods, antique furniture, and the bookshelf full of paperback romances. "I hoped there'd be instructions somewhere in here. I mean, if other people brew tea at home, maybe Talia sends an instruction manual with them or something."

Eddie nodded. "Okay. I'll take that back storage room if you take this one. If either of us finds an instruction manual or notes or just—something labeled In Case of Tea Monster, Break Glass, then we shout. If Teafin jumps out at us, we should . . . probably shout louder."

Fin stepped hesitantly toward the counter. Her gaze slid over the broken jar, the empty ones, their labels half tugged off. To see it in such a state made her guilt all the worse. Fin tiptoed around to the hallway closet, where she found an assortment of vintage coats and even a fur stole. But at the very back, as Fin had hoped, there was an old broom. She found a heavy metal dustpan and carried both back to the counter. She swept up the broken glass and stray leaves of tea. Most had been taken, but there were a few bits of Ceylon and Assam beneath the wooden shelves and a tight curl of gunpowder green that had rolled behind the curtains.

A small metal bucket had been overturned, gray dirt spilling onto the floor. FOR ASHES, read an old label. Fin tipped it upright. It would serve well enough. She swept up everything, dumped it all into the bucket, and carried it outside to the garbage bin. Then she picked up the intact mason jars and put them in a row on the lower shelves. The FOR ASHES bucket went back behind the counter where Fin had found it.

It was good, putting things right. Or at least as right as she could make them.

Behind the counter was the cash register, and a few drawers. Fin found three notebooks and flipped one open. It held receipts and tax forms. Fin blinked at them; she'd never considered that a magical shop would have to worry about taxes. She reached down to one of the lower drawers and pulled it open. It looked like a series of bills. The next drawer was full of office supplies: paper clips and pens and envelopes. Another drawer had dog treats. *Probably for the ravens,* Fin thought, as Talia didn't own a dog.

There was no giant spell book. And perhaps it was foolish of Fin to hope for such a thing—to think there might have been an instruction manual or even a pamphlet. *Magical Tea for Beginners,* she thought, and had the wild urge to laugh. With a sigh, Fin leaned against the register.

Her fingers must have hit a button, because the cash drawer popped open with a small *ding*. Fin jumped, startled. She glanced down and saw dusty dollar bills gazing up at her. Ones, fives, tens, a few twenties—and even a little slot for foreign bills too. Fin had never seen so much money in her life. Talia must sell normal teas too, the kind that weren't bought with whispered memories. She was about to close the drawer when she saw something poking out of one corner. Fin frowned, lifting the drawer. It slid up easily, and beneath the cash section were scattered notes. She picked one up, heart throbbing with excitement.

Milk, it read. *Coffee creamer. Whole wheat bread. Cucumbers.*

A shopping list. Not the spell that Fin had been hoping for. She checked a second note and saw a list of chores; a third note contained a scribble about needing to call someone called Eudora. Fin shut the cash drawer.

Disappointed, she leaned against the counter. At least

Teafin hadn't touched the money. Well, the money *and* the mortar and pestle. Fin supposed it had been too heavy for Teafin to mess with, and Fin was glad for that. She liked the mortar and pestle—the veins of pink and white running through the heavy stone, smooth and cold against her fingers. Teafin had said it held the echoes of many memories, that such things weren't so easily destroyed.

Fin straightened. She had always thought the tea was magical—but what if it wasn't? What if the mortar, not the tea, was the important part?

Fin looked up at the mason jars. There had always been a lot of tea there, but surely there had to be more. Talia couldn't have relied on a few jars' worth to run her shop.

Heart beating a little too quickly, she turned and strode toward the back room. Eddie was on the floor beside a pantry, searching through what looked like old envelopes. "No magic spell books," he said. "Not even a copy of the witch's almanac that Mom keeps in the bathroom. Maybe—"

But Fin wasn't listening. She went right to one of the cupboards and pulled it open. It was full of boxes. She yanked one free and ripped at the cardboard, withdrawing what looked like a metal tube. It was vacuum sealed and on the side was a printed sticker label that read EARL GREY.

Teafin hadn't found all the tea. She hadn't even found *most* of it. She'd gone for what was obvious, in the front room. But this stuff looked like it was bought in bulk off the internet. Fin gazed at the metal tin of tea. Talia bought it elsewhere. Of course she did—because she didn't have giant gardens where she could grow her own plants. Now that Fin thought about it, it was obvious: the tea itself came from outside of town.

Which meant it was just *tea*.

"What's up?" said Eddie, standing. "You look like someone hit you over the head."

Her fingers gripped the tin even harder.

"It isn't the tea at all," said Fin aloud. "It's the mortar. The mortar infuses the tea with its power. It feeds on the memories that people give it. Talia buys tea off the internet. I know this brand—I've seen it at Brewed Awakening."

"And she puts it in mason jars to look more homemade," said Eddie, wrinkling his nose. "Well, that's kind of disappointing."

"It's not, though, because the mortar is the real magic," she said. "They take the memories, infuse the tea with magic, and then the used tea leaves must be like . . . the magical equivalent of nuclear waste or something. They have to be destroyed afterward."

"But how, though?" asked Eddie.

Fin shrugged. She put the tea back on its shelf and returned to the front room. The mortar sat there, silent and gleaming.

One hand resting on the countertop, Fin gazed out the window. A flicker of movement caught her eye. There was a good view of the town. She could see Mr. Hardin's grocery store, Brewed Awakening's rooftop, the edge of Mrs. Brackenbury's porch, and—

And a thin stream of something gray rising from the house beside it.

Fin frowned and took a step closer to the window. It looked like smoke, but it couldn't be. Aldermere had strict rules about burning. It was one of those things that was drilled into them even at school; fires could too easily catch in the dry forest, and after several years of drought, California's fire season threatened much of the state. Last summer, a nearby fire had muddied the horizon and left the sky a strange color of orange. Most of the town's older occupants had stayed inside or worn medical masks.

"What is it?" asked Eddie.

Fin walked closer to the window, her nose almost brushing the glass. Dark gray twined upward, flickering oddly and—and that was definitely smoke. Smoke next to old Mrs. Brackenbury's home. Fin thought of the old lady and her lumpy bulldog, both of whom were rather hard of hearing. Would they know?

"Smoke," Fin whispered.

Eddie jerked in surprise, and he followed her to the window.

"Maybe someone burned popcorn or something," he said, sounding hopeful.

A bell rang out—clanging so loudly that the sound emanated through the walls and the floor. Fin had only heard that bell once before: when a tourist kid had gotten lost in the woods. It summoned the volunteer firefighters.

"Okay, not popcorn, then," said Eddie. He glanced from side to side, racking his brain. "The house beside Mrs. Brackenbury is that small cabin. The guy living in it works at the inn, at the front desk."

"Ben," said Fin. Ben—who was always smiling and nice to her. She hoped nothing had happened to him. "Come on."

Fin made for the door; she checked that it remained unlocked before she pulled it shut behind Eddie. She had no idea where that spare key was—probably in Teafin's pocket. If a monster had pockets. And Fin might still need to get back into the tea shop.

Eddie was the faster of the two; he tore down the gravel driveway, over a neighbor's fence and through a couple of backyards.

There was a terrible acrid scent upon the air. It was bitter against the back of Fin's throat, and she coughed. Eddie skidded to a halt, nearly hitting a man watching from the sidewalk.

At least three people had already arrived—one of them had a hose and was spraying at the flames. It looked like the garden shed had caught fire, not the house. Another woman had a bucket in hand and was filling it up at a neighbor's spigot. Ben himself was cursing quietly as he jogged out of his home, carrying a very dusty fire extinguisher. He sprayed foam at the flames and they died away, falling back into the shed. Ben pulled the door open and stepped inside the smoking interior, waving away anyone who tried to follow.

A tall woman rushed past the gathering cluster of people. She had white hair streaked with cast-iron gray, and there was a distinctly hawkish look to her eyes and tight mouth. Fin knew her by sight—she was the head of the volunteer firefighters. But to her squirming discomfort, Fin realized she couldn't remember the woman's name. It was something like Pat or Patty or—

The woman moved with a kind of sturdy determination, a fire extinguisher in one hand and her other gesturing for people to get back. "Status?" she barked at Ben.

He jumped. "It's—it's under control. Must've been a wire chewed by one of the squirrels or a whintosser or something."

"We need to cut the power," said the tall woman.

"I *did* that, Mrs. Petrichor," said Ben. "The flames are out. It's all just smoke now."

Petrichor—that was it, Fin thought with relief.

Mrs. Petrichor eyed him with all of the warmth of a hawk looking for mice. "You haven't been burning illegally, have you?"

"What? No!" Ben shook his head.

"I'll have to check for signs of arson," said Mrs. Petrichor grimly, and began to walk toward the shed.

"I'm going to call my landlord," said Ben. He looked exhausted and more than a little shaken, and Fin felt sorry for him. "Let him know."

As if summoned by Fin's thought, Ben's gaze jerked up to meet hers. A strange expression passed over his face, and if Fin hadn't known better, she might have thought it was fear. "Hey, Fin," he said with an attempt at a smile.

But the corners of his mouth twitched uncomfortably. His gaze tracked between Fin and Eddie, and he seemed to be chewing on his next words. "Did you two just get back from school?"

"Pretty much," said Eddie. He wasn't great at lying, but he was making an effort.

"You didn't come back early?" asked Ben.

"No." Fin answered for them both. "Can we help?"

Ben smiled. "Thanks, but no. You should head on home. Fin, if you see your mom, tell her I might be late for my shift, okay?" He turned back toward the shed, but not before sliding Fin one last look.

It was this last glance that did it, tipping uncertainty into surety.

Ben was looking at Fin as if he was afraid of her. Ben had never looked at her like that before.

Which meant—

Fin drew in a sharp breath that tasted like burned wood and plastic. "Come on," she muttered to Eddie, and began pulling him away by the arm. Eddie, who liked a spectacle as much as anyone in town, went reluctantly. As Fin and Eddie walked around the front of the house, a voice called out to them.

It was Mrs. Brackenbury, standing on her porch. Her

bulldog, Mr. Bull, was sitting on the lowest step. Some of his girth overflowed, and he looked at Fin and Eddie with a hopeful wag of his stubby tail.

"What's all the commotion about?" asked the older lady, with a sharp glance in the direction of the smoke.

"Ben's shed caught on fire," said Fin. "He said it was probably bad wiring."

Mrs. Brackenbury puffed up with indignation. "It's those Wilsons," she said with a downward twist of her mouth. "Rich landlords living in the city, ignoring the upkeep of places they rent out. They own three houses on my street, and I know at least one of them's got termites." She sounded as though she was gaining momentum, but Fin didn't have time for a rant.

"See you later," she said.

They were halfway down the block before Eddie said, "All right, what's up?"

Fin shot another glance over her shoulder. "Did you see the way Ben was looking at me?"

"Not really," said Eddie.

"He was looking at me like he was scared," said Fin.

At that, Eddie burst into disbelieving laughter. "Yeah—yeah. You're terrifying. Almost as terrifying as Mr. Bull. We should have you doing security for the inn, you'd be—"

He cut off abruptly. Then he looked at Fin.

Fin looked back steadily.

"Oh, no," he said, finally getting it. "You think . . . ?"

"That Teafin set that fire?" said Fin. "Yeah. Yeah, I do."

FIFTEEN
Ashes and Discoveries

"I have deliveries," said Fin a little despairingly. The thought of traipsing about Aldermere, packages in hand, while some monster that looked like her was wreaking havoc was almost unbearable. But if she skipped out, Mr. Hardin might say something to Mom. And even if he didn't, word got around fast. People would ask why their medications or packages hadn't arrived on Tuesday, as always.

She and Eddie parted ways. He returned to the big house while Fin trudged toward the Ack.

The weight of everything slowed her down. She felt as if there was a visible mark on her, some way for everyone to see that she was hiding something, that she knew more about the fire and the break-ins than anyone else. It was her fault, after all. Surely people would see. But everyone's attention was on the fading plumes of smoke, and Fin found herself standing alone inside the tiny grocery store.

The place behind the cash register was empty. Fin gazed at it for a few moments, feeling even more off-balance. Mr. Hardin was *always* inside the Ack. To not have him here felt wrong. Everything was spinning out of control and she didn't know how to stop it—and now even her normal routine was falling apart.

"He said he'd be back in a few minutes," came a voice from behind her.

Fin turned.

It was Cedar. She gave Fin a small smile. "Mr. Hardin," she said, by way of explanation. "He said he'd be back in a few minutes. He wanted to see what all the commotion was about."

"A fire," said Fin. The words came from far away, not from herself. "At Bellhop Ben's house."

Cedar raised an eyebrow. "Bellhop Ben?"

Fin flushed hotly. She'd never let that nickname slip before. "It's just—Ben. From the inn. I—I had trouble remembering names when I first came to Aldermere, so I sort of nicknamed people in my head."

She half expected Cedar to laugh, but the other girl nodded.

"I do that," she said. "Except I attach a rhyme and a fact about the person. Like, 'Harry Hardin loves to garden.' Stuff like that."

"Do you have a rhyme for Eddie?" asked Fin, unable to help herself.

Cedar's smile sharpened. "Eddie, Eddie, always steady."

That fit. Eddie was always easygoing.

Fin opened her mouth to ask. She thought of all the things that would rhyme with her name—tailspin, has-been, even break-in. But then she forced the question down, because honestly, she wasn't sure she wanted to know.

"So it was a fire?" asked Cedar, and Fin nodded. Cedar gazed out the big front window, through the dusty glass and painted letters.

"Everyone was pretty freaked out about it," said Fin, glad for something else to talk about. "The head volunteer firefighter woman seemed to think that someone had set it."

"Mrs. Petrichor?" asked Cedar. She tucked a strand of hair behind her ear. "Yes, that makes sense. She would have to make sure it wasn't arson."

Fin frowned. "Who would set a fire?"

"Maybe a tourist kid," said Cedar. "Playing with a

lighter. Or someone has it out for Ben."

Fin forced a laugh. "There're some angry customers at the inn, but I don't think so."

"Maybe it was Mayor Downer," said Cedar thoughtfully.

"The mayor?" said Fin, startled. "I mean, I know Ben turned off her mic once at a town council meeting, but I can't see her trying to set him on fire afterward."

"I don't think she'd try to burn *him*. But the magic? She doesn't like unexplained things," said Cedar, as if it was perfectly obvious. "That's why she became the mayor. She wants to make this place *normal*."

Fin thought of Mayor Downer on people's lawns with a ruler, measuring the height of the grass. "Then she shouldn't live here."

Cedar shrugged. "Maybe she's the opposite of Nick—she's stuck in town. Other people go for jobs or shopping, but Mayor Downer never takes vacations." Cedar let out a breath. "Or she's scared to leave. People'll do that. They think it's easier to change a place than themselves."

"I don't know how setting fire to Ben's shed would change the town," said Fin.

"Well, if it got bigger," Cedar said. "It could change everything. Fire purifies. Strips things of their magic."

Burn nothing within the town borders.

Fin had always thought it was because of the threat of wildfires. Every late summer and early autumn, the state would be on high alert for any sign of fires. Fires could tear through dry forests like a match on newspaper. Every building in Aldermere had at least two fire extinguishers, and even matches were heavily restricted. Maybe it was as much to protect the magic as it was to protect the town.

Cedar added, "That's what happened to the old town."

"Redfern?" asked Fin.

"Redfern was caught in a wildfire," said Cedar. "Burned all the magic out of that place." She leaned forward, her voice lowering. "I've heard the adults talking about it. Dad volunteers with the firefighters, so Mrs. Petrichor comes over sometimes. No one knows for sure, but Mrs. Petrichor thinks the fire at Redfern was arson."

"Arson?" asked Fin, startled. "You mean someone tried to make the magic go away on purpose? Why?"

"Because magic scares some people," replied Cedar. "And I think it scared someone so much that they burned Redfern for it."

"I like the magic," said Fin.

"So do I," said Cedar. "It's why my family came here."

That startled Fin. She'd always thought that Cedar must have grown up in Aldermere like Eddie. "You moved here?"

"When I was six," said Cedar. "My parents were cryptozoologists. They self-published a few books, had a website and everything. They were trying to prove that Aldermere was the one place in California where cryptids were real."

"Proving that the magic is real . . . Wouldn't that be bad?" Fin thought of Nick and his raven and his warnings.

Cedar looked down at her shoes, frowning, and Fin's stomach lurched. Maybe she'd offended Cedar by questioning her. She should have kept her thoughts to herself.

"You're right," said Cedar, and Fin relaxed a fraction. "It's why everyone in town avoided us for so long. They didn't trust my parents, thought that every conversation might end up in a blog post or something. I didn't have any friends for the longest time and didn't understand why."

"Oh," said Fin. "I'm sorry."

Cedar shrugged. "By the time I was eight, my parents were kind of running out of money and they hadn't found anything because no one would explain the magic or the rules. So they ended up working at the coffee shop and eventually took it over. After that, people chilled out around us. Figured we were settling in." Cedar let out a wistful breath. "I know we're not supposed to investigate the creatures, but I'd still love to meet Bigfoot."

Fin said, "Isn't Bigfoot supposed to be a monster?"

Cedar's mouth crooked in a smile. "Monsters are only monstrous until you befriend them."

The bell above the door jangled, and Fin looked up to see Mr. Hardin. He wore the familiar apron of the shop, but there was sweat along his brow and he looked a little ruffled. "Ah, Finley," he said, "so sorry to keep you waiting. Were you here long?"

"No, it was fine," said Fin.

Cedar walked up to the counter and Fin saw what she was buying: a bag of cheddar popcorn. It seemed oddly mundane after their conversation.

Once Mr. Hardin had counted her change back, Cedar popped the coins into her pocket, tucked the bag under her arm, and made toward the door. As she passed Fin, she said quietly, "Fin, usually at the inn."

It took Fin a moment to understand—that was Cedar's rhyme for her.

Something tight unspooled in Fin's chest. It could have been much worse.

The door swung shut behind Cedar, leaving Fin alone with Mr. Hardin. The stray cat meandered down one of the aisles, meowing plaintively. Mr. Hardin rubbed at his forehead with a handkerchief. "You here for deliveries?"

Fin nodded. The cat wound around her ankles, and she squatted down to stroke his back. He purred loudly, then leaped up onto the counter.

"The fire's caused a commotion," said Mr. Hardin. "I doubt half the people who have deliveries are even home at the moment, and leaving stuff on porches will be too much of a temptation for the ravens." He looked apologetic. "How about you come back tomorrow or the next day? I'll have everything ready for you then."

She nodded. Again, there was that unsettling sensation that the world was spinning off its axis.

She left the grocery store, hands shoved deep into her pockets.

SIXTEEN

An Unwanted Talk

Mom had a plate of snacks waiting in the cottage when Fin arrived home.

She was still wearing her work clothes—pressed blouse and skirt. Her shoes were neatly tucked against the wall. Fin pulled off her shoes, and Mom said, "If I trip over those again, you're putting them on the porch for a week."

Fin thought of cold shoes in the morning and quickly shoved her shoes against the wall.

"How was work?" asked Fin. She sat at their small kitchen table and eyed the plate of grapes and cubed cheese. Normally this kind of thing meant there was a rare guest coming over. And Fin would usually grab a few grapes and scurry up to her loft with a book while her mom chatted with one of her coworkers or a neighbor.

"Go ahead and eat some," said Mom, seeing Fin's unsure glance.

"For me?" Fin popped a grape into her mouth. "Uh-oh, you're working the night shift again, aren't you?"

"Just for a few more days," said Mom, smiling. "Sofia is getting back from maternity leave, so my hours will go back to normal soon, thank goodness."

The cheese was some kind of white cheddar and Fin ate two squares before saying, "Then what's with the bribery snacks?"

"You don't know they're bribery snacks," said Mom.

Fin looked down at the cheese cubes. They were cut very evenly. Too evenly.

"Aren't they?" she said. She put a square of cheese into her mouth to buy herself some time.

"Sort of," Mom admitted. She sat down across from Fin, folding her hands on the table. "Sweetie. You know you can tell me anything, right?"

Fin stared at her.

She knew.

Oh—oh *no*. Mom knew. Ben must have told her about the fire and how he thought Fin had set it. And now Mom was doing that parent thing where she was giving Fin time to confess. It was like in one of Fin's favorite mystery books, when the police had suspects in custody and were trying to get the truth out of them.

Fin swallowed the remnants of cheese. Abruptly, they were crumbly and dry against her tongue.

She had two options.

Option A: she could confess. Throw herself upon her mother's mercy and beg for her help. Mom could handle pretty much anything; she'd raised Fin, worked several jobs, and moved them here. She was often distracted and busy, but Fin knew that Mom loved her. This option was the brave one, probably the right one.

Or there was Option B: which was to say—

"I don't know what you're talking about," Fin said, keeping her face expressionless.

Mom let out a breath. Her face was grave, which only made Fin's heart beat faster. She could almost feel the tea's magic draining out of her. Panic was like fire—it could burn all of the magic out of a person.

"Sweetie," Mom said again. "I know you sometimes get . . . nervous about things. You have for years. And sometimes people need a little more help and—and I asked your aunt Myrtle to talk to a friend of hers. She's a counselor who specializes in kids, and I think you should talk to her."

All of the dread that had been lurking in her body rose up, threatening to choke the words out of Fin. Mom didn't know about the tea shop or Teafin—but this was almost worse. It was shining a beacon on all the parts of herself that Fin hated and had been trying to hide.

It was the conversation Mom had tried to have with her at the town council meeting—and Fin should have known she would try again. Maybe she could convince Mom that she didn't need help.

"There's nothing wrong with me," Fin said. But even as she said the words, she didn't truly believe them.

"Of course there isn't." Mom reached across the table to take her hand, but Fin jerked back. Mom's frown deepened, but she didn't try to touch Fin a second time. "It's just—we don't talk about some things. We never have. And I think that's my fault, because I thought it'd be better to let you grow up. I'm not sure how much you remember about . . . before. With—"

"No!" The word burst out of Fin. She didn't know why, but she couldn't bear to hear the end of that sentence. It was like seeing the shadow of a monster around a corner, knowing that something was coming. And she had to run before it did.

"Fin," said Mom. She sounded pained. "Maybe it'll be easier for you to talk to a professional, because she'll know the right things to say when I clearly don't."

"I don't want to talk to anyone," Fin said stiffly. She wanted this conversation to end, she wanted to leave the cottage and be alone, she wanted—

Out.

She wanted out of this.

She stood up abruptly, the chair squeaking across the floor.

This was why she went to the tea shop in the first place—so she could be normal, so she could stop being afraid, so no one would know how much work it took to function. But now Talia was in the hospital, the tea shop had been ransacked, a raven had been injured, Ben's shed had nearly burned down, and it was all Fin's fault.

"We aren't finished talking about this," Mom said sharply.

"Yes, we are," Fin said. She couldn't remember the last time she'd argued with her mom—she didn't argue with anyone but Eddie. "I'm not talking to anyone. I'm fine."

She strode out of the cottage. Standing on the porch, her feet bare, she tried to catch her breath. The big house wasn't an option; Aunt Myrtle was the one who had suggested the counselor in the first place. With no place else to go, Fin ran down the steps and toward the woods.

Mom opened the door. "Fin?"

Fin ducked behind a tree and stayed there.

"Finley?"

Fin didn't move. She heard a soft sigh, then the closing of the cottage door. Feeling both relieved and a little disappointed, Fin rose from her crouch and walked into the woods.

The late afternoon sunlight felt good on her bare arms. She tried to focus on the sensations of the ferns brushing her fingertips and the soft redwood needles beneath her bare feet. She wouldn't go far—she couldn't, not without shoes.

The forest was solitude and quiet. It was everything Fin needed. She strode past a tangle of blackberry bushes. The underbrush thinned out and the shadows deepened. There was a fallen log, soft with rot and moss. Fin went to sit on it, clasping her hands around her knees. She was shivering, and she wasn't sure if it was because of cold or nerves.

She sat like that for several minutes, and her heartbeat slowed. Her fear collapsed into exhaustion.

"Hey there."

A familiar voice made Fin look up sharply.

And there she stood—the girl who was not a girl at all.

Teafin.

She was wearing the same clothes, but her hair had brambles in it and something dark smudged her fingertips. Her eyes were the silver of steel and her smile too sharp.

The last of the magic keeping Fin's fear at bay must have crumbled, because something gave way in her chest. She didn't have the lacrosse stick; it was still sitting on the porch of the big house.

"You," said Fin breathlessly. "You—"

But Teafin did not approach. She stood there, arms casually at her sides.

"Going to finish that sentence anytime soon, or should I get comfortable?" asked Teafin, grinning.

"You burned down Ben's shed," said Fin.

Teafin raised one hand to her mouth. Ash—that was what stained her fingers. A breeze tugged at her hair and clothes, and the scents of gasoline and smoke wafted off her.

"I tried, anyways," said Teafin.

"You really are a monster," said Fin weakly.

Teafin shrugged. "I mean, I'm mostly bits of you."

Fin stared at the girl who looked so much like her. Teafin might have been her identical twin, save for her eye color. Her evil twin, for sure.

And again came that pang of bone-deep fear, the one she'd been pushing away ever since she'd overheard her mom telling Aunt Myrtle that they'd left their home because of Fin. But Fin had never known why, never understood.

Unless she *had* once known. Unless she'd taken those memories and traded them for a few weeks of fearlessness.

Perhaps Teafin was a monster because Fin herself had the makings of one.

"Oh, come on," said Teafin. "You're just sitting there, all sad looking. Stop being boring and do something for once." She idly picked up a stray redwood branch. It had fallen with its tiny cones still attached, and Teafin toyed with them, pulling each one off and tossing it away.

Her doppelgänger's words sparked something hot within Fin. This creature had screwed up everything: Fin's life, the town, her neighbor's homes, and even the tea shop. Fin was used to glancing at herself in mirrors, taking in her appearance in half looks and brief moments. She didn't like the girl who looked back at her. And now that person was standing in front of her, every bit as terrible as she'd once feared, and Fin kind of hated her.

"I'm going to stop you," Fin said. She pushed away from the fallen log, hands clenched and brimming with anger. It felt good; she was so full of ire there was no room for fear.

"Are you?" asked Teafin, like she was amused by the thought.

"You should've stayed in the sink," Fin said. "You should've stayed where you belong."

Teafin smiled. But Fin had smiled like that a thousand times. It was how she smiled when she was uncertain. And seeing it on Teafin's face made Fin feel braver.

Quicker than thought, quicker than the eye could see, Teafin moved.

Fin cried out and tried to shove the other girl away, but they stumbled together and Fin found herself on the ground, Teafin crouched above her.

"Fear," said Teafin, "isn't something you can ignore. You can't close your eyes and wish it away."

Her hand closed around Fin's bare wrist—and the moment they touched, it was like being plunged into cold water.

Fin wasn't in the redwood forest; she was in an apartment building. There was water on the floor, shattered glass near her feet. A fish lay amid the water, too still. It was a goldfish, the kind with the bulging eyes, the kind Fin hated but didn't know why.

Fin knelt beside the fish and extended her hands out to the creature—

The world slammed back into her.

Fin was on her back, in the forest, shaking hard.

She forced herself onto her elbows. Teafin crouched a foot away, watching her with silver-eyed interest. "What," Fin gasped, "was that?"

"That," said Teafin, and she wasn't smiling this time, "is what I am made out of: all those pieces you tried to forget. Well, surprise—it didn't work. Not really. And now we've got a problem."

"Yeah, you," said Fin. She staggered upright, recoiling from Teafin. She didn't want those memories, didn't want to know what she'd forgotten.

Teafin took a step forward, but a shout cut through the forest.

"Fin! Fin?"

Eddie.

The sound made Fin want to crumple in relief.

Teafin's mouth twisted into a scowl. "This isn't over, you know," she said. Her feet were also bare, Fin realized. Teafin was dressed as Fin had been the night she made the tea—in a loose black hoodie and jeans, but no shoes. "This isn't going to end until—"

"Fin!"

Eddie walked into the small clearing. For a moment, everything was utterly still.

Eddie gazed at the scene in front of him—two Fins. Confusion flickered across his features. Then he began to cast about, as if looking for a weapon. But there were only fern fronds.

"Hey," he said, pointing at Fin, then at Teafin. "Whichever one of you is—I mean, whoever isn't the real one . . ."

But his voice trailed off, the threats collapsing in on themselves.

"We're both real," said Teafin, her voice icy.

Fin's fingers closed around a handful of dried redwood needles, and she threw them at Teafin's face. Teafin flinched back and covered her eyes while Fin scrambled toward Eddie.

Eddie's hand closed around Fin's wrist and he tugged and then they were running. Running through the forest, through the darkening evening, back toward the cottage and the big house.

Teafin's shouts faded behind them.

They didn't stop running until they were out of the woods, beside the cottage. Fin's lungs were scraped raw and her bare feet stung from the fallen redwood needles. As she caught her breath, she saw Eddie studying her with a line between his brows.

"What?" she said, more sharply than she intended.

"Just trying to make sure it's really you," he said after a moment. "Hard to see your eyes in this light."

She stared at him straight on, her face utterly unamused. A smile broke across his face and he nodded. "Brown eyes," he confirmed. "And you look like your mom when she found us playing with that rusty old rake behind the inn's garden shed. Definitely you."

"I do not look like my mom," said Fin. She didn't want to think about Mom, not right now. While most of her anger was reserved for herself—and for Teafin—there was still some left for Mom and Aunt Myrtle. None of this would have happened if they'd left Fin alone. She'd been fine, she'd been managing, and they'd had to screw it all up by trying to interfere.

"What were you doing out there?" asked Eddie.

"What were *you* doing?" asked Fin, still a little breathless.

"Your mom came to the big house looking for you," said Eddie. "She had to go to work. I decided to test my tracking skills. Good thing too. What happened?"

Fin told him a short version of the truth. She'd had a fight with her mom—she didn't say about what—and gone into the woods, where Teafin had found her. She didn't mention the memory that Teafin had forced on her. That felt strangely personal, like it shouldn't be shared.

Eddie gaped at her. "She actually came out to talk to you? Why?"

"Why do bad guys do anything?" Fin asked.

"Usually because a necromancer has reanimated them," said Eddie. When Fin gave him an incredulous look, he added, "You read the boring mystery books! I play games. And usually fight zombies."

"All right," said Fin. "Well, I'm pretty sure she isn't going to summon a zombie army."

"I hope not," said Eddie fervently. "Because there's a lot of compost piles out there with tea in them. Imagine it. Tea zombies."

Fin shuddered. "Please never say the words 'tea zombies' again. How would you deal with them? You'd have to . . ." Her voice drifted off. "Have to . . ."

The smell of burning still lingered in her nose.

She remembered what Cedar had said about fire, what had happened to Redfern—and a metal bucket behind the counter in Talia's tea shop labeled FOR ASHES.

"I know why there aren't more Teafins running around," Fin breathed. It all made sense now. "Talia—she burns the tea leaves afterward. Fire destroys magic."

"Yeah, I know," said Eddie. "Mom considered branching out into making scented candles, because those are really popular right now, but she thought it was too risky, with the magic and all."

"You knew?" said Fin, aghast. "This whole time you knew how to destroy Teafin?"

Eddie blinked several times. "No—I mean, fire's supposed to cleanse, according to all of those witch almanacs Mom keeps in the bathroom."

"You read witch almanacs in the bathroom?" asked Fin.

Eddie shrugged. "Sometimes I forget a comic book. Point is, fire's a purifier. I never realized that's how Talia got rid of the magicked tea leaves."

"It has to be," said Fin. "I found a bucket full of ashes in the tea shop."

Eddie beamed at her. "Talia must tell everyone who takes the tea home to do the same thing. But kids can't play with fire. So that must be why she never let you take any tea home."

Fin glanced back at the forest. Evening was coming on, darkness collecting in the spaces between the trees.

"Well," she said. "At least now we know how to destroy Teafin."

"Yeah," said Eddie, and for the first time, he sounded

doubtful. "We just—uh. Have to set her on fire."

There was a moment of silence.

"That might be a problem," said Eddie.

"You're right," agreed Fin.

"We're not killers," said Eddie, and at the same time Fin said, "We don't have matches."

They looked at each other.

There was a longer pause. A bit more uncomfortable.

"Well, we can't let her run around," said Fin. "She's already hurting people—well, a raven. She's stolen stuff. And what if she burns down someone's house? We can't let anything happen to the town."

Eddie didn't look convinced.

Fin said, "Come on, you've killed tons of monsters in your games."

"None of those monsters looked like you, though," replied Eddie. "I'm not sure I could hurt another person, when you get down to it."

"She's not a person."

"She looks like a person."

"I saw some of her hair come off," said Fin, "and it turned back into soggy tea leaves. She's made of tea and memories, and she should never have existed in the first place." She took a deep breath. "And I'm going to stop her."

SEVENTEEN
The Raven Returns

Despite its small size, Aldermere had a weekly newspaper.

The *Aldermere Oracle* was about five pages long and normally consisted of a few news articles (local highway closures, accounts of town council drama, and the occasional lost pet), a weather prediction (Aunt Myrtle firmly refused to do it, no matter how much the editor begged her), an advice column for people who wanted to write in about irritating relatives and relationships (author unknown), and a recipe (presumably provided by Mr. Madeira).

Newspapers showed up on doorsteps every Wednesday morning. No one knew how they were delivered—and no one questioned it.

Fin woke early on Wednesday, if only so she could avoid Mom. They hadn't spoken to each other much last night; Fin returned to the cottage and immediately climbed the ladder into the loft. When Mom came back from work late, she had checked to make sure that Fin was in bed, but she hadn't said a word. Fin heard the bedroom door click shut with mingled relief and regret.

She loved Mom—but sometimes it felt like there was a divide between them. Mom was like Eddie and Aunt Myrtle; she didn't understand.

Fin got dressed in the dark and unlocked the front door. The newspaper sat there, tied with twine. Fin picked it up and jammed it into her back pocket. She liked reading it on the bus, and Mom could always get another copy at the inn.

Eddie had slept in and looked both rumpled and half asleep when he met her by the door of the big house. Their walk down to the redwood-carving shop was a silent one; both were lost in their own thoughts. Fin kept remembering the cool, slick touch of Teafin's fingers against her bare skin and the plunge into memories. She kept wondering what parts of herself she'd given up and if those parts were truly monstrous.

Eddie finally woke up when they climbed into the school bus. His jaw cracked as he yawned and said, "You do realize it's this Sunday, right?"

"What's this Sunday?" Fin was half listening as she slid the twine from the rolled-up newspaper. It was a little damp on one side, and Fin took care to pry apart the pages so they didn't tear. CRIME SPREE IN ALDERMERE CAUSES CONCERN AMONG RESIDENTS, went the top headline.

"The science fair," said Eddie. "You know—the thing that started all of this? The reason I've got two lizards in a tank in my room? The reason we've got a half-finished poster about native plants in the living room? I know Teafin matters and all, but failing science isn't going to help things." His hands clenched. "River was bragging that he got his stupid windmill working. I overheard him yesterday at lunch. Green energy's popular right now, so he figures he'll win."

"Oh," said Fin. She'd honestly forgotten about the science fair in the wake of . . . well, everything else. "Right. We'll—uh. We can work on it later. I promised Mr. Hardin I'd go back and finish those deliveries today." She turned her attention back to the paper.

Her heart still throbbed at the thought that Ben had seen Teafin set the fire and could accuse Fin herself of the crime.

A crime spree has struck the normally peaceful town of Aldermere. "It seems residents must begin locking their doors at night," says Mayor Downer, in an exclusive interview this reporter obtained while the mayor was locked out of her car. "We should all be more diligent."

The crimes began with an attack on a well-known pillar of the community. Mrs. Marian Brackenbury was mugged on Tuesday, September 10. "They took my shopping," says Mrs. Brackenbury. "And they left before I could set my dog on them." Known for her olallieberry jam, which placed three times in the county fair, Mrs. Brackenbury seems an unlikely target for such a crime. Many residents were hoping it was a one-off, but then the Madeiras' home was burglarized. Add in a case of suspected arson, and there could be a criminal among us.

Fin's breath caught, and she read on so fast the words nearly blurred before her eyes.

Ben Byrne, whose shed was the target of the arson, refused an interview with the Oracle, *saying, "It wasn't arson, it was bad wiring, and if you don't get off of my lawn I'll make sure you can't come to the next town council meeting."*

Despite the witness's unwillingness to come forward, this intrepid reporter—

Fin let out a long, relieved breath.

Ben hadn't talked to the *Oracle*.

"Are you actually reading that?" said Eddie. He sounded exasperated. "The *Oracle*'s never gotten it right, not since I can remember. It's Ms. Catmore trying to stir up gossip."

"Your mom reads this," said Fin.

"She reads the advice column," replied Eddie. "And she likes the recipes. But the news is always wrong."

"Well, she was right about Mrs. Brackenbury getting mugged and someone setting fire to Ben's shed," said Fin. She continued reading, glad that the curves of the highway didn't make her carsick. Eddie could never read during bus rides. As she read, she let out a horrified little laugh.

"What?" Eddie sat up straighter. "Did something else burn down?"

Fin pressed a hand to her mouth. "Just—the latest crime. Someone vandalized Mayor Downer's lawn."

"No," Eddie said, aghast. "She keeps that thing perfect. Even during the drought months when we're really not supposed to be watering anything, it's always exactly one inch tall and green."

"Yeah." Fin's eyes flew across the words. "Apparently someone snuck into Mayor Downer's yard last night and cut the lawn so it . . . uh, spelled out something very rude."

"If I hadn't seen Mom at dinner last night, I might have thought she was behind it," Eddie said, relaxing back into the bus seat.

Fin grimaced. "Or maybe it's Teafin. Setting fire to a shed, breaking into Mr. Madeira's house, vandalizing Mayor Downer's lawn—I wouldn't put it past her."

"I mean, it's kind of a harmless prank," said Eddie. "Probably one of the neighbor kids."

Fin looked down at the picture of Ben's burned shed. "I wonder why Ben didn't tell the *Oracle* about . . ." She didn't want to say the words aloud.

Eddie looked thoughtful. "He may not have gotten a good look at Teafin. Maybe he caught a glimpse, or . . ." His voice trailed off.

"Or what?" asked Fin.

Eddie shrugged. "Ben likes you," he said. "Maybe he didn't want to get you in trouble. And I mean, your mom is his boss. He isn't going to accuse you without proof."

That was something Fin had never considered. She always thought of Mom in her office, managing giant piles of paper and keeping guests happy. It never occurred to her that Mom was actually someone's boss.

Fin looked down at the newspaper; she was holding it so tightly that the paper crinkled beneath her fingers. The last line of the article read, "Will this crime spree continue?" The school bus jounced beneath her and she gritted her teeth.

"Not if I have anything to say about it," she said quietly.

The problem was getting hold of matches.

Just as Eddie had said, Aunt Myrtle didn't keep them in

the house. Even so, when they got home from school Fin spent a good hour searching the junk drawers of the big house while Eddie looked on in quiet disapproval.

"I still think this plan is kind of evil," he said. "And besides, the grocery store doesn't even sell matches or lighters."

"What about the inn?" said Fin, then immediately quashed that plan. "No, Ben's already suspicious. And if he catches me stealing matches . . ."

"Not a good thing," said Eddie. He rubbed at the back of his head. "Listen, Fin. I still think this is . . . I mean, it's one thing to try and chase a tiny blob of tea through the woods, but it's something else to—"

"Talia's," said Fin, alighting on the idea. "She has to burn the tea. She must keep matches around somewhere."

"So you want to break into Talia's a third time?" said Eddie, exasperated.

"Is it really breaking in if the back door's unlocked?" Fin asked.

"Yes."

"All right, then," said Fin. She was a little pleased that the idea of rule breaking was getting easier. Maybe it meant she was becoming a little more fearless—or desperate.

"No," said Eddie, crossing his arms in a rare show of

irritation. "Nope. We are not doing this now. We have a science fair project, remember? And even if I'm not going to beat River with his windmill monstrosity, I refuse to show up with anything less than a decent terrarium."

Shame flooded Fin's chest. She had been a terrible science fair partner—and Eddie was so cheerful and easygoing that this show of displeasure hit her all the harder. All the chaos surrounding Teafin had sent Fin's life into a tailspin; she still hadn't returned to the Ack for her deliveries, even though it was Wednesday. She wasn't speaking to Mom. And now Eddie was irritated with her.

She had to do better.

She'd call Mr. Hardin and tell him she'd stop by tomorrow—that would give her enough time to finish working on the science fair project with Eddie. She owed him that much. As for Mom . . . Fin would talk to her. Eventually. At some point.

"Yeah, you're right," she said. "Let's work on the science fair stuff."

And maybe, just maybe, if they did well in the science fair, Mom wouldn't bring up the counselor again.

"We should get a few more plant samples," said Eddie. "I want to pin them to the poster and label them."

Fin looked at the lizards in the tank; one was sunning

itself beneath a heating lamp. They appeared to be unconcerned with their temporary gig as science fair displays. Or they were unaware. "Here," said Eddie, giving Fin a hand-drawn picture of a flower. "Bring back a few of these. They grow out back, behind the wood pile."

Fin nodded and took the paper, a little glad to be on her own. Between her mom, Teafin, Eddie, and school, she hadn't had a moment to herself for a while. She stepped out the back door. Aunt Myrtle kept her wood pile on the western side, neatly stacked on pallets and kept dry with a small tarp pinned to a nearby tree. Fin walked around the back, damp grasses brushing at her ankles, and began to search for the flowers. She pushed aside a few ferns and was kneeling beside the tarp when a voice called out to her.

"Ms. Barnes."

Her head jerked up. No one in Aldermere called Fin by her surname. Fin rose from her crouch and saw a man standing about twenty feet away. Fin blinked through the late afternoon sunlight and saw dark hair and a slightly crooked nose.

"Nick," she said, then shook her head. Eddie had called him that, but she didn't know him. "Mr. Elphinstone."

A faint smile tugged at the corners of his mouth. "Nick," he said, "is just fine." He walked forward, and she realized he was carrying something. His long fingers were curled carefully around a small raven. "I thought you should see her off. Since you found her."

Fin stepped closer. The raven, to her relief, was peering around the world with a kind of mild curiosity. The bird didn't seem disturbed by Nick's gentle grip on her.

Unease coiled at the base of Fin's spine. The bird had been hurt by Teafin, and maybe the raven had communicated that to Nick. He did have an affinity for them. What if the raven had told him that Fin was the guilty culprit, and Nick had come here as a sort of test?

Fin forced herself to breathe evenly. "She going to be okay?"

Nick nodded. He tickled the raven beneath her beak, stirring the shorter feathers with the edge of his thumb. The raven made a strange, happy grumbling sound.

"She's all healed up," said Nick. And without warning, he opened his hands and tossed the bird into the air.

Her wings opened at once, flapping wildly as the raven righted herself. She did a loop about the yard, letting out a few excited croaks.

Nick watched her, smiling slightly.

Fin expected the raven to flap off into the trees, but the sound of wings slicing through the air grew louder, and then it was right beside her ear. Fin cried out as the raven's wingtip glanced across her head.

It was attacking. It did remember Teafin, did blame Fin, and—

And then all was still. Fin stood there, eyes squeezed shut and one arm raised defensively, but nothing happened.

There was an odd weight on her shoulder. Fin cracked open one eye and looked to her left.

The raven sat on her shoulder. She made a sound like a chuckle, low in her throat. Fin remained frozen in place, unsure what to do. The raven hopped closer, then ran her beak through Fin's hair.

"Crows and ravens have long been associated with bad luck," said Nick. "But in older traditions, they were often watchers or servants of old gods. They were associated with prophecy and with great deeds. They are death and victory in equal measure. Even today, there's still the superstition that if the ravens ever leave the Tower of London, the kingdom will fall. They're smart creatures, corvids. They recognize people." Fin wasn't sure where he was going with this, but then Nick said, "Hold up your hand to her."

The raven was still perched on her shoulder, and with slightly shaking fingers, Fin raised her hand to the bird. The raven made another soft chuckling sound and began gently nibbling at Fin's fingertips.

"What," said Fin, "is she doing?" She still half expected the bird to attack her.

"She likes you," said Nick. "You should give her a hard-boiled egg once a week. Or raw scraps of meat. She'll appreciate it."

"What?" said Fin, startled almost beyond words. "Am I supposed to keep her?"

Nick laughed, and the sound was low and raspy. As if he was unused to laughing. "No, Ms. Barnes. One doesn't keep a wild raven. But sometimes, if you're lucky—a raven might choose to keep you." He took a few steps back, gave Fin a small courtly bow, and strode back in the direction of his home—outside the town lines.

Fin called after him, unable to help herself.

"I thought—I thought you didn't come into town," she said. She wasn't sure what made her say it. She probably shouldn't have—it wasn't her business.

Nick paused mid-step, then threw a calculating look over his shoulder at her. "Good afternoon, Finley." And then continued on his way, leaving Fin with even more questions.

The raven croaked, then took flight, alighting atop the woodpile.

Fin liked animals, but she'd never had a way with them, not like Eddie. She'd scratch Mr. Bull's ears or pet the cat that lurked around the grocery store, but that was the extent of her animal interactions.

The raven made a clicking sound low in her throat. It sounded like a rusted door hinge.

"Hi," Fin said.

The raven cocked her head, staring beadily at Fin.

"I didn't attack you," Fin said. "I—I think you know that? Is that why you like me? Because I took you away from her?"

The raven clicked again. Then she began wiping her beak along a cut piece of wood. Fin shook her head, unsure of what else to say. "Listen, I have to find some plants or Eddie is going to stay mad at me," she told the raven.

The raven croaked again. Then she spread her wings and took to the air, flapping off toward Main Street. Fin watched her go, still uncertain of what had just transpired.

EIGHTEEN
Shadows in the Night

They finished working on their science fair project that night.

Fin left a note for her mom in the cottage, saying that she was going to spend the night in the big house so she and Eddie could do homework together. It probably wouldn't matter. Mom had the late shift again. And Aunt Myrtle didn't mind her staying over for schoolwork. She brought plates of mac and cheese—homemade, not the kind Fin made from the box—up to Eddie's room around seven. She gazed down at the poster board, which now had bits of greenery pinned to its surface. Fin, who had the neater handwriting, was carefully labeling each one.

"I miss school sometimes," Aunt Myrtle said with a kind of wistful sigh. "All that learning."

Fin glanced doubtfully at the tank, where the lizards were eating a few bugs that Eddie had brought for them. So far all Fin had learned was that these lizards weren't fond of the black beetles but did enjoy grasshoppers.

Eddie was looking up the Latin names for all the plants. ("River's windmill won't have a Latin name," he'd muttered. "Maybe that'll count for something.")

They worked well into the night, only finishing when Eddie rocked back on his heels and looked satisfied. They had ten different native plants, both in the terrarium and on the poster, as well as the lizards.

Fin crawled into a sleeping bag on the floor, exhausted but oddly satisfied by the whole thing. The work had been distracting enough that she'd spent a good few hours without contemplating tea monsters or ravens or the sight of smoke billowing up from Ben's shed. For one whole evening, everything had been normal again.

Sleep came quickly—but when she opened her eyes, it was still dark out.

Her fingers slid against the cool, slick material of the sleeping bag. She thought she'd heard something—a tap or a knock. She rolled over, glancing at Eddie. His arm was thrown over the side of his bed and his mouth hung open. Fin smiled a little, about to close her eyes, when a movement made her blink.

Eddie's bed was beneath a window. Sometimes he'd crawl out of it and sit on the roof, much to Mom's distress. Aunt Myrtle never seemed to mind Eddie on the roof, but Fin never went out there, partly because Mom forbade it and partly because she wasn't big on heights. She wasn't afraid of them—she just had a healthy respect for falling. She had never clambered up the water towers the way some kids did, either.

But now she saw movement out there. A flicker of something through the smudged glass, too faint for her to make out details.

Fin sat up, all thoughts of sleep gone in an instant.

It could be a raccoon. It could be an opossum.

But she knew it wasn't.

Fin slipped out of the sleeping bag as quietly as she could. The room was dark; Eddie couldn't sleep with any real light in the room, so the computer was turned off and there was no nightlight. Fin moved as best she could in the darkness, hands casting about for—yes, there it was. She found the lacrosse stick that Eddie had propped up against his computer desk.

Her fingers tightened around it.

She glanced back to the window, but she saw nothing beyond it.

Even so, Fin did not relax. She was pretty sure Aunt Myrtle didn't lock her doors at night—half of Aldermere didn't. The town was supposed to be safe. The only monsters were the kind that lurked in the mists or stayed in Bower's Creek. If they walked the streets, they passed unseen and unfelt. But now a monster was in the town . . . and possibly inside the house.

She left the bedroom, tiptoeing down the stairs, lacrosse stick in hand. She listened as hard as she could—and she heard a *drip drip drip* that set her teeth on edge. Raising the stick, she edged into the kitchen, fearful of what she would see.

It was the faucet, dribbling water. Fin tightened one of the knobs and the water ceased.

Heart still throbbing, she glanced around the kitchen. Everything seemed normal and calm, but she couldn't believe that. Not after everything that had happened.

She hurried to the front door; as she'd suspected, it wasn't locked. She twisted the deadbolt into place, then headed for the back door. As she walked, she passed by a long window in the hallway.

Something moved outside.

Fin whirled. Something was out there. And it was heading around back.

Gripping the lacrosse stick so hard that her hands ached, she rushed through the dining room. The back door was closed—unlocked, but closed.

Fin pressed her hands to the wood, fumbling for the lock.

The doorknob twitched.

Fin gasped. Her fingers were damp with sweat and slid along the deadbolt lever, slipping.

There was the sound of nails against wood, raking downward.

Fin yanked and the lock slid into place. She stepped back, trembling, half expecting to see Teafin slide up through the crack between door and frame. It was a scant centimeter, but Fin wasn't sure a door would be enough to keep the other girl out.

Nothing happened.

Fin stood there, so fixated on the door that she almost missed the tap at her shoulder.

"Something's out there."

Fin nearly jumped out of her skin. She sucked in a breath so sharply that it sliced at her throat, left her gasping for air. She whirled around and saw Eddie.

She could make out little of his face in the darkness, but she saw a frown and a pinch of his brows. "You scared me," she whispered.

"Sorry." He rubbed at the back of his head. "I woke up and you weren't there. And I heard stuff . . . moving."

"I think it's Teafin." Fin glanced at the door, then away.

Eddie nodded. "That's why you've got the lacrosse stick." His gaze roamed over the windows—some had mismatched curtains and others were left with the glass uncovered. "You want to go back upstairs? Or are you going to go hunt her?"

"Upstairs," Fin said.

Fin followed Eddie to the bedroom, forcing herself not to look over her shoulder as they went. She breathed easier with Eddie awake and the bedroom door shut behind them. She settled back on her sleeping bag. "We should tell my mom," said Eddie. He stood by his bed, peering at the window. Fin could see nothing but smudged glass and darkness.

"No," said Fin at once.

"If Teafin is trying to get into the house, we should tell someone," said Eddie. He sounded slightly exasperated, and Fin's heart hammered. She didn't want him to be mad at her, not ever. And especially not now, with so much on the line.

"If we tell your mom, she'll tell my mom," said Fin. "And then . . ." She squeezed her eyes shut.

"And then they'll figure it out," said Eddie impatiently. "That's what adults do."

"No, they'll know I did something wrong. And Mom'll move us again," Fin blurted out.

Eddie went still with surprise. "What?"

Now that the words were out, now that she'd said one of her worst fears aloud, Fin had to look away. Tears pricked at the back of her throat and eyes, and she swallowed hard. She wouldn't cry. No matter what, she wouldn't cry.

"We moved here because of me," said Fin. "I heard Mom talking about it the first week we were here. She didn't know I was listening, and she was talking to your mom. The way she said it . . . it sounded like there's something wrong with me, and I don't even know what." She rubbed at her forehead. "Maybe I forgot. Maybe I wanted to forget, that's why Teafin won't stop stalking me. She's the worst parts of me, and she won't go away."

Eddie looked as though she'd hit him upside the head with that lacrosse stick. "That's—that can't be true."

"I'm not lying," snapped Fin.

"No," said Eddie. "I know you're not. But I mean—kids can't do that. Force parents to move. And definitely not you.

I don't care what Teafin has done or what you did—I know you. You couldn't have done anything that bad."

"*I* don't even know me," said Fin. "Teafin's made that perfectly clear."

"You're not bad," said Eddie firmly.

But what if I am? She wanted to say it but didn't. Because she was afraid of the answer.

She went to the bathroom instead, telling Eddie she needed to pee. It was down the hall and Fin closed the heavy door behind her, sliding the lock into place. Then she sat on the fuzzy toilet lid, her knees drawn up to her chin.

Eddie was sure she wasn't bad, but Fin couldn't be certain.

A tapping sound rang through the bathroom. Fin flinched, lowering herself to a crouch. There was only one window in the bathroom—high up, above the showerhead. It was tiny, just big enough to let sunlight into the room. It was also very dirty, being too far up for easy cleaning.

Someone had drawn words into the dust of the window.

Fin recognized the handwriting—the slightly crooked R and too-loopy D. It was hers.

No, it was Teafin's handwriting. Fin steeled herself, rose to her feet, and read the message.

Stay indoors tonight.

Heart hammering, Fin retreated from the bathroom. With one last backward glance, she hurried to Eddie's room. Setting the lacrosse stick beside her sleeping bag, she buried herself in it. The sleeping bag felt a little like safety.

She lay there, listening, waiting for the sound of something—anything—invading the house.

But nothing ever did.

NINETEEN
A Well-Placed Trap

Thursday afternoon after school, Fin finally returned to the Ack. She carried the weight of her exhaustion like a too-heavy coat. She trudged to the grocery store without seeing much of the town around her.

Shouting was coming from inside the Ack. Fin went still, unsure if she wanted to go inside. She'd heard more than one tourist get into an argument with Mr. Hardin about him not selling matches or barbeque equipment.

But it didn't sound like one of the normal arguments.

"—out of your mouth! Put that down! No, do not—"

Fin pushed open the grocery-store door and blinked at the sight before her.

Mr. Hardin had a broom in hand and appeared to be trying to shoo something out the back door.

"Shut the door," he said, a little desperately, and Fin pulled it closed behind her. There was a scampering sound, claws on linoleum, and then the cat raced by in a blur of tail and whiskers. Fin nearly leaped atop the counter in surprise.

"What's going on?" she said.

"Whintossers," he said, exasperated. "Someone left a boxful of them. I thought it was a delivery, so I opened it and—and there's a family of them, and now I'm trying to—come on!"

Fin saw the telltale shape of a small, gray, rodent-like creature scurrying through the dry goods aisle. "If a tourist sees them, they'll think we have rats," said Mr. Hardin. "I'm trying to shoo them out the back but the cat won't stop—come on!"

The cat tried to pounce on one of the tiny whintossers. The creature scurried up a wall and hung there, apparently at ease with its ten legs.

Fin blinked a few times. She should help. Before any tourist came inside.

She wasn't Eddie or Nick. She wasn't going to grab for the magical creatures. Which left only one option.

The cat sprinted around a corner, raising his paw. Fin

made a dive for him, catching the cat around the middle and hauling him up to her chest. It was like holding a very wriggly stuffed animal.

"Good!" cried Mr. Hardin. "Okay, you hold him. And I'll get these lads out of here." He gently pried the whintosser from the wall and then used the broom to herd the others out the back door. Fin listened to the sound of the claws—ten legs meant a *lot* of claws—as they clicked against the floor.

Once the creatures were outside, Mr. Hardin shut the door. Fin dropped the struggling cat, which looked up at her with an expression of deep betrayal.

"Thanks, Finley," said Mr. Hardin. He leaned against the counter, wiping at his brow with a handkerchief. "I don't know who would do that. Just left a box of those creatures on my doorstep. When I opened it up, they all sprang out."

Fin's stomach sank. She knew exactly who would delight in such a trick. The same person who had carved rude words into Mayor Downer's lawn and set Ben's shed on fire.

"What can I do for you?" said Mr. Hardin.

Fin pulled together a smile for him. "I . . . I came back, since I couldn't do deliveries on Tuesday. I called, remember?"

"Oh, right," said Mr. Hardin, tucking his handkerchief into a pocket. "Of course."

She rocked back on her heels, then mustered the courage to ask, "Is there any more news about the fire?"

Mr. Hardin shook his head. "Ben said it was an accident, but Petra's still been patrolling the town. She's . . . ah. A bit overzealous when it comes to her work. Sees arson in overturned candles—even if they're just the electric kind." He snorted and gestured at the row of camping equipment at the back of the store. Sure enough, there were tiny battery-powered tea lights. "Someone needs to get her a puppy or something."

"What about the cat that you refuse to name?" asked Fin.

Mr. Hardin chuckled. "Doubt he'd go. I think he's decided this is the best place to get every passerby to pet him." He stretched and his back gave a pop. He winced, then strode behind the counter. He reached down and emerged with four deliveries—two medium, one small, and a padded envelope. Then he slid a candy bar atop the pile. Fin blinked, opened her mouth to protest, but Mr. Hardin said, "I added this week's payment to your mother's account. But this one's on me—for being so flexible with the deliveries this week."

Fin was torn between accepting the candy and refusing it. Years of her mother's words—*"We don't accept handouts"*—still rang in her ears. But she hadn't had a snack after school.

"Thank you," she said. It was one of her favorites—dark chocolate studded with dried cherries. Mr. Hardin waved her off, and Fin shoved the candy bar into her pocket, took the packages, and walked back out into the autumn sunshine. She hopped over the cat and then glanced down at the first address. Brewed Awakening. Fin turned to her right and set off down Main Street.

There were two tourists sitting on a bench, a hiking map spread out across their knees. They must have been camping nearby; one of them had twigs in their hair. Another tourist was meandering down the sidewalk, stepping over the protruding tree roots and glancing into shop windows. This was one of the magic seekers; there was a necklace of beads and half-moons draped around their neck and they smelled of incense. Fin gave them a polite nod.

Tourist season was winding down, and while part of Fin was grateful—particularly after hearing Nick's story of the kidnapped raven—late fall and winter were hard seasons for Aldermere. Without the tourists to keep them bustling, most businesses would keep fewer hours. The tiny bookshop would only open on Saturdays and Sundays. The coffee shop would close down an hour early. Even the Foragers' Market would shut down. It was the time Mom always looked more pinched around her mouth, when she worried about budgets.

Fin walked to Brewed Awakening, where the screen door was propped open with a potted redwood cutting. The smells of vanilla and coffee greeted Fin as she stepped inside. Mr. Carver was mixing a drink for a teenager. Fin stood in place for a moment, wondering if she should leave the envelope on the counter. Or—

"Hey, Fin."

Fin glanced over and saw Cedar sitting at a small round table. She gave Fin a smile and waved her over. Glad not to be standing awkwardly by the counter, Fin slid into the seat across from Cedar. "You working on homework?" asked Fin, glancing down at the table. Cedar had several sheafs of paper spread across the table. Fin spotted a few charts and scribbled notes.

"Science fair project," said Cedar. "I'm testing to see what's the optimal temperature to brew coffee at." She grinned. "I'll have some taste tests at my booth. Two of the judges are big coffee drinkers—I've seen them hanging around the shop near school."

Fin was impressed. "Who's your partner?"

Cedar shrugged. She was wearing a sleeveless turquoise shirt with ruffles at the edges, and she looked effortlessly stylish in a way Fin never managed. Today, Cedar's nails were painted a delicate shade of brown. Fin hadn't even known brown nails were a thing.

"No partner," said Cedar. "Just me."

Fin blinked in surprise. She'd assumed—well, Cedar was so cool and nice. She thought Cedar would have had plenty of friends to pick from. But now that she thought about it, Fin could never remember seeing Cedar sitting with many people at lunch. She most often picked a table outside on the sunny days, a book in one hand and a sandwich in the other.

"You could have partnered with me and Eddie," she said impulsively. "I mean, if you wanted to."

Cedar smiled down at her papers. "Thanks." She propped her chin on her hand, leaning on the table. "Is Eddie still obsessed with beating River?"

Fin nodded. "He's getting a little scary about it."

"River once crushed a spider in first grade instead of letting Eddie take it out of the classroom," said Cedar. She shrugged. "After that, they never really got along."

Sometimes Fin forgot that Eddie and Cedar had known each other longer than Fin had. "Really?"

"I hate spiders, so I was with River on that one," said Cedar, "but Eddie's always been good with animals. Even creepy ones." She glanced down at the pile of packages on the table. "One of those for us?"

"Yes." Fin fumbled for the top one, setting the padded envelope on the table. "Would you give it to your parents?"

"Sure," said Cedar. "Why didn't you drop it off earlier, though?"

Fin's fingers froze on the envelope. "What?"

Cedar flicked eraser shavings from the table. "When you came in, like twenty minutes ago."

Fin's mind whirled.

She hadn't come to Brewed Awakening before now—which meant someone who looked like her had.

"You okay?" asked Cedar. She frowned at Fin.

"Sorry," Fin blurted, certain she'd been quiet too long. "I—did I say anything before?"

Cedar's frown deepened, and for a moment Fin was certain the other girl would demand answers. But Cedar said, "Only that you were going to help your mom."

Mom.

Fin's stomach plunged toward her feet.

Fin thought of their conversation a few days ago, of the anger Fin had bitten back and how much she'd just wanted Mom to back off and mind her own business. Could Teafin have overheard some of that? Maybe Fin's darker self was trying to make Mom go away forever.

Terror rose in Fin's chest, and she rose with it. "I've got to go," she said jerkily.

Cedar looked concerned. "Is everything okay?"

But Fin had already turned and rushed from the coffee shop, pushing past a customer as she fled through the door.

She jogged down the steps, turning to her right. The inn was only a five-minute walk from Brewed Awakening, and at a run she could be there in half that time. Fin took off at a sprint, her arms pumping as she raced down the broken sidewalk. Fin knew this way well, and she leaped over the largest of the roots and around the jagged edges. She ran along Main Street toward the inn, keeping off the broken sidewalk. Fin didn't bother to slow as she raced around the single golf cart that inn staff used, nor when a tourist gave Fin a questioning look. Fin only slowed when she reached the front doors.

Her breath came in ragged heaves and her chest hurt. She had to find Mom. She had to make sure Mom was okay, that Teafin wasn't trying to burn down this place as well.

"Hey, Fin." Ben looked up from his place behind the front counter. "How's it—" He cut off when he saw how hard she was breathing. "You okay?"

"Fine," Fin wheezed. She tried to steady herself, so that she wouldn't look as though she'd sprinted through town.

She tried to put him at ease with a smile. "Just—finishing up deliveries. How's your day?"

The tight line of Ben's shoulders relaxed. "Fine. Slow with all the tourists leaving."

"Have—have you seen my mom?" asked Fin.

Ben reached down to straighten a stack of promotional postcards. "Um. I think she's in her office? We had a cleaner call in sick today, though, so she may be helping with that."

Fin nodded in silent thanks. There was no way to ask him if she'd already come this way, not without tipping him off. So she straightened her shoulders, tried to calm her breathing, and strode from the lobby. She walked past the employees-only sign and around toward the kitchen. She could hear Mr. Madeira working on dinner, his familiar rumble of a voice emanating from the swinging doors.

Fin hurried down to the end of the hallway, where there was only a storage closet and her mom's office door. Fin nearly pulled it open, but she realized how weird that would look, her barging in. So she raised one shaking hand and knocked.

She waited.

Only silence.

Fin reached for the doorknob and turned it. The office was empty.

Fin's foot rose as she began to step inside.

"Wait!" someone cried behind her, but Fin was putting her foot down. She glanced over her shoulder and saw Cedar, of all people, rushing toward her.

Fin finished stepping through the doorway, and then—

Then she wasn't in the office at all.

She was somewhere dark and cold and she could not see a thing. She reached out, trying to find something, anything, but her fingers only alighted on damp wood. It smelled like timber and greenery, and for one moment she wondered wildly if she'd managed to screw up the town's magic so badly that she'd warped reality itself.

Then there was a stumble and a crash. Fin whirled, and she hit a wall without realizing it was there. Her hand came up as she tried to steady herself.

"Fin?" said a voice in the dark.

"Cedar?" asked Fin, disbelieving. "Is that you?"

"It's me." There was a clatter of noise, like something falling, and then Cedar said, "Didn't you see the nameplate?"

"The nameplate?" Fin repeated.

"It had fallen off your mom's office door," said Cedar. "It was lying on the floor. I tried to warn you, but you'd already stepped through."

Relief flooded Fin. It wasn't her fault at all—rather, it

was the normal weirdness of Aldermere. The door had been unlabeled. So stepping through hadn't brought her to Mom's office. It had brought her . . . somewhere else.

"Where are we?" asked Fin. Her eyes were beginning to adjust to the dark, and she saw thin slats of light, pale illumination beginning to seep through her vision. It didn't look like a closet or a basement. And it smelled like they were outdoors.

"I think we're in an old water tower," said Cedar.

"A water tower?" Fin repeated, her stomach giving an uncomfortable flutter. She glanced down, imagining how far up they were.

"Yeah." Cedar seemed to be searching for something, moving around in the darkness. "I once went up to one on a dare. I was supposed to stay up there until someone came to get me, but no one ever came. Finally went home when I realized. Ah—there we go." There was a whisper of noise, and then sunlight made Fin blink hard. Cedar had found the curtains on a window and pulled them open. Sure enough, they stood in a small, circular room.

It looked a little like a camping cabin. There was a cot in the corner, an old-fashioned lantern, and a shelf.

"I think someone lives here," said Fin.

Cedar nodded. "Yeah, I think there are only two or three

towers that people still use for water these days." She peered outside. "We're on the edge of town." She gestured for Fin to approach the door. "Come on, let's climb down."

Fin bit her lip, took a breath, and stepped forward. There was a ledge, and Fin took careful hold of the railing before she looked down. They were at least fifty feet off the ground. Fin forced herself to look up; they were surrounded by the boughs of trees. She tried to keep her attention focused on the forest rather than on how high up they were.

Cedar went first, walking to the ladder and climbing down with surprising ease. Fin took one rung at a time, only moving to another when she was sure her grip and feet were steady. It took an excruciatingly long time and she kept expecting Cedar to tell her to hurry up. It was what Eddie would have said.

But Cedar never said a word. She merely stood by the ladder, gazing curiously about the forest. Fin jumped the last two rungs, landing heavily on both feet. For a moment, it was all she could do not to drop to her knees and hug the ground. Then the relief passed and realization settled.

"The nameplate was missing," she murmured.

Cedar looked at her. "Yeah, it was."

For those who lived in Aldermere, it was second nature to check doors before going through them. "I was distracted," replied Fin. She began to walk away from the water tower, trying to get her bearings. If Cedar was right, they'd ended up on the northern end of town, where an old logging road trailed into the woods. If they went farther north, they'd be near the old toll bridge.

"Why were you even there?" asked Fin. Suspicion took hold of her and she looked sharply at Cedar. "Were you following me?"

Cedar fell into step beside her. "Yes," she said, with some dignity, "because you left the rest of your packages at Brewed Awakening. I put them behind the counter, so I thought you might want to come get them."

"Oh." Fin flushed. She hadn't even considered the rest of her deliveries.

"And," continued Cedar, "you looked . . . well, kind of freaked out. I wanted to make sure you were okay."

"I'm f—"

"And to ask who the girl was," said Cedar.

Fin's footsteps slowed. "What girl?"

"The girl who looked like you," said Cedar. "But wasn't."

Fin stopped dead in her tracks.

They stood there, in the silence of the forest, for a few heartbeats. Fin couldn't think of anything else to say but, "How'd . . . ?"

"How'd I know?" asked Cedar. "Because you just confirmed it."

Fin gaped at her.

Cedar said, "I watch a lot of people at the coffee shop. I know that Mr. Madeira always orders chamomile tea for himself on days when the kitchen at the inn is stressful. I know your mom drinks the free coffee from the inn except on paydays, when she comes in for one of our lattes. I know Mrs. Brackenbury's son hasn't been calling her as much because she comes into the shop to talk when she's lonely. And I know that Finley Barnes doesn't wear sunglasses or entirely black outfits, because that might draw attention. Also because when I mentioned that you'd been in the coffee shop earlier, you looked like I'd poured ice down your shirt. Which means it wasn't you." Cedar fixed Fin with a look. "Am I wrong?"

It was the most Fin had ever heard Cedar say.

And none of it was wrong.

"My evil doppelgänger drinks coffee?" Fin said, then groaned. "Of course she does. Because of course she would be a stereotype."

Cedar let out a startled laugh. "You have an evil doppelgänger?"

"It's a long story," Fin said.

"Tell me," said Cedar.

So Fin did. She'd expected it to be difficult, but it felt good to get everything out. She walked slowly as she spoke, laying out everything that had happened since she'd overheard Aunt Myrtle talking about bringing Fin to a counselor: stealing the tea, brewing it herself, Teafin rising out of the sink, the break-in at Mr. Madeira's, Teafin stealing what tea she could find at Talia's, the injured raven, the burning shed, the pranks, and now the fact that Teafin was running around town in black clothes and sunglasses.

"To hide the fact she's got tea balls for eyes," said Cedar. She didn't sound disbelieving; she sounded amazed. "That's . . . well."

"Terrifying?" said Fin.

"Kind of awesome," said Cedar. "I've never had a sister. I wonder if this would be anything like that."

"Teafin isn't a sister," protested Fin. "She's a monster. And when I heard she went to the inn . . ." Her words trailed off as a new, horrible thought occurred to her.

"What?" asked Cedar, seeing Fin's expression.

Fin said slowly, "That nameplate shouldn't have come off. It was nailed to Mom's office door."

She remembered Mom installing it herself. Her mother had been so proud to be promoted, and the two of them had eaten cupcakes in that new office, a blanket spread out across the floor like at a picnic.

"The only way it would have come off was if someone had pried it off," said Fin. She half expected Cedar to scoff, but the other girl nodded.

"It looked like that, yeah," Cedar said. "There were splinters of wood and the nails still attached. I thought maybe—construction or something?"

"Teafin ripped it off," said Fin. "I know she did. Maybe she was trying to get rid of Mom. Or . . . or delay me."

Her steps quickened. Cedar fell behind for a few paces and then caught up. "You honestly don't think she'd hurt your mom, do you?"

"She hurt a raven," Fin said. "She nearly burned down Ben's shed, and who knows what she could have done to Mr. Madeira if he'd caught her while she was carrying a box of whintossers."

Cedar chewed on her lower lip. "She didn't seem—well, when she talked to me, she didn't seem evil."

"I'm not sure how one can evilly say, 'One twelve-ounce coffee.'"

"She ordered a mocha, for the record," said Cedar.

"Not the point," said Fin. Then she blinked. "What's the difference?"

"Mochas have chocolate," said Cedar.

"What did she even pay with? Tea leaves?"

"She had money," said Cedar. "I wonder where she got it."

"Probably out of Talia's register."

They hurried together through the trees, around the back of a house, past a pile of drying wood and a tiny garden. A few pumpkins were visible, curling vines draped over a low fence. Fin didn't dare run; there wasn't a real path. The northern edge of town was more unkempt than the rest—the undergrowth left to tangle and no paths for hikers. Many of these cabins were owned or rented out to those who couldn't afford a house in town.

She needed to find Mom. After all, if that water tower had been in use, Fin would have found herself underwater, unable to find a way out.

A shudder tore through her.

"Who else knows about this?" asked Cedar. She had slightly longer legs than Fin and she kept up easily.

"No one," said Fin shortly. "Just you and Eddie."

Cedar looked surprised and a little pleased by this. "What about your aunt? I know she's lived in Aldermere forever—she'd know what to do."

Fin shook her head. "Aunt Myrtle . . . I love her, but . . ." She trailed off, unsure how to continue. Affection and resentment were a tangle in Fin's chest. "I can't," she said.

Cedar let it go, which Fin was grateful for.

Together, they half jogged up Main Street, back toward the inn. "Come on," said Fin, darting to the left. "There's a side door. If Ben sees me come into the inn twice—"

"Or three times, if he saw your double," Cedar put in.

"Exactly," said Fin. "He's already suspicious—I don't want to give him more to think about. And—and we've been calling her Teafin."

"Teafin," said Cedar with a small laugh. "Well, that's one thing to call her. Evilfin was too much of a mouthful?"

Fin didn't reply; she had reached the service entrance on the far left side of the inn. This was where Mr. Madeira took shipments for the kitchen, and at this time, no one would be here. Fin pulled the door open and gestured Cedar inside.

They moved silently down the hallway, Fin leading the way. It was strange to have Cedar with her, instead of Eddie, but not bad. Just—different.

The kitchen was as busy as ever; the sound of knives and clattering dishes made Fin glance down the corridor before walking toward Mom's office. The door was still ajar, the nameplate on the floor.

"Should we fix it?" asked Cedar quietly. "In case anyone else tries to get through?"

Fin considered. "Not enough time," she whispered. "Besides, what would we put it up with?"

Cedar reached into her pocket and came up with a bit of string. "We could tie it to the knob?"

"Later." Fin's worries were focused on Mom. The fallen nameplate could wait.

They glanced into the custodial closet, into the staff lounge, and finally, into the dining room. Fin's shoulders were tense with worry; what if Mom had already gone through the door and been transported someplace else in Aldermere? What if she was trapped?

"We should tell someone," said Cedar. "Not about Teafin—just about the door not having a label. If people know to be on the lookout, we'll find your mom."

She was about to agree with Cedar, but then she heard a familiar sharp voice.

"—break. Found the phones ringing and—"

"That's Mom," said Fin, her stomach lurching with relief. She turned away from the dining room and hurried toward the front desk.

Sure enough, Mom stood by the main counter, her arms crossed and mouth tight at the edges. Standing in front of her, looking thoroughly scolded, was Ben.

"Can't walk away whenever you feel like it," said Mom. "I found two people trying to call. If they'd been trying to make a reservation—"

"I'm sorry." Ben winced. "I saw—I mean, I thought I saw . . ." His gaze snapped over to Fin and his expression sharpened. "Your daughter."

"Fin?" Mom turned and saw her, a flicker of concern in her eyes. Abruptly, Fin's relief at finding Mom all right collapsed into nerves. Her stomach gave a lurch when Mom looked at her like that—as if she was searching for something wrong with Fin. That hurt—more than finding herself in an abandoned water tower, more than Teafin seizing hold of her wrist.

"Fin," said Mom. "Hey—did you stop by to see me?"

Fin searched for an explanation. "I—I—"

"My parents need tape," said Cedar, stepping forward. "I'm so sorry, Ms. Barnes, but Fin was doing her deliveries when Brewed Awakening ran out of receipt tape. She said you might have some extra. My parents ordered more, but you know how long it takes packages to get here."

Some of the tension went out of Mom's posture.

"Fin said the inn might let us borrow a roll?" said Cedar, making the statement into a question.

"Of course." Mom walked around to the back of the counter and knelt, then reappeared with a roll of receipt paper. "Will one be enough?"

"Yes," said Cedar with a convincing amount of gratefulness. "Thanks, my parents will be really happy and I promise as soon as we get ours, I'll bring a roll back."

"You can send it over with Fin." Mom smiled at Cedar as she handed over the roll. "It's no problem."

It was such a good excuse that Fin threw Cedar a grateful look. Cedar understood; her smile quirked upward at one corner.

"We stopped by your office, Mom," Fin said. "Your nameplate—it's off the door."

"Is it?" Mom rubbed at her forehead, as if it pained her. "Just another thing to fix. Thanks, hon." She reached out, hand hovering over Fin's shoulder, before it dropped away.

There was a wall of unspoken things between them, and Fin didn't know how to climb over it. So she stepped back, gave Mom a tight smile, and said, "I've got to finish my deliveries. I, uh, left my packages back at the coffee shop. Will you be home for dinner?"

"Not tonight," said Mom. "Aunt Myrtle said she was making vegan pizza, and you're welcome to come. Or there are leftovers in the fridge."

Fin nodded wordlessly and walked to the front doors, Cedar at her side. They had done it—found Mom, made sure she was safe—and all without alerting anyone to Teafin's presence.

The tension was finally leaving Fin's shoulders when something dark flashed in the corner of her eye. Fin's head jerked to one side.

Her footsteps faltered.

Standing between two parked cars was a girl dressed all in black. Her sunglasses were pushed back across her hair, and her crooked eyebrows were tilted in a smile.

Teafin lifted a hand, her index finger curving as if to beckon Fin forward.

Fin blinked—

And Teafin vanished between one moment and the next.

TWENTY
Matches

Cedar and Fin walked back to Brewed Awakening.

They made the journey in silence, each lost to their own thoughts. Cedar ran her thumb absentmindedly around the roll of receipt tape. Fin was too busy trying to figure out a plan to ask what the other girl was thinking. Teafin had been at the inn; she had torn Mom's nameplate off, for some unknown reason, and now she was . . . where? She'd vanished from the parking lot.

Teafin moved through Aldermere like a ghost, causing chaos wherever she went. Maybe that was her aim—to disrupt life beyond recognition. Fin couldn't guess at Teafin's intentions, no matter how much she racked her brain.

"You do know we're being followed, right?" asked Cedar.

Fin looked up sharply. "What?"

Cedar nodded and Fin turned in a half-circle, half expecting to see her own face peering back at her. But there was no one.

"Who?" Fin said blankly.

Cedar pointed. "That raven has been following us since we left the inn."

Sure enough, there was a small raven perched atop a parked car. It bounced along, landing on one of the car's mirrors and gazing at them expectantly. It took Fin a moment to recognize the slightly ruffled feathers around the bird's neck. It was *the* raven, the one she'd rescued from Teafin. The raven let out a little chatter of clicks and clacks that sounded like fingernails dragging across an old fence.

"Did your mom forget to pay the ravens?" asked Cedar. "Is this a new intimidation tactic or something? If we don't feed them, they stalk us?"

"No," said Fin. "That's the bird I brought to Nick."

Cedar tilted her head, studying the raven. "She's kind of cute. You think she knows you helped her?"

"Nick thought so," Fin said. "He told me to give her treats sometimes, said that she'd decided to keep me. Whatever that means."

Cedar let out a small, wistful sigh. "That sounds kind of nice, actually. Someone choosing you." Before Fin could say anything else, Cedar walked through the doors to Brewed Awakening. "Come on, you need your packages."

Fin and Cedar dodged around a cluster of teenagers drinking chai lattes.

"Hi, Dad," Cedar said, leaning behind the register. "Just grabbing these—thanks."

Mr. Carver gave Fin a friendly smile before going back to mixing some kind of frozen drink. "Hey, girls. You thirsty? Hungry?"

"No, thank you," said Fin, on reflex.

Cedar emerged with Fin's forgotten boxes. "Thanks," said Fin gratefully. "I don't know what I'd have done if I lost them." She imagined trying to explain it to Mr. Hardin and had to suppress a shudder.

"It's fine." Cedar gave her a small smile. "And—I mean. Thanks for telling me about . . . things. Oh, and here." Cedar picked up what looked like a heel of old bread and forced it into Fin's hand.

Cedar seemed to regard their trip into the water tower like it had been an adventure, rather than a mishap. Fin would have thought Cedar too busy or too . . . well, *cool* to be interested in things like tea monsters or magic.

Fin left the coffee shop with her packages and the decision to invite Cedar over to the cottage at some point. Maybe the other girl liked mystery books too, or they just could hang out.

The raven was still sitting on the car. She hopped closer to Fin, head cocked with interest. It was only then that Fin realized why Cedar had given her the bread crust.

"I think this is for you," said Fin, and tossed the bread. The raven flapped her wings, caught the bread, and fluttered down to the road. She pinned the bread under one talon and began tearing hunks off.

"Glad you like it," said Fin. It was weird to be talking to one of the ravens, but it wasn't the weirdest thing to happen. And besides . . . this was the kind of magic that had endeared Aldermere to Fin. The kind that was a little strange but good.

Fin checked the addresses on the three remaining packages. One was for Mrs. Brackenbury and the others for a house a few doors down from Brewed Awakening. Fin turned left and strode down the street, determined to complete this job without any more mishaps.

The house was old but well-kept, with pruned rosebushes in the yard and moss-covered rocks leading up to the front door. Fin knocked, feeling that familiar flutter of fear as she did so. Knocking on doors never got any easier, no matter how many times Fin did it.

The door opened and a stern-faced woman appeared. Mrs. Petrichor. Her hawk-sharp eyes alighted on Fin. "Oh, good," she said, taking her two packages. "I was wondering if these had gone astray."

"Deliveries were delayed this week," said Fin apologetically.

"Understandable, with everything going on." Mrs. Petrichor reached into her back pocket and withdrew a dollar, slipping it into Fin's hand. Cash tips were rare—most often she received other kinds of things that functioned as currency in Aldermere: cut flowers, baked goods, future favors. Once she'd received a note from the Reyes family that simply said, *Return in time of need.*

Fin pocketed the dollar and walked away.

The last delivery was Mrs. Brackenbury. Fin hefted the package more comfortably under her arm and set off. It was only a two-minute walk down the street, and then Fin saw the familiar wide porch with its swinging seat, suspended with rope and made soft with velvet cushions. As was her afternoon custom, Mrs. Brackenbury sat there, a newspaper between her wrinkled fingers. Her hair was always curled and dyed, and she smelled a little like violets.

"Finley," Mrs. Brackenbury said, rising from her seat. Mr. Bull wagged his stub of a tail hopefully. Fin knelt beside him and scratched behind one ear. His head tilted back, jaw slipping open and tongue lolling happily.

"Hi, Mrs. Brackenbury," said Fin from her place beside the dog. "I've got a package for you."

"Good, good." The older woman opened the door and said, "Come in, I can put a pot of hot water on."

Fin hesitated. Part of her wished to leave the package and return home—Eddie still wanted to go over their science fair presentation; Fin needed to figure out a way to entrap Teafin; Mom was still looking at Fin with that mixture of disappointment and unease; and who knew what Aunt Myrtle was up to. All in all, Fin had quite enough on her mind without making small talk with an old lady.

But Mrs. Brackenbury was already through the door, Mr. Bull heaving himself to his paws to follow, and the door was wide open. There was no way to refuse, not without being rude. Fin sent one last wistful glance over her shoulder, then walked inside, pulling the door shut behind her.

The house was a little cluttered in that way older people's houses were—shelves filled with books and framed pictures, trinkets and memories hugging every flat surface. Fin could tell the house was a mobile home from the faux-wood walls and faded carpets. She and Mom had lived in one for six months once.

"Would you like chamomile, hon?" Mrs. Brackenbury moved about the kitchen with surprising agility, filling two teacups with hot water. She put both on the table, then went to rummage atop the refrigerator for tea bags.

"Sure," said Fin. She hadn't had real tea since—well, since the last cup of Ceylon she'd drunk had crawled up out of a garbage disposal. She didn't think she'd ever have a taste for it again.

Mrs. Brackenbury set out a small plate of packaged cookies and Fin took two, because it was polite and because they were chocolate hazelnut. "So how is school?" asked Mrs. Brackenbury, sitting down.

"Busy," Fin admitted. "There's the school science fair this weekend."

"Oh, that's right." Mrs. Brackenbury beamed at her. "That's at the inn, isn't it? I'll stop by if I'm feeling up to it. It's always marvelous, seeing what young people are making these days. What are you working on?"

"A terrarium and poster of local lizards and plants," said Fin.

Mrs. Brackenbury gave her a shrewd little look. "You're working with your cousin, aren't you?"

"Eddie, yeah," said Fin, startled. "How'd you—"

"Because you've shown about as much interest in lizards

as you have in flying to the moon," said Mrs. Brackenbury. "I'd have expected you to do something more along the lines of seeing what kind of bookmark you could make out of . . . I don't know, what's fashionable these days? Recycled tin cans or something."

Fin shrugged. "It's what Eddie wanted to do, and I . . ." She didn't know how to finish that sentence, so she didn't. Eddie usually took the lead and she followed; it was the way they'd always worked since she'd moved here. She was fine with that.

"How's your mother, dear?" asked Mrs. Brackenbury.

"Also busy." Fin nibbled at a cookie for something to do. Her tea was still too hot to drink. "The other inn manager has been on maternity leave, so Mom's doing both their jobs."

"She works hard," Mrs. Brackenbury said, blowing gently across her cup. "Sets a good example—but I admit, when I think back on those years with my kids, I wish I'd worked a little less and spent more time with my family." She gave Fin a knowing glance, then picked up a cookie. "Maybe it's that way for you too?"

Fin shrugged. There was a doily beneath the sugar bowl and Fin stared fixedly at the swirls of lace.

"Or maybe you don't." Mrs. Brackenbury sighed. She sounded, abruptly, a little tired and a little sad.

She must be lonely, Fin thought. Mrs. Brackenbury's kids were all grown. This was probably why Mrs. Brackenbury sat on her porch so often—looking for someone to talk with. An uncomfortable squirm of guilt went through Fin; she should stop by more often.

"How are things in town?" asked Mrs. Brackenbury. "How's Ben doing after that fire?"

"I think he's okay," said Fin, still looking down. "I saw him at the inn today. He said it was probably an electrical thing." Which was technically true. "Mrs. Petrichor is still suspicious, though."

"Oh, Petra." Mrs. Brackenbury gave a derisive snort. "She's always seeing arson everywhere. She's getting up there in years, and while some of us originals are slowing down, I don't think she ever will." She gently placed her teacup back in its saucer with one quaking hand. "We're all getting old. It's a shame about Talia. I'm going to need to see her when she gets back."

Fin frowned across the table. "I—I didn't know you bought tea from Talia."

"Of course," said Mrs. Brackenbury. "Been going to visit Talia since we were back in Redfern. I remember the old town, you know. It was—different from this one. But still, like no other place in the world." Her eyes focused on something far in the distance. "It was wilder then, you know? People complain about the Bower's Creek monster and the knives here, but this is nothing. Redfern was . . . much, much more dangerous. People were reckless with the magic. They took it for granted. Never bought any tea back then—when I was younger, I didn't really have anything I wanted to change about myself. I'd go to visit, talk about books. But . . ." She let out a gusty breath. "Times change. After I had my kids, it wasn't a good time for me. No one tells you about that, you know. I went to Talia when I needed help. I'd bring the tea home, use it when I needed it. Last time I went was—well, I think it was the day that Talia fell." She touched a finger to her wrinkled lips. "She still puts rose hips and raspberries in my tea. Such a good flavor."

But Fin was only half listening. Her mind had snagged on the last bit of information that Mrs. Brackenbury had told her.

"You went to Talia's the day she fell?" Fin asked. "She—she let you brew the tea on your own? You knew how to do it?"

"Of course," replied Mrs. Brackenbury. She picked up a cookie and dipped it into her tea, nibbling at it. "Brew for four minutes, then toss the leaves into my neighbor's woodstove. She never minds, as long as I bring pastries."

For ashes, Fin remembered. Had everyone else truly

known about the burning of the tea leaves after they were used? Maybe Talia would have told Fin, if she'd been old enough to take the tea home.

"It's a shame my tea was in my grocery bag," said Mrs. Brackenbury. "I've had to go without."

Fin went utterly still. "The tea—the tea was stolen from you?"

"Yes, dear. With the rest of my shopping." Mrs. Brackenbury's thin mouth pursed. "I need to stop by the Ack soon too."

A thought was taking form; Fin sat there in silence while Mrs. Brackenbury talked about her grandkids.

Mrs. Brackenbury had been mugged. But not for her cash or even her jewelry—the thief had taken her grocery shopping. No one had thought to question it, because criminals were supposed to be unpredictable. But now Fin wondered if in fact the groceries hadn't been the target. What if it had been the tea?

Which meant—which meant that the first tea theft hadn't been at Mr. Madeira's home.

It had been Mrs. Brackenbury.

Fin's mind was still whirling when the phone rang shrilly. She jumped in her seat, sloshing tea across her saucer.

Mrs. Brackenbury hauled herself up and walked to the

phone. Fin watched her go. This was the chance she needed to escape. Hastily, Fin picked up her teacup and downed the rest of the chamomile, ignoring the scalding heat down her throat. She took the cup to the sink, intending to wash it out. There were a few open drawers in the kitchen and Fin found herself glancing into one as she walked by. It held the kind of junk that all houses did—stray bits of paper, old letters, pens and—

A matchbox.

Fin went still.

It was a tiny matchbox, the letters faded from age. Without consciously making the decision, Fin pulled the drawer fully open and picked up the matches.

Stealing was wrong. She knew that. She hated to do it. But this drawer was dusty and old and surely Mrs. Brackenbury wouldn't notice, right?

Her breathing coming hard, Fin chanced a look into the hallway. Mrs. Brackenbury was still on the phone, her back to the kitchen.

Be brave, she thought. *Be brave.*

She looked at Mrs. Brackenbury again, then at the matches.

She thought of silver tea-ball eyes, of shadows moving in the dark, of magic that should be put to rest.

And then she slid the matchbox into her pocket.

TWENTY-ONE
The Science Fair

The day of the science fair dawned bright and early.

Mostly because Fin hadn't slept much.

Fin sat up, the worn old quilt falling from her shoulders. She didn't know what had woken her. Then she heard the tapping at the window.

She glanced to her left, breath quickening, and saw the form sitting outside the glass. For a moment, she thought it might be Teafin.

It was a raven. *The* raven, eyeing her beadily through the dirty glass. Fin pushed the window open; there wasn't a screen, and Fin found herself face-to-face with the bird. The raven chittered a greeting and Fin said, "Hi," a little awkwardly. She still wasn't sure how a person was supposed to talk with a raven. She slipped out of bed and went to her backpack for the bag of trail mix she'd taken to school on Friday. She pulled it free and dug out a few nuts, setting them on the windowsill.

The raven began gobbling up the food. For Fin, it was a momentary distraction from her unease.

The science fair loomed before her. She would have thought an evil tea twin would distract her from public speaking, but now that the fair was hours away, it was the only thing she could think about.

She closed her eyes and tried to breathe deeply. But the spaces between each breath seemed too open, too easily filled with fear.

The tea had worn off. Perhaps she hadn't chosen a big enough memory—or maybe all of the chaos of the last few days had burned out the magic faster than usual. Fin no longer felt brave or strong or even remotely calm.

She knew it was irrational—that was the worst part. The science fair was just a school thing, something that in a few months she probably wouldn't even remember . . . unless she said something wrong, in which case the memory would haunt her for years. She remembered when she'd accidentally called her first-grade teacher by the wrong name, when she'd made a joke to a new friend in the third grade that the other girl hadn't gotten, and the times when even Eddie, her best friend in the world, didn't understand why she was afraid.

Fin always found herself biting back words, considering every reply, trying to figure out how other people spoke, how they held their hands, their arms, themselves. She'd tried to emulate other people for so long, she felt more like a mimic than a real person.

The only way to fit in was to saw off pieces of herself.

It had become habit.

Maybe this was why Teafin was so angry. Because she was a mimic of a mimic.

Fin slid her legs over the side of the bed and tried the deep breaths again. She would handle all of this—the science fair and Teafin. She had a poster to read off of if she forgot what to say. She had the matchbox if Teafin showed up. She had Eddie. And she had Cedar—

The raven made a burbling sound.

She also had a rather strange raven that seemed to have adopted her. *Well,* Fin thought, *there were worse things to have.*

Mom was waiting when Fin descended from the loft.

Fin's breath hitched a little, her heartbeat stumbling. It wasn't that she didn't want to see her mom, but the thought of another argument now made her want to turn around and go back up that ladder.

"Hey," said Mom, smiling.

Fin's return smile was more uncertain, faltering at the edges. "Morning."

"I figured you and Eddie would be practicing most of the day," said Mom. She pushed a paper bag—ALDERMERE GROCERY & TACKLE printed across it—across the small table. "So I put together a few snacks for you both."

Fin took it, glancing inside. Sliced apple, some crackers, and chocolate chip cookies, the inn's logo on the bag. "The inn's selling cookies now?" asked Fin.

"Ben put together a proposal about offering guests some fresh dessert item when they check in," said Mom, with a small laugh. "Got the idea from some other hotel company. It probably won't stick, but Mr. Madeira said he'd try it for a few weeks. Not like we have that many guests to cook for at the moment."

Fin took a cookie, sniffed it. It smelled warm, freshly baked. "Thanks."

Mom's smile faded. "Listen, sweetheart. I just—"

Fin drew in a breath.

"—wanted you to know that I'm very proud of you," said Mom. "You and Eddie have worked hard on this, and

I'm sure you're going to do great." She leaned forward in the chair. "But even if everything goes wrong—if the lizards escape and run rampant or if someone's papier-mâché volcano explodes—it doesn't matter. I'm still proud of you."

All of the tension in Fin's body gathered in her throat. It was too tight; she could barely speak. "Thanks," Fin managed to say again.

Mom rose from the chair, then leaned down and kissed the top of Fin's head. "Love you. Everything's going to be fine."

Fin nodded and hugged her mom tightly for a moment before going into the bathroom to shower.

For once Eddie was as keyed up as Fin.

He was checking and double-checking the lizards—moving a few rocks around in their terrarium, adding fresh leaves, murmuring quiet reassurances to the lizards. He wasn't nervous, Fin knew, so much as he was determined. He wanted to beat River at this science fair more than she'd seen him want anything in a long time.

"All right, guys," said Eddie quietly, into the glass. "We've practiced this. When the judges come by, I'll give you the signal and . . ."

He snapped his fingers.

The lizards stared at him.

"What are they supposed to do?" Fin asked. "Dance?"

"Come on," groaned Eddie, leaning his forehead against the glass. "Guys."

One lizard licked its eyeball. Another blinked.

"You didn't train them to sabotage River's project, did you?" said Fin.

"No, of course not," said Eddie. "That idea's way better. I should've done that. I've been training them to eat crickets on command. It's like at the zoo when the animals actually do stuff—it makes people excited. I thought if the lizards did more than sit there, it would up our chances." He lifted his head; there was a smudge against the glass, and he hastily wiped at it with his sleeve.

Aunt Myrtle was trundling about the kitchen. Mom had gone to the inn, preparing for the science fair. If this had been any other event, any other day, Fin might have gone there with her to help fold linens and set out chairs. But now all Fin could do was stand beside their poster board and try to remember exactly which lizards were native to California and why Eddie thought they preferred one type of bug to another.

Finally Fin and Eddie hauled their science project to the inn. "I'll see you two soon," Aunt Myrtle called cheerily as Eddie hefted the terrarium into the small wooden wagon that

Aunt Myrtle used to get her table to the Foragers' Market. The lizards looked rather indignant about the move, and Eddie murmured quiet reassurances. Fin carried the poster.

The walk up to the inn was shorter than normal. The world moved too quickly and too slowly, all at once. They were walking past the Ack, then striding past Mrs. Brackenbury's home, then Brewed Awakening, and then the inn loomed before them, looking more intimidating than Fin could ever remember.

The front door was closed, and Fin had to push it open with her foot and stand there so Eddie could angle himself through with the wagon and terrarium. Ben saw them from the front counter and took a few steps closer.

"Those are shut in, right?" asked Ben, squinting at the lizards with a worried line etched across his forehead. "They're not going to escape?"

"They won't escape," said Eddie with confidence. "Not unless lizards suddenly figure out how to unlatch things."

"Well, this *is* Aldermere," said Fin, speaking without thinking.

Ben threw her a startled glance, and she couldn't tell if it was because she sounded more dour than normal or if he truly was worried about a Great Lizard Escape. "Is the room ready for projects?" she asked him.

Ben nodded. "Just finished it up an hour ago—tables ready to go. We'll put out juices and water before it starts." He rubbed his hands together.

Eddie went on ahead, pulling the wagon down the hallway. Ben watched him go, still looking wary. "I liked your cookie idea," said Fin. She offered the words like an apology, since she couldn't utter a real one. He hadn't deserved to have his shed set on fire, but it wasn't like she could tell him she knew who'd done it.

Ben glanced at her before stepping back behind the counter. "Oh, your mom told you?"

Fin nodded. "You think cookies will make more guests stay here?"

Ben reached for one of the brochure displays, straightening the lines of crisp paper. "I don't know," he said. "We need *something*. With the wildfires lately, we're getting fewer and fewer tourists every year. Only a few weeks ago, I heard your mom talking on the phone with the owners about layoffs during the winter season." He touched a hand to his forehead, rubbing as if he had a headache. "Sorry, I shouldn't even be telling you this."

"It's fine," said Fin, and meant it. She liked it when people talked to her like she wasn't just a clueless kid. "Would you stay in Aldermere, if you couldn't work here?"

"I don't have anywhere else to go," he said, sounding tired. "I used my college fund to pay for my mom's medical bills. Can't afford to move. Can barely afford to stay here."

Fin winced with sympathy. "Sorry."

"Not your fault." He nodded in the direction of the conference room. "You two break a leg. Or—whatever people say before science fairs."

"Good luck?" Fin suggested.

"Good luck," he replied.

Fin took a better grip on the poster and walked toward the conference room. It had been set up with long folding tables and white linens, and there were numbered spaces. The room wasn't empty.

A boy with sandy-blond hair and pale hazel eyes stood beside what looked like a tiny wind turbine made out of Popsicle sticks. Wires were twined out the bottom, connected to what looked like a small electric hotplate. The turbine was spinning because the boy had also set up a fan, making a tiny wind stream.

"River," said Eddie, sounding as disgusted as the time she and Eddie had cleaned mold out of the bottom of the fridge.

"Edward," said River, with a cool glance at Fin and Eddie. Eddie bristled visibly; he didn't like anyone using his full name without permission. "I see you decided to go with animals again? Pity it won't get you first place. I thought you'd have figured that out by now." He cast a cold look at Fin. "Good idea getting someone with legible handwriting, though. At least the judges will be able to read your disappointing project this year."

Fin blinked at him. She'd never talked to River before; she had seen him at last year's science fair, but her grade hadn't been required to participate, so she'd stood at the back of the room. And they didn't hang out with the same people, so he'd never spoken directly to her. He reminded her a little of a villain in a mystery book. One of the bad ones, with the flimsy plot that Fin could usually figure out by the fifth page.

"Your windmill going to last the night?" said Eddie, with a chin nod at River's table. "It looks kind of flimsy."

"It's a wind turbine, not a windmill," said River coldly.

"Still looks like it might fall apart," said Eddie. "Come on, Fin." He turned on his heel and strode to the front of the room, where they would be easily seen. Fin's stomach squirmed uncomfortably, but she followed.

"So that's River's windmill," Fin said, once they were out of earshot. She set the poster down, making sure none of the attached samples had come free.

"Yeah," said Eddie, glowering across the room. "He thinks he's so special because he can make electricity."

"Technically, he's using electricity," Fin said. "He needs a fan to get the windmill-thing to run."

"I hadn't thought of that. Maybe it'll count against him." His mood brightening, Eddie began carefully straightening the terrarium. Fin set up the poster beside it, then glanced about the room. A few other people were beginning to trickle in—kids from school with their parents in tow, carrying papier-mâché volcanoes, model airplanes. . . . One girl had a weird globe with holes poked in it. Fin watched as they set up.

The fair would officially start at five: speeches would commence, the kids would present their projects, and then awards would be given out at seven. Fin checked the clock above the door—there was enough time to visit the bathroom. She didn't need to use it, but she also didn't want to stand beside her table, feeling awkward.

"I'm going to walk around a little," she said to Eddie.

He was barely listening; he was staring daggers at River, who had set a kettle of water on the small hot plate. "He's going to serve them hot chocolate or something," said Eddie under his breath. "He's going to bribe the judges with wind-powered beverages."

Fin gave up on trying to talk to him. Eddie was too consumed to notice her restlessness. She left their table and strolled down another row of projects. The room was beginning to bustle with students and parents, the noise level rising to a steady thrum. A boy was setting up a row of paper airplanes, complete with a chart on how he'd folded each one and how far they would fly; another girl had a poster that smelled strongly of fish and had pieces of seaweed taped to it. Fin hastened past that table.

There was no sign of Mom or Aunt Myrtle yet—Aunt Myrtle would arrive around five to watch the presentations, and Mom would be in a frenzy, trying to make sure the refreshments stayed fresh and no student accidentally spilled something dire onto one of the good linens.

Cedar was by herself at one of the tables, near an exit door that had been propped open to allow for air flow. She had several thermoses labeled with temperatures and a poster with pictures of green coffee beans and a map of where they'd been grown. "Hey," said Fin, glad to see a friendly face.

Cedar looked up, startled, then broke into a grin. "Hey, Fin. You all set up?"

Fin nodded. "Eddie's at our table. I think he's giving our lizards a pep talk."

Cedar pressed a hand to her mouth to hide a smile. "You never know. If anyone could get those lizards to do tricks or start talking, it'd be Eddie." Her hand fell away, her expression steadying. "How are you?"

The question carried more weight than it usually did.

"I'm fine," said Fin, after a moment's hesitation. If she said it enough, maybe it would be true.

"Any sign of . . . ?" Cedar made an odd movement with her shoulders, one that Fin interpreted to mean *your evil twin*.

Fin shook her head. "I heard some weird noises the other night, but she never showed."

"That's scary," said Cedar. "You think she's out there? Watching us?"

Fin's gaze fell on a wrinkled corner of the tablecloth. It was something to look at, other than Cedar. "I don't know what she wants. I've got . . . I think I might have a way to defeat her, if she shows again." She reached into her pocket and withdrew the small matchbox. She flashed the label toward Cedar, who blinked in surprise.

"Where'd you get matches?" she asked, voice quiet.

"Mrs. Brackenbury had them," said Fin, surprising herself with an honest answer. "They were in her junk drawer. I didn't think she'd miss them."

Cedar appeared impressed by Fin's theft. "Wow. So you're just going to set her on fire if she shows again?"

"I think so," said Fin. "But part of me hopes that she will fade away or something. Like the magic of the tea does."

Cedar fidgeted with one of the thermoses. "Is that what it's like?"

"You know," said Fin. "The magic doesn't last forever."

Cedar set the thermos down, lacing her fingers together as if wanted something else to do with her hands. "I don't know. Before they took over Brewed Awakening, my parents didn't know about Talia's place. No one told them—or me. And by the time people trusted us enough to let us know, Mom and Dad had given up the whole cryptozoology business."

"You never went to the tea shop?" asked Fin.

Cedar shook her head, eyes downcast. "I . . . No. I never went there." Something in her voice made Fin think that Cedar had gone elsewhere, but before Fin could ask, Cedar looked up. "Can I ask what was it like? When the tea worked normally, I mean."

Fin thought of those times in the tea shop when Talia had been there—when the shop had been a haven, rather than a source of fear. Those redwood-paneled walls, the smell of incense and tea, the vintage furniture and old paperback romances arranged on a bookcase. Fin found herself relaxing, the memory a comforting one. "My mom told me not to go, so I never told her about it. But Talia was always really nice—and she'd put the tea in this mortar made of rose quartz. That's where the magic was, actually. I found that out later. It wasn't the tea at all. I'd whisper a memory into the mortar, and then the tea would . . . make me feel normal. Not anxious. For a few weeks, I wouldn't . . ." She searched for the right words. "You've seen those videos of big snakes squeezing their prey, right? It's kind of like that." She waited for Cedar to look confused—or worse, pitying. But Cedar nodded.

"Yeah," said Cedar softly. "I get that. I mean—everyone's got different issues, I know. But I get how it feels to be invisible." She looked both sad and a little wistful. "You ever thought about . . . I don't know. Talking to your mom about it?"

The familiar panic squirmed low in Fin's belly. Instinctively, she drew her arms tight around herself, as though shielding herself from accusations and attention. She wanted to be normal, but even more than that, she wanted other people to *think* she was normal.

Before she could answer, something clattered behind them. Fin and Cedar whirled around, gazes drawn to the emergency exit door. It had been propped open, a foot-wide gap allowing the damp autumn air to swirl into the heat of the conference room. Fin had barely taken notice of that door. Now all she could think was how easily someone could be hiding behind it.

Or something.

Fin and Cedar shared a glance, and Fin knew they were thinking the same thing. Fin's hand delved into her pocket, fingers closing around the matchbox. She took a step around the table, then another.

Her heart pounded hard, but she forced herself to reach for the door, to step into that open space and peer outside.

The back of the inn faced the redwood forest, and the overhead trees were so thick that even now the sunlight was beginning to dim. It took a few seconds for Fin's eyes to adjust. Then she saw a familiar figure. Ben was emptying a blue recycling bin into one of the larger dumpsters. He glanced over his shoulder and saw Fin through the doorway. He waved with his free hand.

Well, that was a relief. Fin took a step back. "It's just Ben taking out the trash."

"Bellhop Ben," Cedar said, and Fin nodded.

An electronic shriek of feedback made them both wince. The sound system was being turned on, and two of the science teachers stood at the front of the room, beaming at everyone. The room was bustling now, filled up when Fin hadn't been paying attention. For those few minutes she was talking with Cedar, Fin had forgotten to be nervous. She'd forgotten where she was, what she had to do. Now it all came rushing back.

"You should go to your table," Cedar said quietly as the science teacher began to speak, his booming voice welcoming everyone to the annual fall science fair.

Fin's feet moved without her say-so, back toward her table. She could see Aunt Myrtle, her hand on Eddie's shoulder. Mom was nowhere to be seen. Maybe it was better that way—one less pair of eyes on Fin.

All she had to do was give a quick speech about the names of the plants and what purpose they had in the wild. Eddie would talk about the lizards and how their eating patterns played in to the ecosystem. As she moved through the crowd, Fin caught a glimpse of something. A flash of black clothing and unruly hair. Fin halted in place, scanning the students and parents. Her heart throbbed without her truly knowing why.

Then she saw it a second time—and her pounding heart sank into her belly.

It was Teafin.

Teafin was at the science fair.

She moved through the crowds with a liquid grace, a prowling step that made Fin want to recoil. Teafin strode toward the main exit, something tucked under her arm.

It looked like part of a windmill.

Fin's mouth moved silently, forming Teafin's name. Her fingers tightened around the matchbox in her pocket, and a flare of panic and anger churned within her. She shouldn't have to deal with this now—she had her presentation to worry about. But Teafin was here, and it looked like she'd sabotaged River's science fair project. Maybe River had seen, maybe he hadn't, but either way, Fin needed to make this right.

She glanced up at the podium, at the teacher reading aloud the local businesses that sponsored this event every year.

Fin had ten minutes before the presentations began.

It would have to be enough time.

TWENTY-TWO

Things Stolen

Fin stumbled through the crowded banquet room, then dashed down the hallway and out into the parking lot. Anger and apprehension swirled within her. She had to get to Teafin, she had to get that windmill back before River figured out who had taken it, and she had to—

There. She caught a glimpse of a slim figure moving through the parked cars.

Fin gritted her teeth, clenched her fingers around the matchbox, and tried to move as quietly as she could. Teafin didn't know she was being followed. She didn't look back, didn't so much as glance in Fin's direction. The windmill remained under one arm, wires trailing behind her. Teafin looked like a piece of the night made real, slipping through shadow and darkness with ease. She was heading back into town, past the coffee shop and toward Mrs. Brackenbury's home. Fin frowned, unsure of what Teafin meant to do with the science fair project. Maybe she'd put it somewhere and frame Fin for the theft. That seemed like her.

Teafin darted between two houses and vanished from sight. Fin drew in a breath and leaped over a low fence, trying to keep her in view. If she could just get Teafin away from the houses, she might deal with her without anyone seeing.

After all, setting a tea monster on fire in public would probably draw attention.

Fin jogged around Mrs. Brackenbury's home and realized where Teafin had been heading.

Ben's house.

No—not the house. The shed.

Teafin had returned to the scene of the crime.

Fin kept low, trying to make herself small as Teafin walked into the shed and vanished from sight. The door had been left unlocked.

She swallowed hard and straightened. She could go in there after Teafin, deal with her alone, and then return to the science fair with River's project. That was the right thing to do. The brave thing. She could do this. She had to do this.

Tiptoeing closer, Fin glanced around the edge of the shed's open door. Teafin stood there, the windmill piece on the floor. Teafin had her arms crossed, and she appeared to be waiting for something.

Fin drew the matchbox free and stepped into view. It was time to end this.

"Good," said Teafin, smiling. "You kept up."

Fin drew a breath, steadying herself. She tore a match free and pressed its tip to the edge of the box. She'd never lit a match before, but she'd seen it plenty of times on TV. It couldn't be that hard. She drew the stick across.

Nothing happened.

She did it again.

Nothing.

Fin bit her lip, wondering how people on TV made this look *easy*. She gazed at the red tip of the match, wondering if it was broken somehow.

"Are you done yet?" said Teafin, sounding bored. "We need to talk. That's why I took this."

Fin gazed at her doppelgänger in disbelief. "You took part of River's science fair project to lure me here? Why?"

"Because you need to see," said Teafin. "And I wasn't sure if you'd follow me—you didn't the other day in the inn parking lot. River's a jerk, anyways." She knelt. The inside of the shed looked normal—there were shelves built into the walls and spare gardening equipment scattered in the corner. Teafin ducked and dragged something out from beneath the shelves. It was a singed and dirty tote bag.

"What is that?" said Fin, distrusting.

"This," said Teafin, "is Mrs. Brackenbury's shopping bag."

Fin frowned, and the hand holding the matchbox fell to her side. None of this made sense. Why would Mrs. Brackenbury's shopping bag be in Ben's shed? Why had Teafin lured her out here? Why—

Teafin looked up and her mouth opened, as if to shout.

A hand pressed between Fin's shoulder blades and gave a hard shove. She fell into the shed, and when she looked back, she saw Ben standing in the doorway. He held a heavy padlock in one hand. "So there really are two of you," he said wonderingly, his gaze darting between them.

Fin opened her mouth to explain. "Ben, I—"

But before she could say another word, Ben slammed the door shut and Fin heard the click of a lock.

Fin was plunged into darkness, the smell of burned ash all around her.

TWENTY-THREE

The Truth

For a few moments, all Fin could hear was the rasp of her own breathing. The air sliced into her lungs, sharp and cold and too close. The darkness crowded in on her, and then her eyes adjusted. There were cracks around the door, a few in the walls. Enough to let in a little light. She could see shelves and a few pieces of broken equipment. The black scorch marks were deep enough that she could see them even in the low light. They ran up the wall, to the ceiling.

And in the dim light, Fin saw Teafin.

The creature stood a few feet away, her arms crossed. Fin was trapped in here with her, no way to escape. Fin backed up until her shoulders hit the door. With shaking hands, she pulled a new match from the matchbox and held it up, unlit but at the ready. "S-stay back."

"Oh, stop that." Teafin's voice was sharp with irritation. "We don't have time."

Fin tried to slow her own breathing. Then she could think clearly. "Time?"

"He's going after the tea shop," said Teafin. "Again. Except this time he knows what he needs, because he heard you talking to Cedar."

None of this made sense. Fin found her arm lowering, the match quivering between thumb and forefinger. "What are you talking about?"

"The tea," said Teafin. "The stolen tea!"

"That was you," said Fin. She swallowed; her throat was dry, her tongue clicking as she spoke. "You did that."

"I haven't been stealing the tea," snarled Teafin. "When I left the big house that first night, I came across Mr. Madeira's home and saw Ben sneaking out of it. Then he grabbed that raven and threw her against a tree. She must have tried to warn the Madeiras. I managed to find her."

"That can't be right," said Fin. "You stole the key to the tea shop. You injured the raven so I wouldn't follow you after you stole the tea."

"I wanted someone to *help* the raven," said Teafin. "But

I couldn't deliver her to Nick myself because he's beyond the town borders. So I kept her until I could give her to you. And anyways, I've been kind of busy following Ben everywhere. He was the one who stole the key—the town council meeting was the perfect cover to break into your cottage, then the tea shop."

A few times at the playgrounds in the city, Fin had gotten into a swing and twisted the chain around and around. Then she'd let it spin free, laughing as her legs swung out. She remembered staggering off the swing, the world still whirling.

That's what this felt like. The world was spinning and she didn't know how to make it stop.

"Mrs. Brackenbury," Fin said, feeling numb. "She was mugged—before you were . . ."

"Born?" said Teafin, with a wry twist to her mouth. "Created?"

"Whatever," said Fin.

Teafin nodded. "Yeah. I tried to stop him after I saw him break into the Madeiras' place—he's been storing the stolen tea in here. I thought if I could burn it down, make the magic go away . . ."

"The fire," said Fin. "That was you. He saw you."

"I had trouble starting it," said Teafin. "It's hard to set something on fire when fire can destroy me. I had to find an illegal barbecue lighter at some tourist's cabin."

"What about Mom's office door?" asked Fin desperately. "You pried off the nameplate! You could have lost Mom somewhere."

"I was trying to keep Ben from going into her office again." Teafin scowled. "I saw him digging through her things—I think that's how he managed to break into the cottage. Mom usually puts her key chain in the top drawer."

"I ended up in a water tower," said Fin angrily. "I was looking for you. Trying to stop you."

"And I was trying to stop Ben," said Teafin, sounding exasperated. "You've been so fixated on me, you didn't realize that there was someone else running around."

Fin gazed at the girl that looked so much like her. "Why?" she said. "Why would Ben do this?"

"How should I know?" said Teafin. "You've talked to him more than I have."

Fin remembered her last conversation with Ben. "He was talking about people getting laid off at the inn," she said. "He—he must have found out he was going to be one of them." She thought of the cookies, of Ben saying that there had to be another way to lure tourists to Aldermere. Of his quiet desperation when he'd said he couldn't afford to leave Aldermere.

A chill settled in her stomach. "He's going to try and sell the magic," said Fin quietly. "He wants to sell it to tourists."

Teafin rocked back. "You think?"

"That's the only reason he'd rob the entire tea shop," said Fin. "If he wanted to use it on himself, all he'd need was a little." Even as she said the words, Fin felt the full weight of them settle on her shoulders. "But if the tourists find out the magic is real, everything would change," she said quietly.

A whole new future opened up in front of Fin: one in which Aldermere was swarmed with people. Some would be tourists, yes, but others would want to stay. She imagined the town crowded, its original occupants being shoved aside. It wouldn't be a few newcomers a year, like Fin and Mom or Cedar and her family. It would be *everyone* who'd ever dreamed of magic. Every Bigfoot hunter, every scientist looking to disprove magic, every person who had a flaw they wanted to change about themselves. It would be exactly what Nick had warned her about.

A shudder rolled through her.

"He didn't know about the mortar," Fin said. "Until he heard me talking to Cedar. He's going after it. That's why he locked us in here."

Teafin snorted. "Does he think a lock is gonna stop me?"

Fin glared at the other girl. "You're snarky for a soggy clump of tea and fears."

"I'm not only your fears," said Teafin. "I'm—well, everything you traded away. Those memories, I still have those. I tried to show you in the forest, but you were being stubborn."

Fin gaped at her. "Aren't you supposed to be evil?"

"You're the one who called me evil," said Teafin tartly. "I prefer 'spirited.'" She spread her hands, gesturing at herself. "I'm you, don't you get it? I'm those pieces you tried to get rid of. The memories, the sadness, the fear, the anger. And maybe I'm wilder than you are—"

"You're an arsonist."

"You're the one running around with matches," said Teafin. "Stolen matches."

Fin considered, then said, "Fair."

Teafin took a step closer until Fin's back was to the door. "Don't you want to know? All of those things you're afraid of, there's reasons. You buried them. But I remember."

The match was still in Fin's hand; she glanced down at it, then at Teafin.

"What did I forget?" she asked, voice quiet.

Teafin held out a hand. "Let me show you."

Fin didn't want to touch that hand. She must have

chosen to forget all of those memories for a reason. If Fin was bad, if she was *truly* bad enough that Mom had to keep moving her, then maybe it was better she didn't know.

But another part of her yearned to reach out.

Be brave.

Fin took a deep breath. When she released it, she acted on impulse. With her free hand, she seized Teafin's wrist.

The moment she touched the other girl, the images flooded into her.

And she was no longer in the darkened shed.

She was in a room, pressed tightly into a corner, hands around her ears. There was shouting from the next room. She had to be quiet. Mom had told her to be quiet, but the phone had rung and woken him up and now there was shouting.

The scene shifted and changed and—

She smelled something stale and burning: cigarette-stained fingers reaching into a pocket and coming up with a lighter. The shadow of beard against a jaw as someone looked over at her and said, "Thought you were at kindergarten."

Then everything blurred again and—

A goldfish. Her goldfish that she'd fed every day for months because Mom said they couldn't get a dog.

It was flopping on the floor, surrounded by shattered

glass, water spreading out across the linoleum. The fishbowl had been smashed in an argument. She scooped the fish up, trying to find a glass of water—

Another shift.

Mom in the bathroom, putting makeup over a bruise on her cheek.

Fin listening at her bedroom door, trying to see if he was awake, if she needed to stay hidden—

Again, a new memory.

She was outside school, waiting near the line of cars where parents picked up kids. Mom was late again. Only then a security guard wearing an orange vest was there, taking Fin by the hand and saying that she was going to wait inside. As Fin glanced over her shoulder, she caught sight of a tall man staring after her.

And then—

Hands on her, rousing her in the middle of the night. "Come on, sweetie," said Mom, and she was younger, with less gray in her hair and fewer lines around her eyes. "We're going for a ride in the car, okay?"

"It's bedtime," Fin said sleepily.

"I know, but we're going."

They had gone.

No, Fin realized. They had *run*. They'd been running for

years. From apartment to apartment, never in the same city for longer than a year. At least until—

They'd come to Aldermere.

Fin jerked her hand free. She drew in ragged breaths of air, so hard her chest hurt. She looked at Teafin. The other girl was still and calm, her silver eyes on Fin.

"You remember now, don't you?" she asked quietly.

Fin's hands were shaking. She put them in her lap. "Dad." And it only now occurred to her that it was strange she'd never said the word aloud, never even thought it. "He used to yell," said Fin numbly. "He used to break things. I learned how to be quiet, but it wasn't enough, and Mom—she took me and ran."

"Yes," said Teafin. "And after we came here, when the fear didn't go away, we decided to trade those memories for a cure. If the magic didn't work, then maybe forgetting them altogether would. But it didn't. Because even if our mind forgot, the rest of us didn't."

"All those little habits," Fin said.

She couldn't help but think of her list of fears and how all of them matched up with the memories she had glimpsed. For the longest time, she had been afraid. It wasn't until now that she realized there might have been a *reason* for it. "Avoiding the phone, not answering doors, not wanting to draw attention to myself—I thought it was because there was something wrong with me."

"No," said the other girl. "That was how you survived."

It was a revelation, like seeing herself clearly for the first time. Fin examined old memories, turning them over for new details. This was why she'd never had a pet, why she'd changed schools so many times, why Mom had always looked over her shoulder, as if expecting someone to be following them. Maybe he had been.

"That's who Aunt Myrtle didn't want to come to Aldermere," said Fin, remembering that first night. "And that day outside the school . . ."

Teafin nodded. "Dad came to find us at school. And that night Mom brought us here."

"How?" said Fin. "How did I never talk about this? How did Mom . . ."

Teafin shrugged. "She started running from Dad when we were really young. That's why we never stayed in one place too long—because she was afraid he'd find us. She works hard so that we can stay here. But I think . . . I mean, adults are people, too. They're not perfect. I think she hoped that our problems would go away."

Fin took one shuddering breath after another. Suddenly it all made sense—why Mom looked at Fin with those half-sad, half-fearful glances. She was probably wondering how much Fin remembered of those early years.

"Listen, we'll talk more about this later," said Teafin. "But right now, we've got to stop Ben."

Fin shook her head despairingly. "He'll already be at the tea shop. We can't get there in time."

"Not if the ravens found him first," said Teafin cheerily. "I told our raven to keep an eye out for him."

Fin blinked at her. "You talked to *our* raven?"

"Yup," said Teafin. "And I can get us out of here. But you're going to have to trust me."

Fin looked at Teafin—at the girl made of all the parts of herself she had tried to discard. She still had the matches in her hand. She could use fire on Teafin; the flame would destroy her. Fin could try to destroy her fear and memories. All it would take was a single match.

But hadn't she already done that? Hadn't she spent years trying to forget, to be someone else? And what had it gotten her?

In the end, she was alone with herself. All of herself. Even the pieces she didn't like.

Especially those pieces.

And now . . . she could use them to do some good.

Fin drew in a sharp little breath. "Okay." She lowered the

matchbox. Her thumb ached where it had been pressed into the cardboard. It was like she'd put down a heavy burden. "What do we have to do?"

Teafin nodded at the door. "Move. I can get through there."

Fin glanced down at the scant space between the door and the floor—it could only have been a quarter of an inch.

"Nothing could fit through there," she said uncertainly.

Teafin just raised her crooked eyebrows. "You saw me crawl out of a sink and you still think I can't fit through there?"

"Good point," Fin admitted, and stepped aside. Teafin rolled her shoulders, and it reminded Fin of a diver taking her place over a high pool jump. She stretched and considered, then lowered herself into a crouch.

Teafin changed.

She became formless, a shifting mass of damp tea leaves. A few of them fell away, spattering wetly to the floor. But most slipped under the door, leaving a slick trail behind. Fin watched in amazement as Teafin slid through that small space and vanished from sight.

Then there was nothing.

Fin's heart pounded. She'd made the wrong decision. She'd trusted Teafin and she shouldn't have—not when the girl was made of bad memories and fears. She was made of everything monsters were made of, and Fin should have known better, should have—

The doorknob rattled, then shook. As if something heavy was being bashed against the lock. Then a click, and the door swung open.

Teafin stood there, a smirk tugging at her mouth.

"Ready to finish this?" she said.

Fin nodded.

TWENTY-FOUR

The Team

One thing was certain: Fin could not do this alone.

She had her double, of course. Teafin wasn't a monster or Fin's evil twin or even the worst parts of herself. Because while Teafin had been running around, causing all kinds of chaos—it had all been to save Aldermere. And while it was reckless, it had also been brave.

Fin very much wanted to believe that she had that bravery in her.

But right now, she needed more than Teafin. She needed Eddie. And Cedar.

Fin leaped over the broken cracks in the sidewalk and the stray tree roots. She took a sharp left turn and cut through a backyard. The scents of autumn were crisp in her nose, and a chill crept up her bare arms.

Teafin moved alongside her, every step in unison. She didn't move quite like a person—more like Fin's shadow. She didn't seem affected by the run, not even when Fin's lungs began to burn. There were some advantages to being magical.

Finally the gleaming lights of the inn and that full parking lot came into view. Fin sprinted up the driveway, nearly colliding with a parent who'd slipped out to check a cell phone, unaware they didn't work in Aldermere. Fin dodged around the adult, slowing as she approached the building. That side door was still propped open. "Stay out here," said Fin. "I don't want anyone else to see you."

Teafin crossed her arms. "I look like you."

"Exactly," said Fin. "And if someone sees two of us, there'll be some awkward questions." She slipped through the door, her heart hammering against her rib cage.

A timid voice echoed through the speakers. Fin saw a girl she didn't know at the podium, haltingly explaining her poster on climate change. The parents were watching—some more raptly than others—while most of the kids were fidgeting with their own projects. Eddie stood beside their lizard terrarium, fingers tapping anxiously against his thigh.

Fin pushed through the crowds until she stood beside him. Eddie's shoulders slumped with relief. "Oh. You're here. I thought—I thought you'd run off and thrown up in a trash can and decided to stay away and let me do the speech—"

"Come on," she said, tugging on his sleeve. "We've got to go."

Eddie gaped at her. He gestured vaguely at the podium. "We're up after two groups!"

"Aldermere is in danger," she said in a low whisper, trying to infuse every word with urgency. "I need your help."

Eddie went silent, his mouth still half open. But he nodded.

She turned and started walking, and Eddie followed. She squeezed between two parents and began angling herself sideways, darting between tables until she was nearly at the door.

Then Cedar was there, a line between her brows. She must have been watching. "What's wrong?" she said.

"No time," Fin said desperately. "I need—outside."

Cedar didn't hesitate; she pushed the door open wider and the three of them spilled out beside the dumpsters. Fin shut the door behind them and the speakers went abruptly quiet.

"What's going on?" said Eddie. "What's—whoa!"

Teafin stepped out of the shadows.

Eddie whirled his arms around, like someone trying to catch his balance, and it took Fin a moment to realize that he was trying to do some kind of martial arts.

"Oh, stop that," said Teafin. "You look like one of those 'how to spot drowning people' videos we had to watch in swimming class."

Eddie dropped his arms. He looked between Fin and Teafin, clearly expecting something to happen.

"It's a long story," said Fin, "and I promise to fill everyone in later, but right now—Ben's after the magical tea. He knows about Talia's mortar and he's going to steal it. We have to stop him."

Eddie blinked a few times. He looked as though Fin had asked him to solve a complicated math problem. "What?"

"Ben's behind all of it," said Fin. "He was the one who mugged Mrs. Brackenbury, who broke into Mr. Madeira's house, who stole from the tea shop. I think he wants to try and sell the tea himself, making it into some kind of touristy thing."

Cedar looked frightened. "But if the entire world finds out—"

"Aldermere will be flooded with people," said Fin. "People who won't care about protecting the magic. We have to stop Ben. If we could get to the mortar first—"

"We should get Mom," said Eddie. "She ran to the bathroom, but she'll be back soon. Or . . . I don't know. Aren't we supposed to go to police officers or something?"

"The nearest police station is thirty miles away," said Cedar. "And I'm pretty sure they wouldn't help much right now."

"You mean when a twenty-something decides to break all the unwritten laws of the town and sell magical tea to everyone he can because it'll make him rich, regardless of the consequences to the town and its people?" said Teafin scornfully. "Yeah, that sounds exactly like something the cops would deal with."

Eddie squinted at her. "I'm sorry, aren't you evil?"

"I'm just uninhibited," said Teafin, unabashed.

"And she's on our side," said Fin.

Cedar looked in the direction of the tea shop. "We have to get there first."

Eddie rubbed at his forehead. "But we—Fin, we have to give our presentation in ten minutes. If we run . . ."

Fin's stomach sank. If they did leave, then they wouldn't be back in time. They'd miss giving their presentation. And they'd probably end up with a failing grade.

She'd never failed a project or a test. Those times she'd gotten lower grades, she'd worked herself up into a frenzy of extra credit and sleepless nights because the idea of letting people down, of having the adults think she was failing—it had been unbearable.

"There are more important things than grades," said Teafin.

Fin looked at the other girl. Teafin's steel-silver eyes were full of understanding, but her mouth was set. She'd made up her mind. Which meant some part of Fin's mind was made up too. She said, "Cedar—you try to find my mom or Aunt Myrtle and tell them to meet us at the tea shop."

Cedar nodded. She touched her fingers to Fin's bare arm, a brief little pressure. "You be careful," she said, then turned and vanished inside.

Fin turned to face Eddie. His expression was creased with worry and . . . indecision. He clearly wanted to stay, to beat River. But Aldermere was his home too.

"Eddie, please," she said softly.

Eddie glanced between Fin and Teafin. It felt like an eternity stretched out in those scant moments, and then he nodded. "I'll help."

Her shoulders slumped in relief. "Thank you," she said, meaning it.

Eddie slid another wary look toward Teafin. "You sure she's on our side?"

"She's me," said Fin. "I tried—I guess I tried to push that away, but she's still part of me."

Teafin gave Eddie a sharp little grin.

Eddie did not look reassured. "All right then." He straightened his shoulders, mouth set. Fin knew that look—once he'd made a decision, he'd stick to it. "What can I do?"

Fin took a breath, then another, trying to steady herself. "Get Mrs. Petrichor and tell her that Ben's about to set the tea shop on fire." Fin remembered the way Ben had shied away from Mrs. Petrichor; if anyone could frighten him off, maybe it was her.

Eddie blinked. "*Is* he going to set it on fire?"

"Once he gets the mortar, who knows?" said Fin. "But it'll get her there fast."

Eddie nodded. "What are you going to do?"

Fin hesitated for a moment. "Stall Ben, if I can. Get the mortar if he hasn't already."

"You can do it," said Eddie. He reached out and squeezed her arm for a moment. Then he turned, pushed the branch of a redwood aside, and vanished into the forest. He would get to Mrs. Petrichor's house faster cutting through the backwoods.

Distantly, Fin heard the sound of feedback from the speakers. She winced, her heart lurching in her chest. There was no winning all of the battles, not tonight. She had to choose: her mask of normality or her town.

She picked Aldermere. She would always pick Aldermere.

"Come on," she said to Teafin.

Teafin grinned.

Together they ran toward the tea shop. They cut around the back of several houses, through the underbrush. Teafin moved like liquid dark, slipping in and out of the shadows, silver eyes focused ahead.

Ben. Ben had been lying to her this whole time—all those friendly smiles, that courteous demeanor. He had been waiting for his opportunity to use the magic to make money, never caring what would happen to the town. Talia had gone to such lengths to protect the tea shop and the magic. And now it was all for nothing.

No, Fin thought fiercely. It wouldn't be for nothing. Her steps quickened. Branches hit her bare arms, redwood needles brushing as they sprinted through another backyard.

Finally the tea shop came into view. They were coming at it from the back; Fin caught sight of that familiar back door, the overgrown ferns, and the peeling paint.

"Looks empty," said Teafin. "The raven must have found Ben. Come on, we need to get the mortar to a safe place."

"Will the back door still be unlocked?" asked Fin.

Teafin shrugged. "I think so. The real question is, what do we do if Ben shows up?"

Fin glanced over, saw the silver gleam of Teafin's gaze on her. "He wants magic," said Fin. "Maybe he'd like to meet a tea monster."

Teafin smiled so wide that Fin thought she could feel the echo of it behind her own teeth.

And together they stepped from the forest.

TWENTY-FIVE

Choices

Evening came early in the redwoods.

There was no true sunset. Once the sun fell behind the tall trees, dusk settled at the forest floor, darkness filling up the spaces between Aldermere's buildings. Fin wasn't afraid of the encroaching dark, but she was aware of every moment passing—how each minute could bring Ben a little bit closer.

Teafin reached for the tea shop's back door, but her fingers froze on the doorknob. Her head tilted to one side. "Someone's coming," she said quietly.

Fin's heart throbbed. She clenched both hands into fists.

She wouldn't let her fear stop her from doing the right thing.

Ben emerged from between two houses. His hair was mussed and he scowled as he walked. His shirt was torn in several places, and he kept glancing at the sky. Looking for ravens, Fin realized. He kept underneath the house's eaves, moving with furtive haste. He strode up the driveway, gravel crunching beneath his feet as he reached into his pocket, producing a small flashlight. He twisted it to life, piercing the dusk. He fumbled in that same pocket for a key—the key. The one with the crescent-moon key chain. With one last glance upward, Ben strode forward.

Then he saw the two girls by the back door and went still.

Shock flashed across his features. The key dropped from his fingers, vanishing into the gravel road. "How'd you get out?" he said.

Fin had been right to trust Teafin. Ben was clearly here for no good reason. And she felt a little more powerful at the sight of Ben looking so shocked. She had spent so long trying to make herself invisible that she'd never imagined there could also be a fierce pleasure in being seen.

"Hi, Ben," said Fin.

The flashlight yanked one way, making Fin's eyes ache, then back toward Teafin.

Fin crossed her arms. "What are you doing here?"

He gathered himself together. Fin watched as he straightened, his mouth hardening. She was a kid in his eyes, easily brushed aside.

"That is none of your business," he said crisply.

Teafin eased forward; her arms were held loosely at her sides. She looked like Eddie when he was catching lizards: ready to pounce at a moment's notice. "Where'd you get that key, Ben?" Her voice was all mocking and brittle humor. "Let me guess—out of our bedroom?"

"That's funny," said Ben, in a wholly unamused tone, "coming from someone who tried to burn down my shed. Or was it you?" He nodded toward Fin. "She's some kind of magic gone wrong, isn't she?"

"I'm what happens when the tea is brewed, then tossed aside," said Teafin. "Of course you'd know all about tea gone wrong, wouldn't you?"

Ben's irritation flared. "It wouldn't work for me. Not the stuff from Mrs. Brackenbury, not Mr. Madeira's, and not even the stuff from the shop. It wasn't until tonight that I knew why."

"Because you hadn't paid for it," said Fin. "For the tea to work, the person has to pay the mortar with a memory. You never did, so the tea was just tea for you."

"Probably a good thing," said Teafin conversationally.

"Otherwise you'd have a bunch of Tea Bens running around." She frowned. "Teaben? Bentea?"

"Bentea sounds like a brand of frozen yogurt," said Fin. "What do you think, Ben?" She spoke airily, trying to hide her own fear. They had to stall him. Cedar or Eddie would bring help. Fin just had to delay him.

"I think," said Ben, "that you made a mistake coming here." He took a step forward.

Fin held her ground.

"Maybe," she said. "But you made a bigger one when you decided to sell out the magic." It was still a guess—but Fin thought she was right. Color flushed across Ben's face.

Keep him talking, Fin thought. "Why the tea, Ben?" she said. "Of all the ways you could try and make money in this town, why did you pick the tea shop?"

Ben threw her a derisive look. "What else was I going to do? Sell tourists tickets to walk through an unmarked door? Take bets on where they'd come out? Or try and teach the whintossers tricks and hope they didn't bite someone? At least the tea's predictable, once you know how to use it."

"But if everyone knew," said Fin, "then Aldermere wouldn't be Aldermere. The magic—"

"Magic? What has the magic done for any of us?" Ben snapped. "Nothing. We protect it—and for what? It's never made any of our lives better. Instead, some monster eats our pets and we have bloodthirsty knives and doors we can't trust. Magic couldn't save my mom. It couldn't keep Mrs. Madeira from getting Alzheimer's or even prevent Talia from falling. Magic doesn't help any of us. The best we can do is get what we can from it before some wildfire burns it all up."

"That mortar belongs to Talia," said Fin.

"I tried to include her," he said, and suddenly his voice was sharper and clearer. It wasn't the same soft tone he'd used when he opened doors for her or answered the phone at the inn. This was the real Ben—sharp and brittle and angry. "Do you know what people would *pay* for that kind of thing? How much money they'd give to be more beautiful or confident, or to stop being in pain or depressed? People would even pay to have certain memories taken away, whether they gained something else or not. So I went into the tea shop after my mom died, tried to convince Talia that she was sitting on a fortune. I was studying business at college—I could've made her rich. Put this town on the map. You know what she did? She threw me out. The tea shop vanished the next day. I didn't find it again until you and Eddie showed the EMTs where to go."

"Good," said Fin fervently.

"Good?" Ben let out an incredulous laugh. "I know

you're a kid, but you aren't stupid. Fin, you must see how Aldermere is struggling. The inn does well during the summer months, but it's dead in the winter. People don't have enough work. With climate change, with the wildfires, even tourist season can't be counted on like it used to. The town is dying." He took another step toward her, his face open and beseeching. "I'll let you in on it, Fin. If you help me. I'll give you a cut. Talia might never come back. Old people who get hurt sometimes don't recover. What if we . . . made the tea available to anyone in the world who wanted it?"

Fin thought of her mother working tirelessly at the inn, with shadowed eyes and tired smiles. She thought of Aunt Myrtle selling fortunes and postcards and seashell wind chimes. She thought of her own deliveries every Tuesday, so she and Mom had grocery store credit. She thought of secondhand clothes and used books. They'd never lacked for anything, but Fin had seen the new backpacks that her classmates had, the fancy cell phones and clothing that fit just right. And all right, part of Fin wished that Mom was around more, that she wouldn't look so worried all the time.

And if the tea was widely available, she could get it whenever she wanted. Now that she knew what she'd done wrong, Fin could avoid it. She could burn the tea leaves afterward, burn out those memories and those parts of herself she didn't want. She could live in a world where she didn't have to feel awkward and anxious all the time.

All it would cost was Aldermere.

"No," said Fin. "Talia is coming back and I won't let you do this to her. To the town. You're right that people are struggling, but telling the whole world about the magic wouldn't fix things."

Ben let out a heavy breath. "I was hoping you'd understand. People matter more than magic."

"This isn't the way to help them!" said Fin. "Everyone who lives in Aldermere will be pushed out. You said you could barely afford to live here. What happens when the whole world knows this place is magic?"

"Then we'll get rich selling the tea," said Ben, "and leave. There are other towns—you don't have to live here."

Fin shook her head. She couldn't find the words to tell him that Aldermere was the first place she'd ever loved like a home—that with its dangers and strangeness, there came a sense of possibility. Of opening an unmarked door and going anywhere in town, of seeing creatures that shouldn't exist flitting through the forest.

Magic was real, and the world was the richer for it.

Ben knelt, angling his tiny flashlight downward so that he could see where the key had fallen in the gravel. The crescent-moon key chain gleamed, and he reached for it.

Wings sliced through the air as a black shape swooped down upon him.

For a heartbeat, Fin thought it was a bat. But then she saw the shape of the wings and the body, and she recognized it. It was a raven—*her* raven. The small bird plucked up the key chain with its beak and took to the air.

Ben cried out, lunging after her, but he was too slow. The bird landed on Fin's shoulder, the key in her beak. "Get back here," Ben snarled, rushing toward her.

Fin lurched back, but Teafin surged forward.

"No, you don't," she said. For a moment, it looked laughably one-sided: a small girl running at a grown man. Fin's heartbeat throbbed with fear for Teafin, but before Ben could touch her, the girl *changed.*

Because she wasn't human—and Fin had forgotten that. Teafin's edges blurred and she shifted, becoming a monstrous-looking creature with spindly arms and legs, with slick hair that dripped tea water and eyes that were nothing but silver tea balls. She opened her mouth wide, a gaping void. Fin had never thought she'd be so glad to have a monster on her side.

Ben skidded to a halt so fast that he nearly fell over. His eyes flashed wide and he fumbled at his pockets, as if trying to find something to defend himself.

The raven nudged at Fin's cheek and she flinched, surprised by the touch. The raven burbled gently, then dropped the key into Fin's hand. She barely managed to catch it. "Thanks," she said, still unsure if the bird could understand her. The raven chittered, tightened her hold on Fin's shoulder, then launched herself into the air. She flapped until she was out of sight.

Fin looked down at the key.

There were no adults here yet. None at all—which meant she and Teafin had to handle this.

The mortar. If Ben couldn't get that, his plans would fall apart. All she had to do was lock a single door, and Ben would never manage to get them. He couldn't break in, not without the tea shop vanishing. Her breath came in jagged gasps, her body quaking.

She tried to fit the key into the lock, but she had it upside down. Fingers unsteady, Fin jammed the key into the deadbolt and twisted. She heard the lock click into place and hope lit hot inside her chest. She'd done it. The tea shop was safe.

An inhuman cry rang out behind her.

Fin looked over her shoulder, and her eyes widened.

Ben stood there, holding what looked like a small torch.

No, it wasn't a torch—it was a barbecue lighter.

"Shouldn't have left this by the shed," he said, panting. He lunged at Teafin, driving the lighter toward her like a fencer with a sword.

Teafin darted away, but Fin saw that the other girl was limping. She'd returned to her Fin form, out of that monstrous shape. She was glaring at Ben, angry and—and afraid.

It was the first time Fin had ever seen her double look frightened.

"Get away from her," Fin said, voice tight.

"Then give me the key," said Ben. "I don't want to hurt either of you. I just want the mortar." He edged closer to Teafin, who stumbled back. The flame looked too bright in the dusk.

The key was the most important thing. She couldn't give it to him.

Ben lunged. He seized a handful of gravel and tossed it at Teafin. She ducked, holding up her arm to protect her eyes. While she was distracted, Ben seized her by the arm. He dragged her close, and the tiny flame illuminated her face.

For all that she was a monster, Teafin looked vulnerable and angry about it. Her tea-slick hair writhed against her cheeks, like one last act of defiance—and Fin remembered that old Greek myth of Medusa dying at the hands of Perseus. "Do it, then," Teafin said.

A tangle of emotions flashed across Ben's face—anger, regret, and fear. Fin's stomach lurched; she knew how fear could drive a person to do bad things. She'd stolen tea from the shop, lied to Mom, and created Teafin, all to escape her own fears. If Ben was afraid, it meant he was more dangerous than Fin could handle.

Ben lowered the flame toward Teafin, his mouth set in a grim line.

"Wait," said Fin urgently. She held out a hand, begging. "Don't hurt her."

She couldn't let anything happen to Teafin. They were part of the same whole. If Teafin was lost, so were those memories.

"Give me the key," snapped Ben. "Give it to me now and I won't hurt whatever this thing is. Choose—her or the tea shop."

She couldn't give it to him. She had to give it to him.

She had to give it—

She had—

Teafin shook her head frantically. Fin ignored her.

"All right," she said. Then she tossed the key at Ben. The

crescent moon glittered in the air and Ben had to let go of Teafin to grab it.

Teafin staggered away, turning toward Fin with a wide, accusatory look. Then she went still.

Because Fin hadn't only tossed the key toward Ben. She had also reached down. She seized a rock that fit snugly against the palm of her hand. It was cold against her skin, the edges sharp.

She couldn't let Ben have the magic.

Even if it meant she couldn't have it, either.

Fin spun around and threw the rock as hard as she could.

Not at Ben—but at the tea shop window. The rock sailed through the air, its shape stark in the flashlight's beam, arcing perfectly. It had been a good throw, aimed true.

The rock crashed through the glass of the window.

For a heartbeat, everything was suspended in silence. The world was frozen and still, as though it was holding its breath.

And then the air pressure changed. The hair on Fin's arms stood on end and her ears popped. Something was changing, an unseen tide was rushing toward her, and then—

The tea shop vanished.

TWENTY-SIX
Explanations

The silence lasted a few moments. Then Ben sucked in a breath and whispered, “No.” It was a broken little protest. He took a step toward where the tea shop had stood—but now there was only dead grass and crushed ferns. The space was empty. Not even the foundations remained.

Fin stood there, barely able to believe what she had just done. She’d made the tea shop vanish—and she didn’t know if it would ever be found again.

“No!” Ben repeated, his voice rising. Astonishment hardened into anger and he rounded on Fin. “You little—” He dropped the key and grabbed Fin by the shirt, giving her a hard little shake.

"GET YOUR HANDS OFF HER."

The voice cracked through the darkness with such ferocity that Ben let go immediately. Fin stumbled and looked up.

Mom came rushing toward them, her expression one of utter fury. Ben retreated, bumping into Mrs. Petrichor. The older woman looked as hawkishly stern as ever, but now there was a new gleam to her eyes. She reached down for the barbecue lighter. "Well, well," she said softly. Her gaze snapped to Ben.

Ben tried to run.

Mrs. Petrichor seized him by the arm, putting it behind his back and driving him down to one knee. He grunted with pain. "I knew it was arson," she said. "The moment I saw your shed."

"It wasn't me," snarled Ben. "It was Fin's magic twin."

"Sure it was," said Mrs. Petrichor, marching him away.

Mom reached for Fin, touching her shoulders, her arms. "Are you okay?"

"I'm fine," Fin said. "Mom, I'm fine." She glanced around and saw Aunt Myrtle, Cedar, and Eddie a few steps away. Cedar was looking at the expanse where the tea shop had once stood, her eyes wide. Then she slid that look toward Fin, raising her eyebrows in a silent question.

Fin's own gaze darted around, but she saw no sign of her double. Teafin must have made a run for it the moment the other adults showed up. Fin shook her head at Cedar and Eddie, who both seemed to understand.

Everything was chaos and explanations for nearly an hour afterward. Mrs. Petrichor locked Ben in her car—a minivan, with one of those child-proof systems—and asked what had happened. Fin cobbled together a story that was half truth and half lie: that she'd overheard Ben talking about the tea shop and realized he intended to steal the mortar, that she'd seen him with a barbecue lighter, that Fin had come here to delay him while she sent Cedar and Eddie for help. The others simply nodded along with her story, and no one mentioned Teafin. Ben snarled something from inside the minivan, but Mrs. Petrichor only slid him a look that was mingled disappointment and pity.

"This is a mess," she said. "I'll have to speak with the town council." She pressed a hand to her forehead, rubbing as though she had a headache. "He's not the first to try something like this. He won't be the last."

"What'll happen to him?" asked Fin.

"Banishment," said Mrs. Petrichor with an exhalation too sharp to be a sigh. "I've no doubt. Council won't have a choice. Nick will see him out and he won't return."

Fin didn't know what banishment entailed—or how they'd keep Ben from ever coming back. She considered asking, but part of her didn't want to know.

"What about the tea shop?" asked Fin. "Is it gone forever? Or will Talia be able to find it when she comes back?"

Mrs. Petrichor shrugged. "No idea," she said frankly. She was one of those adults that never softened her words, not even for kids—and Fin appreciated that. "It'll be a right mess, either way." She gave her minivan a dour look. "He's going to see the council tonight. Even if it means I have to drag Mayor Downer out of bed." Her car keys in hand, she walked away.

Mom and Aunt Myrtle fussed over Fin and Eddie, saying that they'd been brave but foolish. Mom leaned more heavily on the foolish side, while Aunt Myrtle was more on the brave side.

"You missed your school presentation," said Aunt Myrtle, and Fin's stomach sank. "I'll talk to your teacher," Aunt Myrtle continued. "We'll get it smoothed over—for all three of you."

Cedar brightened; she had stood a few feet apart, looking a little unsure of her place in the conversation.

"Come on," said Mom, putting her arm around Fin's shoulders. "Let's get you all home."

They all went their separate ways. Aunt Myrtle and Eddie headed toward the inn to retrieve the terrarium, and Fin could hear Aunt Myrtle complimenting Eddie's bravery in the same breath as she mentioned he should have found an adult sooner. Eddie threw Fin an exasperated look.

Fin nodded. Then she gave him a half-hearted grin, because she wasn't sure how badly they'd be grounded for the next few weeks.

Cedar began to slip away in the direction of Brewed Awakening. "I'll see you later," she said quietly, and before she could leave, Fin reached for her.

"Hey," said Fin, and Cedar went still. There were so many things Fin wanted to say: *Thank you for believing me, thank you for hiding Teafin's existence, thank you for not thinking this was all ridiculous and just staying at the science fair.* But all she said was, "Thanks."

Cedar understood. She gave Fin a small smile before she left..

Mom and Fin walked home to the cottage. Something moved in the dark and Fin's heartbeat quickened—but not with fear. It was probably Teafin, lurking out of sight.

Mom unlocked the door. Every movement was slow and careful, and she flicked on the light with a small sigh.

"Let me guess," said Fin. "You're going to tell me I should've told an adult and not gone after Ben, even though he might have managed to break in before—"

"I visited the tea shop when I was younger," said Mom abruptly, and Fin fell silent. The words were so shocking that all she could do was stare. Mom walked into their small kitchen, turning on the gas stove and setting a kettle atop the flame. "I was a teenager and I was young and—and growing up in a place like this, in any small town, you end up either loving or hating it. Your Aunt Myrtle loved Aldermere, even then. Our parents knew she would stay. But I . . . I had no such attachments. I wanted more than this town could offer."

Fin didn't move, afraid it would break the spell of this story.

"I went to the tea shop when I was nineteen," said Mom. "Talia was there, even then. I asked her if the teas could help me find love—and she said that love couldn't be created, but that I could make myself more appealing. So I used the tea to make myself more outgoing, friendlier, and happier. I used it to become the kind of girl I thought that I should have been. And it worked—a tourist, a young man, was passing through. I caught his eye. We fell in love. But now I can never be sure if I truly loved him or if I wanted to love him. He left Aldermere—and I went with him. We went south, got married, found work and an apartment, and . . . he wasn't a good person. I hadn't seen that before, because he hid it well."

Fin swallowed hard.

"After you were born, I tried to stick it out with him," continued Mom. "I thought he'd try, for you. But he didn't. Things got worse and . . . Fin, I know you were young. I don't know how much you remember. But it wasn't a good time."

Fin still didn't remember—not all of it. Just the flashes that Teafin had shown her, small snippets. "We left," she said.

Mom nodded. "Yes. Because you will always be the most important thing to me, you got that? It's why we came to Aldermere. Your dad kept tracking us down, and one time he almost got to you at school. So I decided we'd be safest here. And I wanted you to have a real home, the kind of place you'd enjoy growing up in." She squatted in front of Fin. "I know you're anxious a lot. Sometimes I worry it's because I didn't leave soon enough . . . or it's the way you would have been, regardless. You're a smart girl, and I love you so much. But it's not wrong to admit that sometimes we need help. Do you understand?"

Fin took a breath. It wasn't weakness, she decided, to accept help. She'd accepted Eddie and Cedar's help—even

Teafin's. But none of them could help her with this. "I'll see the counselor," she said.

Mom's face broke into a smile. "I'll make an appointment," she said. "And we can drive up together. There's a mall in Eureka, and we could even buy you a few new school clothes."

It sounded nice.

Fin nodded. "Okay."

Because Teafin was right. Fear wasn't something that could be pushed aside.

Mom went to bed, and Fin went up to her loft. She picked up one of her books and flipped it to the back page. Tucked between the pages was the handwritten list of all her fears. She'd brought it with her, from apartment to apartment, and it was only now she understood how those fears were part of her.

She crumpled it up, paper crinkling between her fingers. Then she yanked up the window and threw it as hard as she could.

The list vanished into the darkness.

Relief swept through her. Then, out of nowhere, the list flew back out of the night and nearly hit her in the face. Fin barely managed to snatch it from midair, fumbling with the paper.

"You might want that," said a familiar voice.

Teafin swung up onto the sharp incline of the roof. She was dressed in the same black clothing, and the raven sat on her shoulder. She looked like some kind of dark heroine. She looked fearless and daring, and maybe—just maybe—Fin thought she could look like that someday too.

"Sorry about that," said Teafin, "but the last time you tried to get rid of your fears, it didn't end so well."

"It's a list," said Fin. "What's it going to do? Grow legs and start eating people?"

"This is Aldermere," said Teafin. "It might."

Fin's mouth twitched into a genuine smile. "Are you sad that the tea shop is gone?"

"Naw," said Teafin. "I get why you did it. After spending almost two weeks running around trying to keep Aldermere safe, I'd have been mad if you let Ben walk in there." She squared her shoulders. "Aldermere is our town. We keep it—and the magic—safe." She touched a hand to her own collarbone. "Speaking of . . . I think it's time we figured out what to do with me."

"What to do with you?" Fin frowned.

"The tea magic is temporary," said Teafin. "I've been losing leaves for days. And when Ben burned me, that sped things up." She held up a hand, squinted at her own fingers.

The shape blurred, became something formless and soggy, then reformed into a hand. "I'm disappearing."

Fin felt a pang of sadness. She'd never thought the prospect of losing Teafin would hurt her. But her double had become an ally instead of a threat.

Teafin must have seen the look on Fin's face, because she laughed. "Oh, come on. You couldn't keep me, not forever. Just like you couldn't keep the tea's magic forever." She rocked back on her heels, and the raven chittered and took flight, alighting on the rooftop. The bird began grooming her feathers, grumbling quietly to herself.

"So what are you going to do?" asked Fin.

Teafin shrugged. "We've got two options. First: you let me go. I can hang out in the forest or play with the raven for a while. I probably won't last more than a few more days and—and then there'll be a lump of soggy tea leaves somewhere in the forest. It'd be peaceful and I wouldn't mind it."

"Or?" asked Fin, frowning. She didn't like the idea of Teafin leaving.

"Or," said Teafin, "you can take me back."

Fin blinked. "Take you back?"

"Your memories," said Teafin. "A bit of anger. A dash of recklessness. I'm not exactly pleasant, but I could be part of you again. Or not. I mean, you did get rid of me for a reason."

"And look at how well that turned out," Fin murmured. She considered the other girl—crouched on the rooftop, comfortable and at ease with her surroundings. That wasn't Fin, but maybe it could be.

And besides, it was wrong to lose Teafin. To have those parts of Fin vanish into some forest and never emerge. A few weeks ago, she would have done it. But now . . . now she wasn't sure she could.

Maybe the first step in not being afraid was to accept that fear could not be buried. It could not be hidden away or ignored.

Sometimes it had to be felt.

"Okay," she said.

Teafin grinned suddenly—a wide smile that curled the edges of her mouth. It was the kind of smile that promised all sorts of trouble and mischief, and Fin wondered if she'd ever look like that. "Good," said Teafin.

"You don't seem surprised," said Fin.

"I'm not," said Teafin. "I'd have done the same." She held out her hand. Her nails were painted black.

Fin shook her head. "Evil twinning it to the last fashion statement?"

"Try plum when you finally paint your nails," said Teafin. "That's more our color."

Fin shook her head, amused. "Just tell me one thing."

"What?" asked Teafin, tilting her head.

"I can understand why you burned Ben's shed," said Fin. "But why sabotage River's science fair project? Or ruin Mayor Downer's lawn? Or put those whintossers in Mr. Hardin's shop?"

Teafin laughed. "I mean, like I said before. River's a jerk. If I had to lure you out of that gym by sabotaging someone's project, it might as well have been him. As for Mayor Downer . . . I mean, come on. Who hasn't thought about ruining her perfect lawn?"

"And the Ack?" asked Fin.

"The cat gets bored," said Teafin, shrugging. "And he likes chasing whintossers. I thought I'd give him some fun."

"You are trouble," said Fin, but this time she said it like a compliment.

Teafin beamed.

Fin thought back through the last few days. "One last question," she said.

Teafin looked expectant.

"That night," said Fin. "When Eddie and I were at the big house after working on our project. You were moving around outside, making noise. Then you wrote on the dust in the window. 'Stay indoors tonight.' What was that about?"

Teafin touched a finger to her lips thoughtfully. "Because," she said, "I wasn't the creature making the noise."

Fin drew in a sharp breath. "What was it?"

"I don't know," said Teafin. "It was big, I can tell you that much. Like a shadow had fallen across the house—but I couldn't see what cast it. One thing's certain, though. I wasn't the only one keeping an eye on you." She leaned forward. "Be brave, Fin."

Fin lifted her chin. "I'll try."

Teafin smiled. It was a wicked curve of a smile. Then Teafin's hand covered Fin's eyes. Fin shut her eyes on reflex, the cool slickness of damp tea leaves against her cheek.

And then all of the things she had forgotten came flooding back.

TWENTY-SEVEN
The Aftermath

The gossip about the vanished tea shop sustained Aldermere for nearly a month.

Fin wasn't sure how the story got out. But somehow people knew the bare bones of what had happened.

No one was surprised the tea shop had vanished. After all, it tended to do that.

What had surprised people was Ben's involvement in a conspiracy to make the magical tea into some kind of corporate entity. There were mutterings of how it was dangerous to let newcomers into the town—which were promptly shut down when it was pointed out that Ben had grown up in Aldermere. Mayor Downer put forth some kind of new town ordinance to regulate business with outsiders, but the debate was long and cited town laws that Fin had no interest in. She spent most of that town meeting in the back, drinking hot chocolate with Mom.

Mom had finally stopped working constantly. The other manager of the inn had come back from maternity leave.

That next Monday, Eddie, Cedar, and Fin found themselves in the principal's office. It was strange to be there—Fin had never even seen the inside of the office, except when her mother had filled out the forms to get her into school. But since the three of them had ducked out of a school-organized event without adult supervision, they were in trouble. Mom couldn't make it, and Cedar's parents were working at the coffee shop, but Aunt Myrtle bustled into the school, all crystal necklaces and swinging skirts and long hair. She took one look at the principal, eyeing him the way the Aldermere ravens tended to eye stray crumbs.

"You three stay out there," she said, and marched into the office with a grim set to her mouth.

None of them knew what was said. Aunt Myrtle never raised her voice, but about ten minutes later, she strode out. "You'll give your presentations to the science teachers at lunch on Friday," she said, walking them out of the office.

"How?" said Fin faintly. She couldn't believe that was all it had taken to get them out of trouble.

Aunt Myrtle let out a throaty little chuckle.

No one asked after that.

Cedar did sit with them at lunch. She brought an empanada from the coffee shop and didn't talk much, but she smiled the whole time.

Fin filled them in on what had happened with Teafin. Eddie seemed relieved that she was gone, but Cedar looked sad about it. "She's gone?" asked Cedar.

Fin shrugged. "No, not really. She's—me again."

Fin wasn't sure how she'd been affected by Teafin's memories. She didn't feel evil or reckless or a desire to set things on fire. She was still anxious. But now she understood why.

"What happened at the science fair?" asked Fin.

Eddie let out a cackle. "River didn't win since his windmill didn't work. The girl with the seaweed display won—something about rising sea temperatures or something." He looked pleased, then sighed. "We didn't win either, though. So it's a stalemate."

"There's always next year," she said.

After lunch, Cedar and Fin walked to English class together. "What about the raven?" asked Cedar. "Is she still around?"

"Yes," replied Fin. "She stopped by the big house and brought me a half-dollar coin. I think she must have found it somewhere."

Cedar grinned. "That's handy. You have a raven friend. You should name her."

"I did." Fin's fingers tightened on her binder. It made her feel vulnerable to admit it. "Morri. That's her name."

"Morri?"

"Short for Morrigan," said Fin. "Nick said that old myths had ravens in them a lot. The Morrigan was one of them, and I liked it better than Badb."

"Much better," agreed Cedar.

Talia came home a few weeks after the tea shop vanished.

It turned out she had been staying with her sister in the Bay area. She came home with a cane and a scowl when she saw the empty space where the tea shop had stood. The moment Fin heard that Talia was back, she raced across town, her heart pounding.

"Well," Talia said when she caught sight of Fin. Her red-orange cane perfectly matched her lipstick. "I heard you kept Ben from making off with my mortar and burning the tea shop down. Mrs. Brackenbury's been telling the story all over town."

"It was my fault," said Fin. It took all her courage to say the words, but she said them. "No one knows the real story. I mean, no one but Eddie and Cedar."

Talia gazed down at her. "What happened?"

Fin told her. When she'd finished, Talia made a disgusted sound at the back of her throat. "Ben. He's wanted the tea for years. It's not your fault he tried."

"But," said Fin, "he only got the spare key because he saw me use it."

For a moment, she was sure Talia would yell at her. But she did no such thing—rather, Talia held out her hand. As if waiting for something.

Fin understood after a few panicked moments. She dug into her jeans pocket and came up with the key.

It had been the raven, Morri, who'd found it. Fin had come home to the bird on the cottage rooftop, the glittery crescent moon in her beak. Fin traded a hard-boiled egg for the key, and the raven was pleased with the exchange.

Talia took the key with a satisfied nod. "All right," she said. "I'll start looking in the morning, then."

Fin perked up. "You mean you can find the tea shop?"

"It's Aldermere," said Talia. "Keys can't exist without a lock."

Fin stared at her. If that was an Aldermere rule, it was

one Fin had never heard. But it sounded as real as the others.

"Where will you live?" she asked.

"Mrs. Brackenbury has a guest room," said Talia. "And I know she's been wanting company. I'll just have to keep Mr. Bull from dozing on my bed." With a sigh, Talia shuffled in the direction of town, her cane flashing in the sunlight.

Relieved that Talia hadn't blamed her, and that the tea shop might be found, Fin headed to the grocery store to begin her deliveries.

Mr. Hardin was at the counter, shooing the stray cat away from a new display of canned anchovies. The cat meowed pitifully at him, ignoring the bowl of kibble a foot away. "Oh, hello, Finley," said Mr. Hardin, glancing up at Fin. "Good to see you. Got three packages for you. One for Mrs. Brackenbury, one for Ms. Catmore, and one for you."

"For me?" asked Fin, frowning. She never got mail; there was no one to send it to her.

Mr. Hardin passed her three pieces of mail: a large padded envelope for Ms. Catmore, a shoebox-sized package for Mrs. Brackenbury, and a normal-sized envelope for Fin. Hers had no address—only her name, written in a tidy cursive. There was no stamp, no return address. Unease curled at the base of Fin's spine, but she resisted the temptation to open the letter right there. Instead she smiled at Mr. Hardin, petted the cat, and carried her deliveries outside.

She stopped on the sidewalk, setting the other packages between her feet. Her envelope was strangely lumpy. She tugged it open; there were three words scrawled on the inside.

Just in case.

Fin held the envelope to her nose and inhaled.

The scent of Ceylon and spice filled her nose. Tea. There was a teaspoon's worth of tea in the envelope.

But who had sent it to her? And what was she supposed to do with it? Shaking her head, Fin folded the envelope and shoved it into her pocket. She'd figure this out later. In the meantime, she had deliveries to make.

She was carrying the package to Ms. Catmore when she heard footsteps behind her. She glanced over her shoulder and saw Eddie. He'd pushed his way out of the forest, leaves caught on his sleeve and what looked like a baby squirrel in his hand. "Hey," he said brightly. "What are you up to?"

"It's Tuesday," said Fin, holding up the packages. She set them down, brushing her hands on her jeans. "Where'd you find the baby squirrel?"

"Fallen from a tree," said Eddie. "Lost his parents, I think. I'll find 'em."

Fin gazed at him—and realized that she'd never asked

one thing. It made sense now, considering the memories she'd been missing for a year. "Hey," she said. "Um, I've never asked about your dad before. Where is he?"

Eddie said, "He's an artist up near Granite Falls, in Washington. He and Mom were good friends, but they weren't really happily-ever-after material. I get packages sometimes, and Mom drives me up there every few years." He frowned. "Why didn't you ever ask before?"

"I don't know," said Fin. "I think I traded a lot of big memories for tea. Just never crossed my mind until now."

Eddie shook his head. "That tea thing is weird."

"Agreed," said Fin. "I think I'll keep my memories from now on." And she meant it. Trying to forget things and lose pieces of herself hadn't made her any happier. All a person could do was learn to live with themself. The best parts and the worst.

"Right," said Eddie. "So when do you think you'll be done with deliveries?"

Fin glanced at the packages. "Ten minutes," she said. "Twenty, if Ms. Brackenbury is home."

"I need to find this guy's family," said Eddie, holding up the squirrel. "Want to come with? I thought I saw some weird tracks. Could be a bigfoot. We could ask Cedar too."

Fin glanced at the forest—at sunlight streaming through

the redwood branches. At the shadows flickering through the ferns—shadows that could be from the wind . . . or perhaps from something else. She thought of a tea shop, somewhere in the woods.

"Yes," she said. "I'm in."

Acknowledgments

When I was young, my family made annual trips from Oregon to the coast of northern California to visit my grandmother. Those long drives through the redwoods—with the curvy roads, audiobooks on cassette tapes, and forests veiled by fog—always seemed like magic. I remember wanting to capture that magic, to find a way to bring it home with me.

Decades later, I set out to do just that. And I couldn't have done it alone.

To my agent, Sarah Landis, for being the best champion that I could ever ask for. Thank you for all of your support and your expertise. I'm so glad to be part of Team Landis. And a big shout-out to the rest of the team at Sterling Lord Literistic.

To my editor, Martha Mihalick, who just *got* me and my writing from that very first phone call. Thank you for your thoughtful guidance, for making this book the best it could be, and for the adorable cat pictures.

To Virginia Duncan, for giving me the chance to be part of the Greenwillow family. And to the rest of the team: Arianna Robinson, Lois Adams, Sylvie Le Floc'h, and my sharp-eyed copy editor, Laaren Brown. To the brilliant marketing squad: Vaishali Nayak, Delaney Heisterkamp, Mitch Thorpe, and all the wonderful people working on Shelf Stuff.

To Izzy Burton, for illustrating my dream cover. I am so happy every time I look at it.

To Ryan O'Rourke, for bringing the town of Aldermere to life.

To the people who have been with me from the very start. First of all, to my mother for being my cheerleader, beta reader, occasional therapist, and assistant cat wrangler. I couldn't have done it without you. To Dad, for all of the motivation. To Diana, for all the sisterly support. To my cousins, Kasey and Roman, for being both friends and family. To Lynden, for being an amazing aunt and one of the few people who could drive Highway 1 without making me nauseated.

And to the next generation of readers: Roland and Floyd. You have many amazing years of reading ahead of you.

Being an author is often a solitary endeavor, so I'm very grateful to all of my friends who've been with me on various parts of this journey. To s.e. smith, for being one of the first people to hear about Aldermere and for explaining how Fin couldn't get locked in a water tower. To Deth P. Sun, for going with me on that train at Confusion Hill despite the conductor announcing that a derailment was inevitable. To Rosiee Thor, for always being there when I need dog pictures or plant advice. To Mary Elizabeth Summer, who listened to a rough draft of Chapter Two and told me I had to keep going. To Catherine Garbinsky, for coming up with the perfect pun coffee shop name. To Katherine Locke, for all the support as I was halfway through a first draft at space camp. And to all the friends I made at Launch Pad 2019—particularly Diana Rowland, for making sure that our van didn't slide off the edge of a mountain.

To all the booksellers and the librarians. You're the ones putting magic into people's hands and I appreciate you so much.

And specifically, to Alysha Welliver, Gabrielle Belisle, Kalie Barnes-Young, Alex Abraham, and Lily Tschudi-Campbell.

To all the bookish people who have promoted/talked/tweeted/instagrammed/reviewed my books, I owe you a big thanks.

And lastly to you, dear reader. Thank you for picking up this book.

May you find the magic you seek.